JAN THE DUTCHMAN

JAN THE DUTCHMAN

MIKE KINGDOM THRILLERS

BOOK 6

DAVID JARVIS

HOBECK

This edition produced in Great Britain in 2026

by Hobeck Books Limited, Unit 14, Sugnall Business Centre, Sugnall, Stafford, Staffordshire, ST21 6NF

www.hobeck.net

A CIP catalogue for this book is available from the British Library.

ISBN 978-1-915-817-99-0 (pbk)

ISBN 978-1-915-817-98-3 (ebook)

Cover design by Jem Butcher

www.jembutcherdesign.co.uk

Printed and bound in Great Britain

ARE YOU A THRILLER SEEKER?

Hobeck Books is an independent publisher of crime, thrillers and suspense fiction and we have one aim – to bring you the books you want to read.

For more details about our books, our authors and our plans, plus the chance to download free novellas, sign up for our newsletter at **www.hobeck.net**.

You can also find us on Bluesky **@hobeckbooks**, Twitter/X **@hobeckbooks** or Facebook **www.facebook.com/hobeckbooks10**.

Just then, they came in sight of thirty or forty windmills which rose up from the plain. And no sooner had Don Quixote seen them than he said to his squire, "Fortune is guiding our affairs better than we ourselves could have wished. Do you see over yonder, friend Sancho, thirty or forty hulking giants? I intend to do battle with them and slay them. With their spoils we shall begin to be rich for this is a righteous war and the removal of so foul a brood from off the face of the earth is a service God will bless."

"What giants?" asked Sancho Panza.

"Those you see over there," replied his master, "with their long arms. Some of them have arms almost two leagues in length."

"Take care, sir," cried Sancho. "Those over there are not giants but windmills."

Don Quixote
***Miguel de Cervantes*, 1605**

PART ONE

CHAPTER ONE

She had her knickers around her ankles when the nuclear attack on London and Washington, DC, began.

On the back of the cubicle door in front of her, there was a sign suggesting she should now wash her hands. Was this a priority as the intercontinental missiles rained down? Perhaps she should wipe the toilet seat ready for the next occupant? That's if anyone was still alive.

Being blissfully unaware she had missed the start of Armageddon, she tore off some toilet paper and pondered what it was about the British that meant they thought that, while seven floors underground in an ultra-secret facility outside Bath in Somerset, she needed to be reminded about personal hygiene.

A few minutes later, while walking back into the main room, she was struck by the contrast between – at least to her American eyes – the crudely whitewashed concrete walls, with their rows of pipes suspended by brackets, and the banks of wafer-thin screens and displays representing the cutting edge of technology.

"You missed it," said Leonard, her boss, as she sat down and began putting on her headphones, which were the old, padded version.

"When you gotta go, you gotta go."

"If you take a look at the screens, I think you'll see that, while you went, most of the population has already gone - about 30 million of them," he explained in a gentle Alabaman accent, using a hand on the back of her chair to steady himself.

"Oh great," she said rather unsympathetically while trying to rejoin the joint Five Eyes exercise aimed at testing communications between the spying agencies in the group of English-speaking countries during a simulated nuclear attack. It was called Operation Silver Lion. Whether this meant anything in the USA, UK, Canada, Australia or New Zealand or it had randomly been generated wasn't explained.

Michaela 'Mike' Kingdom (an analyst) and Leonard de Vries (her chief of station) were part of the team of eight from the CIA (aka the Agency) in London who'd joined their British colleagues deep underground in a system of mines that had originally been converted in World War II as the RAF Command and Control Centre.

Since that time, some of the rooms and corridors in the network had barely changed, apart from the liberal application of the ubiquitous white paint. Sadly, nowhere was the beautiful oolitic limestone visible; this being the reason the blocks had been cut from these strata in the first place to build the Georgian terraces of Bath.

Although they weren't scheduled to spend the night underground, Mike had been shown the bunks and the dining area – all of which were, in her opinion, basic in the extreme. The British were weird. Who in the MOD was continuing to specify metal-framed beds and chairs? They must be sadists. Her only satisfaction came from the fact that, in a real nuclear attack, the procurement department would have been wiped out.

Actually, the thought didn't give her any joy. It was so depressing.

She had taken off her paisley bandana and rested it on the

small Stars and Stripes flag beside one of her monitors; everyone down there had a flag to show their nationality. Mike was concerned that if the thirty-five people in the room couldn't work out she was American, should they be down here in the first place? On surveying their faces, she wondered if this was the best gene pool the human race could assemble, should it need to repopulate the world following devastation by nuclear war.

Although everyone had only been below ground for five hours, she was missing her fiancé, Wazz. There was something about the fact that she might survive while he was one of the millions on the surface who'd be vapourised by the bombs that affected her deep down – ninety feet below the surface, to be exact.

Mike was sitting there bald-headed and needed to rub her scalp periodically. The room was stuffy, which was caused by the air-conditioning and filtration system doing its best to remove anything harmful – although this appeared to include oxygen. It was fighting against the heat from all the computers to keep the temperature at a steady 21°C.

Sitting in a seat for hours at a time hadn't been good for her ever since the accident in the Netherlands over seven years ago; her left calf was damaged, and it ached if it wasn't exercised frequently. This and her hair loss served to remind her constantly of the worst day of her life: the day her husband, Dylan, had been killed on an undercover Agency operation.

"Here we go," Leonard declared as the banks of screens indicated that the communication systems of the five agencies would switch over from their normal configuration to one that avoided those wiped out in the imaginary attacks. Across the globe, the facilities on sleepy military sites or in mountaintop listening posts, which had seemingly been mothballed, kicked into action to remake connections, avoiding the damaged synapses.

Mike's screens all came to life, and she spent an hour checking that everything she usually received was continuing to come in. While the scenario was imagined, this was real data and real intelligence on her projects, which was being diverted to her new location via various alternative routes.

Something caught her eye. It was the code number of a project long finished and archived. Leonard was walking behind her just then, so she didn't open it, but she put it in her secure folder to be looked at when she got back to her house in the village of Rodbourne, a little under an hour's journey away. Fortunately, Leonard had discovered over several years that Mike was the most gifted analyst he had ever employed. Not wanting to lose her, he allowed her to work from home four days a week, which was a luxury he didn't offer to any of the others.

The old clock on the wall was one minute slow. Why leave it up there? The screens throughout the room displayed the time, accurate to nanoseconds. Either way, she had another two hours before she could breathe fresh air again and ride her Italian motorbike south through Wiltshire and across Salisbury Plain.

While Mike had been reading the notice on the back of a washroom door seven floors underground, a man 2,500 miles away to the south took in a deep breath, instantly regretted it and, despite coughing, strode forwards with enthusiasm.

He was clutching a crude walking stick as if it would save him from falling. It did not. The surface was uneven, and the sun was beyond blistering.

Arthur, his fourteen-year-old guide, had given it to him as they emerged from the beaten-up Datsun, but he still managed to trip after less than 100 yards. All this was watched by the taxi driver, who had made it clear that he thought they were mad, and he would take them no further. As Terry regained his footing, the car was turning around, ready to park at the side of the track with the engine running.

They were walking across the unpredictable surface of a rubbish tip alongside a dirty, white wall. Strange sounds emanated from beyond and contributed to the assault on all their senses. Added to these noises were the sickening stench, the dust filling their lungs and the blinding African sun shining directly into their eyes. He had also collected his own swarm of flies, which were attracted to his sweaty, grey polo shirt. It was hard to decide if his faded, green baseball cap was of more use on his head or as a fly swat.

Terry Bailey wasn't your average British tourist, and he had found Arthur by chatting to locals in a bar. He wanted a bird-watching guide who wouldn't simply take him for a walk around the grounds of his hotel or the local kickabout area, even though there were dozens of exotic species to spot, such as the red-eyed coucals and the turquoise bee-eaters. His first request to his guide had been, "Take me to where *you* go to watch birds, and if I see lots of new ones, I'll give you these binoculars."

Arthur had been very suspicious of a sixty-year-old tourist offering him presents, but he needed the money and had noticed immediately that the binoculars were Zeiss from the factory in West Germany, not the one in Jena. "I go to the lake behind Mile 2 Prison to watch the flock of sacred ibis. It's the biggest in The Gambia."

"The flock or the prison?"

"Both."

"Then let's go there. I've never seen a flock of sacred ibis."

"We'll need a taxi."

"No problem."

The next day, they'd met up and found a taxi. Terry had asked its driver to take them to the prison – an instruction that had needed to be repeated as the driver had stared in his rear view mirror at the sweating, overweight man in the back; this wasn't one of the usual tourist destinations. Arthur, while sitting in the front passenger seat, had tried to explain where they wanted to go, but he had given up, and when they had eventually reached the prison, he had simply pointed out the track next to the white walls and observation towers of the jail.

Terry was unfit, having spent his life sitting on his backside and, more specifically, on barstools; however, in his retirement, he was determined to indulge his passion for ornithology. The Gambia was the best place in Africa for this, and next year, he intended to go to Costa Rica, which was the best place in the Americas if you excluded the Amazon, which didn't appeal to him. The distance between drinking establishments was too large.

"Here, take this stick." Arthur had found a length of acacia branch and, with a few deft strokes of his penknife, had removed some spines to make it usable. "It's very difficult to walk. Stay close to me."

Despite the initial stumble, which had temporarily dispersed the flies, Terry made reasonable progress, managing to avoid the bags of domestic refuse and the various sharp objects. The biggest problems were the voids, some of which were large enough to take human beings. This was immediately demonstrated when two men completely covered in matt-brown dust leapt out of a hole, brandishing machetes.

Terry raised his stick as an automatic defensive reaction to their sudden appearance.

"Easy, boss!" Arthur calmed him by putting a hand on his arm. "These are my friends. They live here."

He proceeded to introduce them, and Terry, despite his life working all over the world, felt the very British need to offer a handshake. After Arthur had asked them what they had found today and about a mutual friend who was in hospital, the bird-watchers set off again towards the dense vegetation that formed the rear edge of the landfill.

"How many people live here?"

"There are about 100 who live near or in the tip and survive by ..." Arthur didn't know the word for 'scavenging', but he articulated this by motioning with his hands. "It's their life," he concluded with a shrug.

Terry resisted the urge to keep turning around and staring at the people who periodically popped up from below ground, like prairie dogs, to see what was happening. It was as if he were in a *Mad Max* movie. Finally, caked in pale-brown dust that had mixed with the sweat and dried on their skin, they approached a foetid, dark body of water, which had been dammed by the advancing rubbish tip. Arthur indicated that they should be quiet and proceed a little more slowly.

Terry took in his surroundings and thought to himself how utterly wonderful his life was now he no longer worked in the secret squirrel world. Retirement suited him, although not everyone would savour his current location on a rubbish tip next to a sulphurous lake behind an African prison. He had been in far worse places and felt far more threatened.

And there in front of him was the most wonderful flock of sacred ibis, waders with down-curving bills, which began to walk away from him *en masse* around the edge in the shallow water. It was one of the most beautiful things he had ever seen.

Despite both of them standing still with their binoculars raised, the birds took off, and the sky was filled with flashes of black and white, which also reflected in the surface of the water. They flew around and landed on the other side of the small lake, where they were watched for a quarter of an hour by the unwelcome visitor.

"Thank you," Terry said before they turned around to retrace their steps across the lunar landscape and back to the track.

This took twenty minutes. As they approached, the taxi driver reversed fifteen yards towards them as if this would make the slightest difference to his client. If he were hoping for a bigger tip, he would be disappointed. Terry wasn't interested in him, but in anticipation of finding a good guide, he had purposely brought two pairs of binoculars with him and handed over his Zeiss ones to Arthur, who hadn't really believed that he would get them. The boy beamed enthusiastically as he held them in his hands. They slid into the taxi and savoured the air conditioning as it took effect. The windows had been open and half a dozen flies had found their way inside.

This trip to Africa was more than a holiday; it was symbolic.

Being a case officer for the Secret Intelligence Service, or MI6, had been Terry's life for almost thirty years, mostly in Europe and particularly in Spanish-speaking countries. He had possessed no burning desire to join MI6, just like he had never felt a burning desire to read Spanish and history at Nottingham University; these things simply happened. His father was a pilot, and his mother was a flight attendant on the first cheap airlines flying to Spain. They bought a villa near Alicante and learnt the local language, as did their son. It was one of the few things he was good at.

He was a functioning alcoholic and probably hadn't been a good spy; he couldn't remember. Instead, he had been what Napoleon desired in his generals: not good but lucky – well, mostly. Even having a mini stroke didn't end his life. When it had happened, he had been at a police station in Central London, filling in some forms at 2.00am, when he suddenly froze and stared at the document in front of him. He had forgotten how to write. A doctor attending someone else recognised what was happening and stepped in to help. By breakfast time, he could just about do joined-up writing again, although only by using his entire energy and concentration. It wasn't simply mental frustration; it had physically hurt as well. This had all contributed to the file that Human Resources had assembled, which led to the service having to "sadly consider letting him go".

Within days, he had retirement imposed on him at the age of sixty, and a life of leisure and increasing boredom loomed ahead. This had been months ago, and his African holiday was meant to be a reset. So far, this had worked, and he had begun to relax.

On the way back to the hotel, he was distracted by a pied kingfisher sitting next to a clump of moss growing on a telephone wire. Was The Gambia where he would like to be if there were a nuclear war? He could think of many worse places and had worked in a long list of them.

At that moment, he caught a glimpse of a man he thought he recognised, driving in the opposite direction, but this wasn't possible – the man was dead.

Terry should know; he had killed him.

CHAPTER TWO

For the rest of the taxi journey, he had replayed that moment over and over again.

He could, of course, have been mistaken. It wasn't as if the man known as Jan the Dutchman had distinctive facial features or skin colouring. Jan was a nondescript white man in his forties with mousey hair and brown eyes. In the shadowy world in which he had operated, it would have been an advantage to be eminently forgettable.

It also helped that his name was not Jan, and he was not a Dutchman.

Whoever was in the car, Terry didn't think that he himself had been spotted by the man, whose eyes had firmly been looking forwards as he concentrated on his driving. *And what would Jan be doing driving a car in Banjul, given the inconvenient fact that he was dead?* After all, Terry had seen his body sprawled over the sofa, his white shirt soaked in blood. Terry had shot him, firing two bullets. Oddly, he had never known Jan's real name. Nobody did.

Yet there was still a nagging doubt, and if Jan had somehow survived, there could only be one logical reason why he was in

The Gambia, and that would be to follow Terry. *But why?* Well, apart from the fact that Terry had shot him.

He dismissed the idea, putting it down to frayed nerves, too much red wine the night before and the tropical sun on the bird-watching trip across the rubbish tip.

Once back in the cool of the hotel lobby, it didn't prevent him going into work mode, and he walked over to a noticeboard promoting river cruises, visits to local villages and trips into the jungle. While pretending to read, he watched to see if anyone was acting suspiciously, but no one was paying him any attention. At the reception desk, he asked if he had any messages and if anyone had been looking for him. The man he'd asked shook his head.

Despite the fact that nobody was hanging around and nobody appeared to have followed him, Terry still took the stairs instead of the lift and checked out the corridor before approaching his room. After opening the door, he kept it from closing with his foot and threw his small leather bag onto the bed while he waited for any response. There was none.

Once the bathroom and wardrobe had been searched, he went out onto the large, red-tiled terrace, which was shaded by the room above. There was no sign of life apart from a pile of ants devouring a black beetle the size of a World War II grenade.

He went back inside, cranked up the air conditioning and grabbed a glass from the shelf by the kettle. After having opened a bottle of gin from the fridge, he took out a can of tonic – although there was only room in the glass for a splash. The damp, grey polo shirt felt refreshingly cold on his back, and sitting on the edge of the bed, he tried to calm down while gulping the drink.

If anything, his neurosis had got worse since he retired, which rather surprised him, as the pressure should have eased. Perhaps, after a lifetime of looking over his shoulder and suspecting everyone, it was too deeply engrained and would remain with him for the rest of his life.

His shoulders dropped, and he peered down into the glass he was holding in both hands. If he wasn't careful, he would start jumping every time a car backfired or someone was walking behind him. *Relax ... just relax. Think it through.*

Firstly, Jan was dead. Secondly, Terry had only told one close friend that he was going to Banjul birdwatching, and even if Jan were miraculously alive and had followed him to Heathrow, he couldn't have jumped on the plane. Finally, and most importantly, it was impossible for Jan to know who had shot him or anything about a man called Terry Bailey.

Anyone thinking logically would know that it couldn't have been Jan the Dutchman in the other car.

Unfortunately, after his mini stroke, Terry no longer thought logically, and this was without the influence of alcohol. After another drink, he decided to tell someone so if anything befell him, they could work out what had happened. Only one name came to mind, and he sent her a cryptic message. He hoped that she was still with the Agency and remained in London.

She had ridden for an hour across Salisbury Plain, enjoying the breeze and the open views – unlike the Earl of Pembroke who, in the eighteenth century, had a tree planted every mile so he could count them to alleviate the boredom on his way back to Wilton in his carriage. Mike had to use the twenty-first century version: yellow-painted railway sleepers marking the tank crossing points used by the military.

She had hoped that the journey would be long enough to completely blow away the dank smell of the underground facility, but this hadn't happened. A shower was high on her agenda.

Reaching the main street in Rodbourne, she had passed The

Green Feathers before turning into Church Lane. The terrace of cottages was still standing, and this felt especially wonderful having spent so long imagining a nuclear attack. On arriving home, she stopped the bike, got off and wheeled it around to the back of her cottage. Once the bike was under its cover in the rear garden, she headed to the house and opened the kitchen door.

"How was the holiday?" Wazz asked as soon as she walked in carrying her matt-black motorcycle helmet.

"Unlikely to feature highly on Tripadvisor. I need a beer and a shower. Beer first." Being unable to tell Wazz what she was actually doing, she had made up some story about being on a field trip.

He started his own thread of conversation: "I was on a military camp."

Mike was always slow to ask him about his day. "Really?" This wasn't what she was expecting him to say.

"I was laying turf in the gardens of some new married quarters at the Land Warfare Centre."

"Where's that?"

"Warminster."

Mike had never heard of it, but she was pleased Wazz had finally settled into a job. It hadn't been easy spending two and a half years in prison, but he had knuckled down on his release and had subsequently been employed for some time as personal security to rich women in Spain and then as a bouncer at a strip club in London while completing his degree. After this, and despite trying for six months, he couldn't land a job that paid more than minimum wage; the degree counted for nothing. As he had gradually been losing his self-confidence, Mike had suggested that he should start his own business.

From that breakfast table conversation, 'Wazz with a van' was born, and he now had a mixture of clients requiring landscape contracting and building maintenance. It surprised him, but for no obvious reason, the turfing side of his business had blossomed, and his reputation locally had grown. While he was now earning a reasonable living, it was the freedom of being his own boss that was the most important aspect. His prison time was no longer a weight around his neck.

He kept himself fit, mostly worked outdoors and was back at a reasonable hour to share a normal evening with Mike – something they had never experienced before. Only on Wednesdays did she set off for London, where she stayed with her friend Carol, then she worked all day on Thursday in the Agency office before setting off on the long journey back to Wiltshire, arriving about 9.30pm in time for a light meal and bed.

This was the new rhythm of their life, and they were glad to be away from some of the traumas that had plagued them – principally when Mike went off on wild goose chases to places such as Morocco or Oman, forgetting that she was an analyst not a case officer. Hopefully, all that was in the past; however, Wazz could read Mike like a book.

"Wazzup?" he asked, keeping it light.

"Nothing ... well, nothing serious. I do want to check something for half an hour, though. Oh good, you're cooking. I'll be back before you can say 'meatballs'; it is meatballs we're having?"

"That's what you asked for."

"I'll be back in twenty minutes or ten if I can have a Peroni."

"Whatever."

The need for a shower had been forgotten, and she disappeared into the lounge to set up her laptop and gizmos; the latter were supplied by the Agency so she could work from home with them offering a range of protection and security. The room was small but cosy, with the house being part of a terrace of old thatched houses. Everything was a contrast to anywhere she had lived before – either with her parents in Oregon, in a dorm at university, at the Agency's Langley HQ, in an Oxfordshire cabin deep within a wood or sharing Wazz's flat in West London.

Number 3 Church Lane, Rodbourne, was hers, and she had no mortgage, but she did have a live-in boyfriend who had become her fiancé. How did that happen? Well, of course, she knew how it had happened; nevertheless, it had rather crept up on them both. They were well-suited to each other, which in reality meant that he was able to put up with her and her low tolerance to, well, everything.

Sitting on a small sofa, she logged in and opened the secure file to which she had quickly copied across the message – the one that had come in while she was bizarrely ignoring a nuclear war raging above her.

It read thus:

173/17/Jan 2026/20/7

Mike,
I'm not sure if this will reach you.
I've now retired and would love to catch up.
Are all our old friends still around? I think I spotted one of them recently, but I was probably mistaken.
Give me a call; I'm at the same address. I'm sure you can find my number.
I'm abroad at the moment, but I'm in the UK from Wednesday.
Terribly excited!
X

She sank back into the cushions and stared at the ceiling; it wasn't far above her head. This was one of the joys of living in a cottage. With her hands clasped behind her neck, her thoughts wandered off, and she realised her whole body was shaking.

How long had passed, Mike had no idea, but Wazz was at the kitchen door holding an opened bottle of Peroni.

"Dinner is served, milady," he said, rocking the bottle gently back and forth as if it were a metronome.

"What? Oh, thanks."

She logged out and walked into the kitchen, where the beer was accepted with a smile. The size of her first mouthful gave Wazz an indication of the severity of the problem. They had an unwritten code that had been developed to cope with the impossible strain on their and any relationship where one party works for a secret organisation and details can't be revealed. It was a simple mathematical scale to give an indication of mood, difficulty, life expectancy, etc.

"On a scale of one to ten, I'm going to guess you're at about seven?"

She took another swig and stared at him with a strange look. "Let's call it an eleven, and we should eat the meatballs before I go into meltdown."

"I'll give the chef a kick up the backside." Wazz knew when he needed to let air gently out of her tyres. He jumped into the air, doing some strange hitch kick as if he were trying to deliver the necessary blow to the chef's ass, which ended up looking like he was flamboyantly riding a hobby horse. This was all the more odd as he was a large man with well-defined muscles under a tight, orange tee shirt.

Mike smiled and sat down at the table. She didn't say anything, which was also a sure sign that something was up.

"My Italian meatballs aren't going to put the world to rights, I feel."

"No, probably not."

He waited for her to give him some general idea of the problem while he served the two plates of food. She said nothing and sprinkled grated parmesan cheese onto the tomato and onion sauce.

"I thought we'd left all this behind. It seems I've moved on, but your work continues to mess you up."

"I'm sorry." She put a whole meatball into her mouth and breathed out fast to cool it down.

He noticed that, in truth, it was the beer she craved and not the food. She was obviously nervous, frightened or disturbed by something she had seen on her screen. He faced an evening walking on eggshells. "Can you tell me anything?"

"Not really. It's something from the past ... my past."

"Something personal?"

"Work ... and personal."

They continued eating for a while, but without enthusiasm. Eventually, she stood up and walked to the sink, carrying her dirty plate.

"It's OK. I'll wash up. You go and find out if it's all as bad as you think." He took the plate from her and pointed to the lounge.

She gave him a rather forced smile. "I don't deserve you. You could have done so much better."

"Maybe you should resign and join me laying turf? It's therapeutic."

"I'm not sure I should be allowed near anything living, but thanks for the offer. I envy your contentment."

"The grass is always greener ... but that's turfing for you."

She managed a genuine smile and went into the lounge, where she again stared at the message, rereading every line and between every line. Anyone could see it had purposely been written in a very cautious way in case it was read by others. It appeared a harmless contact by an old friend who had retired, but it was so much more than that.

Firstly, the reference at the top meant she knew whom he was referring to in the text: someone she knew as Jan the Dutchman. Using an apparent date of Jan 2026 would mislead any reader into thinking this was all about something discussed months ago.

Secondly, "173/7" was the code for a project now finished but from which she still bore the scars – literally. The skin may have healed on her left calf, but there wasn't a day that went by when her leg didn't ache; the deep, long gash was a constant reminder of the ambush. Every day, she relived the shattering of the windscreen as the bullets hit; Dylan swerving off the long, straight road and down the bank; and the vehicle bursting into flames. She had been thrown out of the passenger door and rolled down the grassy bank near a line of poplar trees. All around was a Dutch landscape at its most benign.

"I think I spotted one of them recently, but I was probably mistaken" could only mean that he had seen Jan, even though they both believed him to be long dead.

"Terribly excited!" told her more than an indication of the sender's emotional state. He hadn't signed it, but he had used an anonymous "X", which gave no hint of his identity – but that didn't matter. She knew where it had come from.

When they had first been introduced on the project almost eight years earlier, she had misheard his name. She had thought that he had said, "Terribly," not "Terry Bailey," and this had become a running gag between them.

Now, after all this time, her avenging angel had made contact again. She would have to find his phone number and leave a message. This needed to be done urgently.

CHAPTER THREE

"And when will the factory be fully fitted out?" the reporter was asking.

"Over the next few weeks, and then there will be a further three months of testing, testing, testing." Keith Herring, the managing director of Commicron, was hoping this was the last question from the dozen or so members of the press corps gathered outside the new building. It wasn't.

"How big are these microchips?" someone from the local *Hereford Echo* piped up.

"Well, a microchip is about the size of your little fingernail, but what goes on this chip is almost beyond comprehension. Imagine a dinner plate as thin as a wafer. They come from Japan and cost $1 million. Over four or five months, we fire UV light tens of thousands of times through a droplet of molten tin, which is refracted in specialist mirrors. The machines come from the Netherlands, and the mirrors are from Germany." Keith stopped to look at the reporter; he was using his tried-and-tested barrage of mind-numbing facts to stun his audience. "When we've finished our processes in this factory, that dinner plate will have 14 trillion transistors on it, and this means each microchip we produce from it will have billions of transistors, each a four-billionth of a metre – what we call a 'nanometre' – in size. They're ridiculously small. It's why they're called microchips ... they're in everything such as that Samsung phone you're holding."

The reporter looked at his phone, hoping it was recording all this because he had completely lost track of the numbers.

"May we see where all the action is going to take place?" This came from someone on a national newspaper who was keen to get a look inside.

"Sadly not, and that's even before the important pieces of equipment are installed. You have to understand that the chips we're going to produce here, apart from being commercially sensitive, are physically sensitive as well. They'll be produced in a small room within another room within a big room to which no humans will have access once it's set up. There won't be one speck of dust in the inner sanctum. It'll be the cleanest place on earth." He tried to emphasise this using his hands, which were in the pockets of his black jacket under a tight-fitting hi-vis waistcoat. "Thanks to everyone for coming. I believe you've all been given the artist's impressions of the factory and the foyer; if not, ask Milly here. Now I need to look inside myself. It's all very exciting."

He turned and walked towards the sliding blue-glass doors.

Once through them, there was a sense of relief from being inside the structure and away from the press pack, despite having to wear hard hats and protective equipment. It was still technically a building site, but the enormous scale of the operation was very evident. The building and internal rooms were all complete. With him were a private security guard; someone from the Foreign, Commonwealth and Development Office (FCDO); someone from scientific liaison at GCHQ; a major from military intelligence; and the senior partner from the consultants in charge of project management.

Milly had remained outside to make sure the newspaper reporters and TV crews were happy and had been provided with all the quotes, shots and PR materials they required.

Keith Herring was quietly impressed with what he saw, even if the interior of the vast building resembled a beehive, with workers everywhere. He walked around some of the completed internal spaces, still amazed that the production of something billionths of a metre in size required so huge a factory.

As he'd been flown in by helicopter, he'd been reminded again of his debt to a nineteenth-century industrialist who had decided to build a paper-making factory in some of the most beautiful rolling countryside in England. There was no way he would have obtained permission to locate his new plant here on a greenfield site, but this had proved possible as he was demolishing and redeveloping the derelict paper factory. Although, of course, the fact this would be delivering one of the government's top five projects on a list of priorities not made public had helped the process considerably. As with the current US administration, his task was to make Britain resilient against foreign supply chains and control.

His helicopter had flown in over the mature parkland of The Rolls of Monmouth golf course – which was based at the home of Charles Rolls of Rolls-Royce fame – and over a cricket ground that was now looking very orange in the middle where an attempt had been made to hide a two-word expression that had been written using weed killer a few weeks previously. Love for the landowner who had now demanded rent from the local cricket club was in short supply, and its members had made their feelings public in thirty-foot-long letters across the pitch.

He had seen, or at least glimpsed, the small barracks nearby where a dedicated missile system would soon be installed to ensure the new facility was protected from aerial attack by malevolent countries. The fact that the base of the 22nd Special

Air Service Regiment (SAS) in Credenhill, near Hereford, was less than twelve miles away was pure serendipity.

Mike spent the Wednesday morning not working on her main project but searching for Terry Bailey. She had the house to herself, which gave her the freedom she needed. Wazz was at work, cutting the grass on the lawns of two of the larger houses near Rodbourne, which was probably the easiest money he could earn, using their own ride-on mowers while listening to Green Day through his earbuds.

It was seven years since she'd had any contact with Terry, after which their paths had never crossed again; a common occurrence in the world of the secret services.

Back then, he had felt an enormous guilt that he had trusted Jan the Dutchman, an informant she remembered he had cultivated remotely, who had betrayed the British and American team investigating the smuggling of cocaine into Rotterdam. It was Mike who had originally discovered the use of false floors in shipping containers, but the Dutch authorities had never caught the ringleaders, who had been tipped off by Jan.

This would have been bad enough for Terry to bear, but the betrayal didn't stop there.

Leonard had thought it would be more credible if Dylan, as the on-site CIA liaison officer with the Dutch narcotics police, had a wife with him in the house that had been rented near where the Colombians were living in a suburb of Amsterdam. Mike would be there primarily to provide the very latest intelligence in real time, particularly if there were last-minute changes of plan by the drug traffickers. She was a desk officer, untrained in field work and wouldn't take part in the raid with the police. It seemed fairly straightforward, and she would get to be with

Dylan for a week or more. Unfortunately, it didn't work out like that.

Four days before the predicted arrival of the container ship, it was passing to the north of the Azores and making good progress across the Atlantic Ocean. Dylan and Mike were taking a few hours off and driving along a quiet, tree-lined road next to a canal on their way to have a picnic. They had just overtaken a lady on a bicycle when the occupants of an oncoming car opened fire.

It was their one day off, and they never suspected the vehicle coming towards them. The shots shattered the windscreen, killing Dylan instantly, while she was half-thrown out of the passenger door as the car careered down the bank and hit a poplar tree.

She had dragged herself onto the grass as the car burst into flames. The only witness to her screams was the lady whom they had just overtaken, and she had also crashed; her bike had lost its front wheel and was lying on its side.

Terry never forgave himself.

Mike had been in hospital for two weeks, but when she had returned to England, she drew comfort from the fact that Jan the Dutchman was dead, and she could move on with her life. Somehow, Terry had found out that Jan was in room seventy-eight of a particular hotel. He had never told her how he had traced Jan. Terry had called it his 'extracurricular project', although he didn't use that adjective often on account of the increasing amount of alcohol he was consuming.

She was the desk-based analyst, and he was the very experienced case officer – albeit from a sister service. When he had told her privately that he had made the breakthrough, she had expected him to share this with his colleagues, but this didn't happen. Terry had taken matters into his own hands, and a week later, he had met her in a pub in Chiswick, where he had told her he had shot and killed Jan. The matter was closed; the debt to her repaid.

Already in a fragile state and with a severely damaged left leg, this had placed an almost intolerable burden on Mike. He had asked her to forget all about it and never mention it again. With every week that went by afterwards, it had become harder for her to tell anyone about it. The moment had passed. None of this was helped by her hatred of her boss Leonard, who had sent her out to the Netherlands in the first place, ostensibly for a week's holiday but really to support Dylan on a live operation.

Then it was too late. The years went by, and no reference ever came up to the shooting of Jan the Dutchman. She put it to the back of her mind – or at least she tried to do this. That Jan was dead didn't keep her awake at night.

The thought that he might still be alive and had been seen by Terry in Africa had, however, kept her awake the previous night. What did Terry mean?

It hadn't taken her long to find a new telephone number for Terry; after all, she knew his Chiswick flat's address. It took longer to pluck up the courage to call him and decide what to say. It was mid-morning on Wednesday when she walked back into the kitchen and started a chain of events of which she could never have conceived.

Earlier, she had taken out her personal burner phone, which she kept in a sugar jar on the highest shelf on the wall, and put it on charge. There was no way she would use her work phone and no way she would leave any trace. She dialled.

"Hello," a male voice answered, not identifying who it was.

"Terry?"

"Yes."

"It's Mike. It's years since we spoke. Do you fancy a drink?"

"Does the Pope shit in the woods? Great idea" – perhaps he had been drinking already? – "How about that pub we met in a couple of times?"

"No problem. I'm coming to London later tonight for work, so how about tomorrow evening at 6.30pm?"

"It'll be great to see you after all this time."

"See you tomorrow. Bye."

Without any preparation, they had purposely kept the conversation banal and of no interest to anyone. Despite this, she immediately felt the need for a drink, but she forced herself to return to her computer and her main project for the rest of the day.

Later, with her rucksack already packed, she was ready to leave at about 6pm for the two and a half-hour ride to Carol's flat. There was plenty of time for her to run through scenario after scenario, none of which had a happy ending.

On Thursday morning, after a short ride to the office from Carol's house, Mike handed in her phone and bag at the security desk and walked through the body scanner. She took the lift and made her way past the drinks station to the room she shared with five other analysts. Only Morag and Chuck were already at their desks.

"Hello, stranger." Morag always missed Mike for the four days a week she was in Wiltshire. "Watch out for *Mein Führer*; he's not in a great mood. I worry about him. Anyone would think that the Russians were halfway up the Thames."

Mike didn't bother to say that, on Tuesday, she had been underground with Leonard, imagining the Russians wiping out London. Not everything in the exercise had gone according to plan, so perhaps it wasn't surprising that Leonard was under pressure to sort things out. Morag was smiling innocently, unaware she would have been one of the tens of millions exterminated.

Mike's phoned buzzed, and she was summoned up to the top

floor. She headed up there, and when she arrived, she waited outside of Leonard's door to be called in. The red light above the door turned green, and she stepped inside.

"I see you survived the nuclear winter," he said, indicating that she should take a seat opposite him.

"Being in that bunker isn't really where I want to spend my last days on earth ... even with you."

"I'm not offended."

"What's that?" She was staring at what looked like a leathery body part on his desk.

"Relax."

"I hope that's not what I think it is."

"It's a signed basketball. Some jerk didn't deflate it before getting on the plane. Now it's gone flat."

"Can you blow it back up?"

"Not personally, and it's not top of my to-do list today." He moved it to the side of the desk, where it began to resemble a Dalí painting. "I've just had a message from POTUS via Langley."

"Really?" She wondered how often the President of the United States sent a personal message to a station chief, even London.

"He's worried about his pet project in Arizona. He doesn't want anyone screwing it up. What's the latest? I'm depending on you."

"There have been no more conversations and no other background noise. I'm still not sure that it's a real threat and we haven't got the wrong target."

"They've never mentioned microchips specifically, have they?"

"No, but what other new multi-billion-dollar factories are being built in Arizona?"

"Keep me in the loop. I need to tell him something later today when he wakes up. You've got four hours."

With that, the meeting was over, and she went downstairs to her desk, where her mind wasn't wholly on a group of apparently European terrorists who were intent on targeting the new Taiwanese-funded microchip factory near Phoenix in Arizona. This was a flagship project demonstrating how the President was bringing key manufacturing back to US soil. He had picked up on the threats and wanted them identified and eliminated.

Throughout the day, she pursued every new lead and avenue, but she was no closer to identifying the group behind the threat. By the time she left the office, she was excited about the meeting at 6.30pm with Terry.

The journey west to Chiswick took twenty-five minutes, and after arriving early, she locked up the bike on the road. She walked across the wide pavement, removing her helmet. The Leather Bottle hadn't changed. It was a drinkers' pub, and she was greatly relieved that it hadn't been converted into a trendy wine bar or restaurant. The memories of her time when she had been seconded to Five Eyes nearby flooded back.

CHAPTER FOUR

If wine bars are always bright and cheery, the pubs frequented by serious beer drinkers are always dark and melancholic – or perhaps this only applied to those patronised by Terry Bailey.

The Leather Bottle had diamond-pattern leaded-light windows that were clearly, or not so clearly, there to keep the daylight out. Anything wooden inside was painted in a heavy, brown gloss paint that, according to Terry, hadn't been available since William Hogarth lived nearby.

It had a bar halfway down one side wall, which created a back corner hidden from those entering. It was here that Terry liked to sit, with a large mirror giving him an early glimpse of anyone coming in before they saw him. Some habits never die.

He saw her reflection. She was carrying her helmet, unzipping her leather jacket and wearing a bandana on her head. There were only about twenty customers, but they had managed to create a warm atmosphere with their chatter and laughter. At the bar, she ordered an alcohol-free beer; once received, she carried it towards the back of the room.

She sat down opposite him after putting her helmet on the

padded bench. He was holding a half-finished pint with an empty packet of crisps neatly flattened and folded before him. Terry didn't get up, but he looked at her bandana, which triggered memories he had spent years suppressing. Neither offered any friendly words of welcome.

"You look brown."

His tanned and haggard face was hard to miss. "I've been to The Gambia ... birdwatching."

She thought he had aged terribly, with veins on his cheeks, bags under his eyes and a mop of dirty, grey hair. "Through choice?"

He smiled, remembering how she had never taken any prisoners and always shot from the hip, even in gentle banter, but this only served to remind him that he also hadn't taken prisoners, which was probably the reason they were having to meet.

"Yes, it was something on my bucket list ... now I'm retired."

She was thinking, *It must be a very deep bucket,* but she said, "I didn't know you'd retired."

His eyes dipped to the table, and it looked as if he were going to say something profound – perhaps an apology for the umpteenth time. He bit his lip, collected his thoughts and moved on. "Birds weren't the only thing I spotted in Banjul." He lifted his gaze, one hand on his pint glass.

She waited, hoping what he said next would be something other than what she had been dreading since receiving his message.

"I'm pretty sure I saw Jan driving a car. Relax, he didn't see me."

"But why would he be in Africa – especially as he's dead?"

"I don't know. I keep doubting myself."

"You're seeing ghosts. He's dead. You told me how he died. Remember?" She looked around, but there was no one in earshot.

This conversation wasn't what Mike needed. She had got through the last seven years in the knowledge that Jan was dead and there was nothing she could do. It had given her closure and had helped her cope with the death of her husband and her own injuries. The stress from the accident was part of the reason she had ended up bald.

It had affected her in other ways too. She was angrier, more intolerant to injustice and less precious about her own life. This had led her into serious danger on at least three occasions. Now what? She felt unnerved.

"I've had a couple of days to think about it. I'm ninety-nine per cent sure it was him."

Taking this all in, she picked up her beer bottle and took a large mouthful. "Jeez, Terry. If you're right, what was he doing in The Gambia? Following you seems to be a pretty high likelihood, don't you think?"

"But how? He doesn't know my name or anything about me apart from seeing my face for a split second in that bedroom before I shot him."

"Why? Why now after all this time?"

"I've been thinking about nothing else."

She lowered her voice and said, "But you saw him in the hotel room ... dead. How has he risen from the grave?"

He leant forwards. "I didn't stay to check his pulse or attend the funeral. I nicked his phone off the table to make it look like a robbery and got out of there ... and then I disappeared – fast."

"What can we do? What should we do?"

"Only you and I know what happened in Amsterdam. Shit, it was over seven years ago. There's no way he should be able to find you or me. I've been trying to stay calm." The shaking in his hands tended to suggest he hadn't been entirely successful, and drink was playing a big part in that.

"Did you ever discover his real name?"

"No. I found the room number at the hotel in a live report by" – he hesitated, avoiding referring to MI6 out aloud – "my bosses into what had happened to you and Dylan; that's all I needed."

He looked over beyond her, and she swivelled around to see who had come in, now on edge.

"We need to relax," she said, mostly to herself, "but stay alert."

"I hadn't intended to spend the rest of my life looking over my shoulder. I'd rather hoped for a quiet retirement. I wanted you to know for your own safety."

As they finished their drinks, they discussed how they should stay in touch. In this, Terry's experience in the field came to the fore, and he ended by saying he was moving out that evening. He was going to stay with his best friend, Brian, until this was all sorted.

"Leave it with me. I'll do some very discreet searching, and I mean *discreet*." She couldn't conceive of where to begin. Accessing the MI6 report on the whole episode using her CIA work laptop was not an option. It would trigger so many alarm bells. However, Mike always enjoyed a challenge, even if this might stretch her to the limit. She was looking for a man who supposedly died over seven years ago, and all she knew for certain was that he wasn't called Jan and he wasn't a Dutchman.

At 9.45pm, she arrived at her cottage in Rodbourne and wheeled the bike through the tunnel to her back gate. The lights were on in the house, and this was strangely reassuring after her meeting with Terry. For the whole journey, she had been looking in her mirrors and had even pulled off into a service station for a few minutes before rejoining the motorway.

She let herself into the kitchen. Wazz had prepared a ham salad for her, which was covered with cling film in the fridge. She was ravenous and thirsty, so the salad barely touched the sides once she sat down to eat.

They never stayed up late on Thursday nights after her long ride from London, but before going to bed, she preferred to take a little time to let her food settle. As she sat at the kitchen table with Wazz, she was faced with a dilemma: did she tell Wazz that someone was after Terry and, potentially, her? She decided to stay quiet until she knew if this was all real. After all, Terry may not be the most reliable witness, and it was seven years since he had seen Jan at the hotel.

"More stressful than usual?" Wazz asked.

Without mentioning the personal relevance, she said, "Well, on top of my main project, I've been asked to look for someone who died many years ago, and they don't even know his name."

"You mean find his grave? What are they going to do? Exhume him?"

"Who knows? Finding the grave would be a great result."

While they were having this general conversation, and despite her leaving out key facts, Wazz had given her an idea. Jan, if he had died from the shooting, must have been buried soon after. It was generally agreed that he wasn't a Dutchman, and therefore he could have been buried locally or his body flown anywhere in the world.

Tomorrow, she said to herself, *I'll start this fresh tomorrow with a clear head.*

After Wazz had told her all about his day spraying weedkiller from a backpack, they went to bed.

Mike boiled eggs for them both and put the bread in the toaster. She transferred the salt, pepper, and pots of marmalade and peanut butter to the table. The cutlery, plates and eggcups were already in place. Wazz could sense she was keen to start the day. It was June, and through the kitchen window, the elderflowers in the hedgerow at the end of the garden were in full bloom. It had been a hot, dry spring.

Ahead of him, he had a day replacing fence panels before the winds of autumn and winter began. He wasn't in a rush to set off, but he picked up the vibe that Mike wanted to search for this man or where he was buried.

With breakfast eaten, she jumped up to clear the table.

"So while I'm putting up fence panels that may well avert World War III, you'll be searching records of graveyards?"

"How did we end up here?" She shook her head.

"The Chapman and Derwent families have been feuding for decades, so they tell me. The fence between their two properties is a critical line: the Berlin Wall of Rodbourne."

She bent over and kissed him, envying his problems.

Twelve minutes later, she was alone and setting up her system. All night, she had thought through her plan of attack. This was perhaps one of her strengths while at work: the ability to place parts of a complex problem into a hierarchy of importance. For the task ahead of her, there was absolutely no way any human could investigate all the potential avenues, especially as she couldn't use most of the Agency infrastructure normally at her disposal.

Where was she to start? Particularly, where was she to start so as not to draw any attention to her searches?

She began with the burial records, obituaries and 'In memoriam' from local media around the Amsterdam area in the weeks after the date when Terry shot Jan. It wasn't complicated, but it was tedious plodding through the deaths of nonagenarians, babies, road-traffic victims, and the expected mix of the mundanely normal and frankly bizarre. The collapse of a circus tent killing a clown rehearsing his act delayed her for a few minutes.

To her surprise, she spotted a newspaper article on a suspected robbery where the victim had been shot. On digging deeper, she found it had happened in the hotel whose name Terry had discovered in a MI6 report. The name of the deceased was Henk Visser.

For hour after hour, Mike followed every mention of events that day, building up a mental picture. According to the assistant manager at the hotel, the maid had discovered the body of a male guest at 10.40am, and he had called the police.

From the coroner's report, she read that the victim had died from two gunshot wounds fired at close quarters. The coroner had assessed the time of death as twelve to eighteen hours before discovery, and there were no signs of a struggle. The police had noted there was no indication of forced entry to the room, so Henk Visser must have opened the door voluntarily. The reception desk at the hotel confirmed no duplicate keys had been requested or issued. They assumed the victim knew his killer or was happy to open the door to them.

CCTV footage from inside the lobby, outside the lifts and in the corridor outside room seventy-eight revealed a middle-aged man with curly, blond hair and black-framed glasses, who was wearing a coat but not carrying a bag. The man wasn't staying at the hotel, had never been seen before and was never identified. Mike could well imagine that it was Terry in heavy disguise.

There was insufficient data for the authorities to use facial recognition, and beyond the footage of the killer entering and leaving the hotel, there was no clue as to how he arrived or left. Searches of CCTV from nearby streets had revealed nothing.

Identifying all mobile phones used in the hotel or nearby at the critical time also showed up nothing. The marks on the bullets didn't match any on record.

Mr Visser was originally from near Bruges in Belgium and was described as a family man with one child. He lived with his wife near Leiden in the Netherlands, where he worked for an import-export business specialising in fruit and vegetables shipped from Africa and the Caribbean. The police were unable to establish a motive beyond theft. His phone couldn't be found, but his wallet hadn't been stolen, and searches of his laptop revealed no other leads. Mike knew immediately that Henk Visser was Jan, the man who had organised the shooting on the dyke.

The press, however, picked up on something else – his conviction as a teenager for exposing himself at a bus stop – but this fact had led the investigation nowhere.

As far as Mike could see, the case had never officially been solved or closed. Henk Visser was buried in the Groenesteeg cemetery in Leiden, the city where his family still lived. His wife had never remarried.

Wazz put his head around the door. "Am I disturbing anything?"

"What? Oh, no," was the automatic response, but it wasn't entirely accurate. Now Mike knew Henk Visser's name, she wanted to spend several hours confirming he was Jan the Dutchman, but this would have to wait.

"Mrs Derwent gave me two chicken pies, so there's no need to cook."

"Great," she replied, but she had forgotten all about the Derwents and where Wazz had been working today.

"Was today good or bad?"

"Actually, good." She allowed herself to accept that a huge weight had been lifted from her shoulders by discovering that Terry Bailey hadn't been lying or deluded, and he really had shot Jan in room seventy-eight. In truth, having seen the state of Terry, she was beginning to doubt everything he had ever said. It was difficult to work out what was real, fantasy or had been generated in some drunken stupor.

"Wow." Wazz wasn't used to this sort of answer; he always expected the worse.

"I haven't eaten." This was a much more typical response.

"I'll heat the pies."

CHAPTER FIVE

It was Saturday morning, and Wazz had driven off in his van to do the weekly shop at Tesco. Mike had asked him to buy burgers and buns as the weather forecast was good, and it might be one of the rare weekends when they could have a barbecue.

The moment he left, she dialled Terry's number. He picked up, and when he said his name, he sounded reasonably sober.

"Hi, I've got some good news. You can relax; Jan is long dead." She wanted to put him out of his misery as soon as possible.

"Really?" There was relief in his voice.

"I'll give you all the details when we next have a drink, but I thought you'd like to know."

"Thank you ... thank you. I'm sorry I panicked. It would be great to have a drink under less stressful circumstances."

"His real name was Henk Visser, and he was a Belgian, if you're interested. I can give you the plot number in the cemetery if you really need to check for yourself."

"No; no, thank you. I'll take your word for it." He let out a long breath. "I've never heard or seen that name."

"Terry, you don't have to keep thanking me. It's me who should thank you."

"Actually, I have something I'd like to give you. Are you up on Thursday? I could meet you at the pub."

"You don't need to."

"I want to."

"I hope it's nothing big, as I'm on the motorcycle?"

"No, it's very small."

"OK, 6.30pm as before. I can't stay long. It's a long ride home."

"Excellent. I can go back to my place now. Brian will be pleased. He's a painter contributing to a big exhibition coming up at the Hayward Gallery. The house is full of his work, and I'm in the way."

"Now I'll get back to my day job. See you on Thursday."

The call ended, and she settled down in front of her laptop, on which a series of messages and new leads on her microchip project had come in. She scrolled through them, but nothing was urgent, and everything could wait until Monday. It was too easy in her job to get sucked in and end up working twenty-four hours a day, seven days a week. Despite the praiseworthy objective of enjoying her downtime, she still managed to spend over forty-five minutes undertaking what she called 'scrolling through'.

At this point, a loud tapping could be heard from the kitchen.

She ran out of the lounge towards the back door, shouting, "*Shoo!*" and waving her arms.

The peacock, a regular visitor who was in love with his reflection, stared in through the lower glass panels. As she approached, it strutted off up the garden path, displaying its affrontery. It slowed almost to a stop before pushing its way through the hedge at the bottom.

Mike needed to clear away the breakfast things before Wazz

returned. She didn't wash up the plates, cups and cutlery, but she stacked them in the dishwasher. This would annoy him, and the conversation about her single-handedly dragging Britain into the twenty-first century might require another airing.

She collected the bread crusts from the drainer, opened the back door and threw them out for the birds. The fact that this sent out mixed messages to the peacock was lost on her. It was perhaps for the best that she didn't have kids.

As she stepped back into the kitchen, Wazz came in through the front door, carrying two hessian shopping bags.

"How was the store?"

"Busy, but I got everything on the list."

She ran over and kissed him.

He lifted the two bags onto the table. "You're in a good mood. Anything I've done? It's always good to know so I can try to repeat it."

"No, the news I had yesterday has taken some pressure off me."

"You mean you've found the grave of the person you were looking for?"

"Actually, yes. I can finally close that case."

Keith Herring let out an oath under his breath and leant on his wedge – a risky business given that he was a big man.

He had attempted a pitch shot onto the ninth green at Staunton Grange Golf Club in Surrey, but he had succeeded only in reaching a deep bunker. There was a rake in the bottom, which should have been left on the grass at the top, and he moved it without awarding himself a penalty. Reaching the green, he stepped out from the hazard and stomped his shoes. There was some sand on his pink-and-white shirt, which he dusted off.

This was a very exclusive club with only 120 members, including half the royalty of Europe. It also had always offered visiting rights to certain high-ranking members of the FCDO, the secret services and the military.

It was Wednesday, 17th June, and he was a guest of Gordon Overton, a senior controller at MI6. They weren't there only for the golf among the pines and heathland. Keith lifted his white sun visor and wiped the sweat from his face, where his cheeks and jowls were almost always showing a blue five o'clock shadow whatever the time of the day, which was a throwback to some Armenian grandfather of his. Gordon, by contrast, was blond with an annoying quiff, which he constantly flicked out of his eyes. Most people would agree that the quiff wasn't the most annoying thing about him; his snobbery and condescension usually came near the top.

"How was Hereford?" Gordon asked as they walked up onto the large, flat green. There was no one in sight and probably no more than ten people on the whole course.

"Good. It's on schedule and almost ready to receive the machine." He didn't need to describe which machine; there was only one that mattered, and it was currently being built in Holland. It was very big at seventeen feet wide – the size of two luxury coaches parked side by side – and incredibly sensitive to movement. Keith had been to the factory site in Hereford to see the floating concrete floor on which it would sit; this would absorb the tiniest vibration, whether from an aircraft overhead or the meekest of earth tremors. When positioned in the inner sanctum, it would be serviced by robots only, as no humans would enter and, more importantly, no dust would either. When commissioned, it would laser the trillions of transistors onto the wafer-thin discs to make the next generation of microchips.

"Do you have a provisional delivery date?"

"No, but I'll discuss that tomorrow. I'm going to Holland.

Whichever date is set, it will be weather dependent. There's nothing I can do about that."

Just outside Breda, two machines were being built: one for use in Arizona and one for Commicron's new factory in Herefordshire. They were identical and weighed sixty tons each. The biggest problem in a long list of difficulties facing both the USA and the UK was how to transport them. They were extremely sensitive to vibration and other damage, therefore sending them by boat across the North Sea or the Atlantic was too risky.

The machines were purposely exactly seventeen feet wide so the Americans could fly theirs in a Lockheed C-5 Super Galaxy from Breda to Phoenix in Arizona. In transit, the machine would sit on a bespoke platform intended to remove some of the movement during the flight. Monitoring the weather – and, in particular, the jet stream – would be critical. The problems would only worsen after it had been unloaded at Phoenix. There would have to be a 120-mile road journey to the factory.

The British had taken a different approach. They were intending to use an airship.

A French company had developed a new helium-filled dirigible, as it was known, which could carry up to sixty tons. It would transport the machine slung beneath it, and it would take off directly from the factory near Breda and travel at up to sixty-two miles per hour to Hereford, where it would lower its load through a sliding opening that had specifically been left in the roof of the new factory. Thereafter, the room would be sealed and every speck of dust removed. While this method reduced all the potential shocks and vibrations to the minimum, it had one huge downside: it was at the mercy of the wind.

To this factor could be added the unfortunate geography of the Dutch coast, English Channel and South East England. The route would take it due west, going across London and through the airspace of at least two major airports – possibly any of Gatwick, City, Heathrow, Luton or Stanstead. It would fly at

10,000 feet and not be as manoeuvrable as an aircraft. In a direct line, the distance was 320 miles, and it would take six hours even in perfect conditions; however, any wind would seriously add hours to this total.

"Have the RAF boys been in contact?" Gordon had taken out his putter.

"Yes, and Air Traffic Control and HM Customs and the Met Office and ..." Keith waved his own putter in the air to indicate that the list was extensive. Nevertheless, he wasn't complaining and welcomed that the military was going to accompany the airship with at least one helicopter for the whole journey once it was in British airspace.

After halving the hole, they walked to the next tee.

"Any more chatter on the airwaves?" Keith was eager to know if there were any more details on the threats that had been identified by GCHQ.

"We're liaising with our American chums in London. They're picking up similar vibes."

Keith winced at the word 'vibes'. Avoiding vibrations from project inception to full operation was costing him over £100 million. "Who's behind these threats?"

"We're not sure." Gordon was big on using the royal 'we'. "They're hiding their tracks well, but I'm sure that, between us all, we have all the bases covered. The fact that you're transporting it from factory to factory without touching the ground makes all our lives easier ... unlike for my American counterparts."

"I certainly wouldn't want to be taking it by plane and road." Keith pressed his tee into the ground, placed a ball on it and surveyed the fairway ahead of him. It was a picture-perfect view, and he had trouble believing he was less than twenty miles from London.

Although he drove straight down the middle and chipped onto the green, Gordon managed to hook it in into the bracken, where he hacked it out but only as far as the short rough. Who would get their ball into the hole first? There were so many routes to the same destination, and some more perilous than others.

While Keith putted off the green and down the slope, cursing gently, Mike was doing a bit of research in her house before setting off for a night at Carol's place in London. Originally, the conversation that had drawn the attention of the main intelligence services to a threat to the new microchip factories was from an intercepted phone call in Arizona. It sounded as if a group was intending to hack into the companies' systems and demand a ransom. However, she and her British colleagues had found subsequent indications that this was more of a threatened physical attack on the new machines or the power supply into the factory.

Mike had taken a leading role for the Agency in this because all the internet traffic was in Spanish, her speciality, and it appeared to originate in London. Leonard was under pressure from on high to identify the threat so it could be dealt with before the US machine left the factory in Breda.

Alone at her kitchen table, she did allow herself to be distracted for a few minutes before she packed up and set off on her weekly bike ride up the A303 and around the M25; the journey always gave her time to think.

Terry Bailey's wild goose chase had proved to be just that – a panic about nothing. Jan, or Henk Visser as she now had to call him, was dead. He hadn't been in The Gambia or anywhere for seven years. However, stirring everything up had meant Mike had begun to think again about what had taken place, about old colleagues whose names she had forgotten and about what had truly happened to the cocaine-smuggling project. Had it really just been aborted by the Colombian cartel? She knew of their new routes into Europe via Málaga and Bordeaux, but there had been no reprisals from the Dutch fiasco – just silence.

Perhaps to achieve complete closure, she decided to phone a Dutch colleague, Jakob, and ask how he was after all this time and if there had been any aftershocks. It took her a few minutes to find a new phone number for him and pluck up the courage to call.

Once the call had been made, there were a few minutes of general gossiping before she asked about Henk Visser. Despite having to talk in a coded way, he said that Visser had been lazy; basically, he hadn't concealed where he was staying from the intelligence services. He had been buried quickly by his family, who had never come to the authorities' attention again.

Jakob also confirmed that the smuggling network had been closed down immediately. That route was never used again to the knowledge of the Dutch authorities and the European Union Drugs Agency (EUDA). All Dylan's and her hard work had been successful in that regard – if at enormous personal cost.

He asked about her health and what she was doing now, but as in all such conversations, there was a level of self-protection and censorship that had to be used. The only thing that mattered was that she now felt complete and utter closure; it was a surprisingly uplifting feeling.

She had, of course, not mentioned Terry, but Jakob wouldn't have known his real name anyway and certainly not about him shooting Henk Visser.

With the tightness around her heart – which she hadn't realised had been there all these years – now loosened, she was looking forward to her trip to London. She would communicate all this to Terry when she met him tomorrow evening at The Leather Bottle.

As she went upstairs to grab her things, she was wondering about this small item he was so keen to give her.

CHAPTER SIX

"Drones." Mike opened her arms wide to show what she was saying was obvious.

"Sheesh." Leonard wasn't receiving her update with any enthusiasm, but he remembered just in time to thank her for her hard work: "But well done."

The deflated basketball was no longer on his desk. Peering around, she realised something else was missing. "What's different in here?"

"This blazer? It's new."

She stared at the dark-blue jacket with its gold buttons and his grey pants. It looked as if he had slept in them. "Your framed basketball shirt has gone."

He'd only had one personal item to accompany the standard issue pair of clocks showing the times in Washington and London on the otherwise bare office walls. Now this shirt had gone.

"New regulations. They've taken it away, along with the basketball, to scan it for microphones or botulism or ... something."

She had previously noted that there weren't even

photographs of his wife or daughter on his desk. His office was where he worked and ate – mostly the latter.

People, however, tended to underestimate him and his methods. He spoke in a soft American accent, he didn't care about his health or appearance, and he gave off an air of being slightly overwhelmed by life, but this belied a very experienced and effective head of station.

Mike thought she had him worked out, but she was never 100 per cent sure.

She continued with her update: "I don't have the name of the group, but we have several references to them buying drones in phone conversations. I can't find who's behind them at the moment."

"Chinese or Russian or Iranian. My money's on the Chinese. Are they going to use these drones at the factory outside Phoenix, or are they hitting the machine while it's being transported on the highway?"

"No idea. We're monitoring the group twenty-four seven. The Brits are on the case as well."

"Is this a terrorist group we've come across before but under a different name?"

"It could be. We've only hacked into some very short telephone conversations that appear to come from somewhere in the southern states: Arizona, New Mexico or Texas. There are dozens of possibilities, but remember that the group communicates in Spanish."

"Mexican? Cuban?"

"We're analysing the messages to see if it's Castilian Spanish or South American. We don't have enough yet."

"Are any of the threats against the Brits?"

"No, but your buddy Gordon Overton is getting excited. Our teams are working together."

"Do we have dates? I want this sorted before POTUS gets interested again."

"No. The Dutch say both machines will be available in three to six weeks."

"That's not much time if we're going to take out this group."

"I'm on it. I'll find them."

"If they bomb that factory or that machine, I'm toast, and you wouldn't want to have to work under a new director, would you?" He beamed like a self-satisfied frog.

"Uh, no." She had experienced a few weeks under an acting director, and this hadn't gone well – in fact, he had suspended her.

Mike knew she was scraping the bottom of the barrel when her attention had been drawn to a message picked up by Danish intelligence. It did indeed contain five keywords, but these weren't quite in the right order and definitely had no relevance to her project. So much of her life was spent lifting pebbles to see what was underneath when she mostly had no idea if she was on the right beach.

She went downstairs, collected her personal belongings and was already putting on her helmet while she was stepping out onto the street. A long bike ride lay ahead of her, but The Leather Bottle beckoned first.

After an easy journey through West London, she parked her bike and chained it up. The sky was overcast, but the weather forecast predicted no rain. Unlike the previous week, she wasn't apprehensive when she entered the pub and was instead wondering what Terry had to give her. The bar wasn't busy, and she recognised some of the faces from last Thursday, who were sitting at their favoured tables. Two men smiled at her.

The barman also nodded to her before waiting for her to choose. He also remembered her, but most people found her difficult to forget with her leather jacket, paisley bandana and carrying the matt-black helmet. He reached up for a glass and poured a non-alcoholic beer, trying not to stare into her dark-tourmaline eyes as he handed it over.

With pint in hand, she took the obligatory sip while walking around the bar to the back corner.

The table was empty. Being the first to arrive, she slid onto the bench to get a better view of his arrival. The interior of the pub reminded her of one in Boston, but something was indefinably different. She decided that it was the smell, which was probably coming from the slightly sticky carpet. The fact that it had a pattern not dissimilar from her bandana made her reconsider what she should wear on her bald head.

On a warm evening, it was tempting to take off the bandana, but the relief wasn't worth all the stares and comments.

Time dragged, the beer had disappeared from her glass, and another one didn't really appeal. It was 6.45pm, and she began to get irritated; after all, he only lived a couple of roads away, whereas she was facing a more-than-two-hour bike ride to Rodbourne.

At 7.00pm, she picked up her phone and called him. His phone was switched off.

Five minutes later, she had reached her limit. Terry was quite possibly drunk at home or in another establishment. She stood up, walked out of the bar and went across the street to her bike. After settling herself on her bike, with one last glance at the pub entrance, she rode off around the corner, heading for Harding Street.

Mike had never visited him at home, but she found it easily. He lived in a so-called 'garden flat' at the back of a Victorian house. His view of the rear garden, if it had actually warranted the effort, would have been achieved only by standing on a stool in the kitchen. In reality, he looked out onto a mossy brick retaining wall and the bumpers of cars parked on some crudely laid tarmac. Even this less-than-desirable view could be seen only through white metal security grilles.

Having pulled up and placed the bike on its stand, she walked down the damp steps to the basement. *If it's as wet as this in June, what will it be like in winter?* she wondered to herself.

After knocking on the door, she took a pace sideways to peer in through the windows. There were no lights and no sign of recent life. What looked like a bird book was open on the table and an upside-down wine glass was on the kitchen drainer; otherwise, the flat looked tidy if unused.

Mike rapped on the door more loudly and waited for a response. There was none.

She became conscious of a shadow above her. Two men in their twenties had emerged from a parked car and were peering down. They were in hoodies and sweatpants. Another knock resulted in no activity from inside.

"Do you know if he's out?" she asked, always assuming it was better to engage and take control in such situations.

"I don't think he's been around for a few days. Who's asking?"

"Mike ... he was going to give me something. He said he'd be in."

"We can give you something."

She didn't like the way this conversation was going. "I don't need anything, thanks."

"Nice bike." The taller of the two was standing next to it.

She was weighing up her options, which didn't look good. Still wearing her helmet was the only thing in her favour, at least she wouldn't bang her head on the floor as they beat seven bells of shit out of her.

"It gets me to work and back." She was managing to keep a level, confident voice.

"Pricey."

Mike had no idea what he was talking about, but she could

see no way out of the situation. Where was Wazz when she needed him?

"How do you know Terry?" the nearest man asked.

"What? We used to work together." She felt her fear ease slightly. There was hope if they knew Terry.

"He's not around."

"Do you know where he is? He was meant to meet me in the pub an hour ago."

"I haven't seen him for a couple of days."

"How do you know him?"

"I live up there." He nodded at one of the upper-floor windows.

"If he turns up, will you tell him Mike was here?" She began to climb the stairs, still waiting to be attacked.

"Sure."

She walked between them, trying to control her breathing. They were evidently out of their heads on something and had been sitting in a car to share whatever it was. The bigger man leant back against one of a row of plastic recycling bins, unsteady on his feet. His face stretched slowly into a strange grimace, but he didn't speak.

Mike swung a leg over the bike, keeping all her movements both slow and unprovocative. She rode out between the houses as a beaten-up car drove in. There were three more cokeheads inside on their way to join the party. She had timed her departure to perfection, although it didn't feel like that. Her heart was thumping inside her leather jacket as she rode to the end of Harding Road.

She stopped by the pavement and pulled out her phone. Terry didn't answer, and there were no messages. She called Carol and asked if she could stay another night. With her heart rate nowhere near normal, Mike made her way northeast for about twenty minutes.

When Mike had first described Carol to Wazz, she had used the words 'short', 'bubbly' and 'lucky'. While the first two epithets were accurate, the third was open to interpretation, which Wazz had pointed out immediately while shaking his head. Both Carol's parents had been killed in a car accident, after which she had inherited a house in London that she could never have afforded on an orthopaedic nurse's salary. Instead of selling it for around £2 million, she had continued working while letting out two of the bedrooms. Another, which was really a small box room, she used as storage, but she let Mike use the single bed within it whenever she wanted, as long as she put up with the cramped space and the piles of stuff.

It was after 8.00pm when Mike turned up, explaining there had been a change of plan. She was pressured into joining the others for a spontaneous meal they had already ordered, which would be delivered in thirty minutes. While waiting, she had called Wazz to explain she would be down a day later, so he shouldn't miss her too much. Nothing to do with Terry was mentioned.

Despite enjoying the meal and company, Mike was on edge. She had a bad feeling.

Would Terry have got so drunk that he missed turning up at The Leather Bottle? It was possible, but she felt he had been excited to give her something. It wasn't like he had to travel far; it was only 500 yards away from his flat. The fact that he hadn't been around for a couple of days – according to his spaced-out neighbours – added to this feeling of disquiet. She told everyone around the dining table that she needed an early night and then made her way to her little room where she had some searching to do.

Sitting on her bed with the laptop on her knees, she looked for anyone called Brian who was an artist contributing to a temporary exhibition at the Hayward Gallery. It didn't take her long; there was only one, and his name was Brian Morton Rosie. Finding his telephone number also wasn't difficult, and she called him immediately.

"Brian Rosie," he answered in a mild Scottish accent, which she failed to notice.

"Hello, Brian, my name's Mike Kingdom. We've never met, but I'm a friend of Terry Bailey. I was meant to meet him this evening at The Leather Bottle, but he never showed up. Do you know where he is?"

"I don't; he stayed here a wee while back, but he told me he had to be at his flat to receive something ... some package."

"Brian, I used to work with Terry, and I'm a bit worried about him. His drinking is getting worse. I've just been to his flat, and it looks like he hasn't been there for a couple of days. Do you have a key?"

There was a pause while Brian thought everything through. "I do. I look after the place when he's on his travels. I've known him a long time. I know where he worked, by the way."

"Good," she said. "It's good you know where he worked. You probably can guess why I might be worried about him. It's also good you have a key."

"He was a wee tad stressed when he was here. He was scared to go back to the flat until someone said it was all clear. After that, he cheered up."

"Brian, it was me who told him it was all clear. I think I'm beginning to regret that."

"Where are you now? London?"

"About twenty minutes from his flat. I'm staying with a friend."

"Shall we go round to his place together?"

"Oh, that would be fantastic. When?"

"I'm in the middle of something right now. I've got a large

painting to finish for an exhibition. Can we meet there at 8.00am tomorrow?"

"No problem, and, Brian, thanks for trusting me and for helping."

"Terry's been a great mate of mine for many, many years. I'm a bit worried too."

CHAPTER SEVEN

Mike arrived around the back of the Victorian house at the same moment that a tall, grey-haired man with a scarf tied around his neck was getting out of a car. She knew this was Brian, having spent some time checking him out online the previous evening. Apparently, he was well known for large oil paintings in a post-modernist style, which incorporated random pieces of fabric. Mike appreciated modern art, but to her eyes, it looked like he had accidentally got paint over the curtains while decorating the lounge wall. *Each to their own,* she had thought, but how long had it taken for him to settle on this style? It turned out he was sixty-two and had graduated from the Glasgow School of Art in 1985. He must have got through a lot of curtains.

Once the bike was on its stand, she took off her helmet and rested it on the seat. She retied a bandana around her head and walked towards him. They shook hands and said hello while he took out a key from his jacket pocket.

"Brian, thank you for trusting me. The world in which Terry and I work makes it hard to have normal conversations. You understand, I think?"

"I do, or perhaps I get how difficult it must be. He never tells me details or where he's travelling, but he always wanted me to know whom he worked for so he didn't need to explain why he was unable to tell me what he was up to. It's been a lot easier since he retired."

"I'm pleased. I hope he gets to do more birdwatching trips."

"Aye, he says that Costa Rica is next. Can't see the attraction myself."

"I've got a peacock that visits my garden. That's enough for me."

"That's lucky until they start screaming at 4am."

"He roosts somewhere else, I think, but I'd better stop encouraging him."

He smiled as they walked towards the back of the building. "All set?" he asked, perhaps for his own benefit.

Mike was fascinated by his beard, which was a random mix of black, white and grey hairs.

"Let's go. Lead the way." She had expected him to ask her a few questions, but he had obviously accepted that she was for real. It was unlikely Terry would have mentioned her name.

At the bottom of the stone steps, it smelled like a public urinal. The partygoers from the night before had probably failed to make it to their cars before needing to relieve themselves.

Brian put the key in the lock and leant against the door, knowing it was difficult to open. They stepped inside to be hit by an awful smell that was far worse than the improvised toilet outside. Mike held her nose, and Brian pulled his scarf up to beneath his eyes. No words were spoken.

The small hallway led to the kitchen. Nothing looked any different from when she had peered in the day before. The bird book was open on the table, and the wine glass had dried on the draining board.

Brian walked through the door to the lounge, but he turned rapidly and retched; he didn't need to say anything. Mike moved to follow him, but she knew what she'd find inside.

"I wouldn't, Mike," he suggested, but she had to see for herself.

Terry's body was spreadeagled on the floor in front of the sofa. There was congealed blood on his temple, but whether this was from hitting his head on the coffee table or from some blow, she had no idea. Neither of them bothered to check for signs of life; he was very obviously dead.

"What do we do?" Brian asked. "Call the police?"

"Yes, yes ... but give me two minutes to think."

Mike was pretty sure he had been murdered, and unfortunately, she had a very good idea who had done it. Her first thought was that the killer might still be in the flat. Her second thought was that, wherever the killer was, she might be next.

Locking the front door, driving off and ignoring what they had stumbled across wasn't a possibility. She had been seen the evening before, and they would both have been spotted today, either out of the dozens of windows nearby or on CCTV. They had to face the police, but should she call Leonard or, God forbid, Gordon Overton at MI6 – someone she hated? He would probably be involved anyway.

Her mind was all over the place, and she wondered what she should say to the police about her past and why she knew Terry. There was no point denying that he was in MI6; they'd find that out pretty fast and involve police officers with different security clearance levels as well as someone like Overton. What should she say was her involvement? Why was she there?

"Mike?"

"Yes, yes; sorry. There are so many things to think through ... complications ... connected with his old job. You understand?" But she had come to a conclusion. There was only one detail she needed to conceal from absolutely everyone: Terry had killed Henk Visser seven years ago and she had known all this time. "OK, you call the police. I need to call my boss. Let's get out of this room."

Brian went into the kitchen and began to dial the emergency services. He moved quickly to the back door.

Mike stayed there a few seconds longer, wondering where in the lounge or bedroom Terry had left the small thing he wanted to give her. She daren't touch anything, but the temptation was overwhelming. It was perhaps a relief that, even if she rummaged around, she had no idea what to look for. The smell swiftly drove her out of the room.

They waited for the police, with Brian sitting in his car, visibly shocked, and Mike standing next to her bike.

Glad of the fresh air and relative privacy, she phoned Leonard's PA, Lana.

Keith Herring had transferred from the private plane, a Cessna Citation, to a helicopter. It didn't land at the factory outside Breda but a mile away. Security was typically Dutch: understated but robust and efficient. No aircraft could fly directly over the factory or in a small exclusion zone, so he had been transferred to a Mercedes car. As he was being driven the short distance, his host, Willem, pointed out the upgraded but well-hidden military facility, which would shoot down anyone or anything that threatened the factory. It was a Category A* site according to the Dutch government.

Very soon, his own facility in Hereford would have the British equivalent protecting the airspace above it. For such an important and strategic project, the government wanted the very latest systems to be installed.

"Why do you need that level of protection, Willem? You aren't producing chips here."

"I know; that's true, but we're making many different pieces of equipment for the Dutch military and secret services. Drones are the new problem, both for commercial espionage and if anyone wants to attack us. If you fly a drone here, it's jammed or shot down."

As they walked into reception, Keith was struck again by the understated interior design of the whole complex. There were no pointless sculptures, no fighter jet slung from the ceiling and no arty photographs of microchips. Every wall was painted in one of two tones of warm grey.

They got into a golf cart, which took them to the end of Zone 1, traversing almost a quarter of a mile along warmly lit corridors. There were no stark fluorescent lights. At the interface with Zone 2, they were required to put on a white coat, safety goggles and ear protectors, although they weren't scheduled to go into any of the critical rooms.

Their next destination was a first-floor viewing platform behind glass, from which Keith was given a panoramic view of three robots at work: machines building machines. He had to peer around to spot a single human being in this part of the factory.

"What do you think?" Willem was keen to hear from his client.

"It's enormous." Even though he knew what to expect, the size of 'Nelly' – which his machine had inevitably been nicknamed – took his breath away. He had seen it at several stages of construction, but this was always as a skeleton, never with the finished outer casing.

"Let's go and have a coffee. We need to speak about dates and logistics."

They returned to the golf cart, and for a few minutes, they were driven around while they discussed the minor refinements that had been necessary. When they were back somewhere near reception, they left the main corridor, stopped the golf cart, and stepped out of it and into the cool of Willem's office.

"So, as discussed, it'll technically be finished on 26th June. That's one week from today. We have two weeks in which we run tests with the machine at full power. I don't foresee any problems, but who knows. I won't tempt fate."

"The French want one week's notice, but it's all dependent on the wind and rain. The long-term weather forecast isn't much use three weeks in advance. Let's set a date and move it back as much as is needed."

"You were checking how long it will take for the airship to arrive here?"

"They say three hours, and they'll leave at 6am. They have to get air traffic control clearance from France and the Netherlands, plus from the UK authorities for the second leg."

"In that case, we'll open the doors at 8.00am and have it outside by 8.30am. They've provided the net already. We'll roll it out in its protective case. They estimate it'll take less than half an hour to attach the twelve cables to the ... what are they called?"

"They call them 'eyelets'. I know, I know; it's a stupid name."

"They're this big." Willem widened his hands to demonstrate. "They'll never fail, I'm sure."

"If we confirm this plan, it means the airship will leave here after 9.30am, and depending on the wind direction, it should be over the factory in Hereford six or seven hours later. That gives us a few hours to lower the thing through the roof and onto its platform."

Willem looked at Keith in admiration. No one had ever moved one of his machines using an airship, but it made sense. It avoided planes, trains, ships and lorries – all of which would bump and vibrate for hours or days. It was that very last stage – lowering it through the roof – that was frightening Willem, but he was pleased to say that this was not his problem. "Do you have a plan B?"

"You mean at Hereford? Yes, we'll lower it onto the car park and bring in a tank transporter or a crane. We have a Liebherr LTM 1750-9.1 crane with a 204-ton counterweight on standby.

Nelly weighs the same as a Chieftain tank, and they lift those easily. However, I'd rather we don't have to use plan B."

"That's why it's plan B."

Keith managed a smile, but while the site at Hereford had so many advantages, its road access was challenging for wide or very heavy loads, and this is what made the airship option so attractive. It would be difficult enough to get the crane there with its nine axles and eighteen wheels.

"We won't know the exact flight path until it leaves here," Keith confirmed. "Crazy, isn't it? A RAF helicopter will escort us in British airspace all the way to Hereford. For the four SAS lads on board, it will be a slow ride home."

"I'm sure the British public will be out in their thousands to watch such a spectacle. It'll be all over social media. They'll be lining the route, cheering and waving."

Under the possible flight path, Daniel Drinkwater was scarifying the lawn in the garden of his red-brick farmhouse near Stratford-upon-Avon. He hated the moss and wanted it removed. It was a thankless task, but he refused to have a gardener, whom he would have regarded as an intrusion. The exercise was no bad thing, and he enjoyed the time to think. It wouldn't take long as the area of grass was small, with most of the garden put down to vegetables. To the side was the chain-link fence surrounding a tarmac tennis court.

He had lived there for over ten years, having bought the place for its privacy; it was surrounded by red-brick walls. In fact, the house, outbuildings and perimeter were all fashioned from the same local brick, along with slate tiles. It had paddocks to the rear and was a very desirable property.

Behind the greenhouse, near a group of birch trees, he emptied the final bag of arisings onto his open compost heap.

While he had been walking back and forth across the lawn, a decision had been made.

He looped the electric cable around the handle of the scarifier several times and pushed it towards a sizeable garden shed and workshop converted from two old stables. Adjoining them, and configured out of two more stables and a tack room, was a man cave. This was his haven. He closed the wooden door and walked to the back, savouring the deadened silence. The room was an eclectic mix of old bits of furniture mixed with bric-a-brac he had rescued or taken a fancy to. Today, he chose an old barstool, which gave him somewhere to perch and look out of a window, but this wasn't until he had tilted an ugly and heavy concrete garden ornament in the shape of a windmill and retrieved a mobile phone that had been hidden in a cavity underneath.

As with many of his calls, it was important that his wife didn't hear and that there was no trace of it.

He plugged the phone into a charger and composed himself. The information he had been sent earlier from the Netherlands had changed everything. Timing; it was always all about timing.

CHAPTER EIGHT

"Sheesh! Mike ..." Leonard was lost for words.

"What do I tell the police?"

"The truth would be good, unless you murdered him."

"I didn't murder him."

"I'll get someone over from the embassy ASAP."

"I don't need counselling."

"Hey, I meant to vouch for you and look after your interests. It's protocol."

"Oh."

"Why were you at his house in the first place?"

"He contacted me out of the blue about ten days ago and said he had something for me, something small. I don't know what it is."

"After seven years? That's a load of baloney."

"It's true."

"Please tell me you did not break into his house."

"No, of course not" – although most people who knew Mike would see this as a valid question – "I rang a friend of his, someone not in the business, who has a key to his flat. We found his body together. He rang the police."

"I'll ring Gordon Overton. He might as well be given the heads-up."

"Why does it have to involve him? Terry was retired."

"Yes, but there are rules, regulations, legacy commitments ... what you'd call 'irritations'."

There were the sounds of police sirens in the distance. "I think I need to go."

"Try not to get involved. Try not to upset anyone. Give the police my name if there's any problem, but hopefully, it won't come to that."

"I have my ID card with me."

Just then, the peace was disturbed by two police officers walking into the car park.

Some hours later, Mike was in a room at Uxbridge Police Station while Brian was being interviewed separately. Both had given witness statements and provided fingerprints to eliminate them from enquiries. It had been made clear that they weren't suspected of anything at this stage and the cause of death hadn't been established. It was a suspicious death of a retired MI6 agent.

The flat had been sealed off, and scene-of-crime officers (SOCOs) were photographing and collecting evidence, in as much as there was any. They hadn't found a weapon, but there was congealed blood on the edge of the coffee table. Officers were searching through the gardens and bins in the area in case a weapon had been thrown away. This had to be done irrespective of the final established cause of death; it couldn't be left for a number of days when any evidence would have been removed or compromised in some way.

Mike was being asked questions by an inspector from Counter Terrorism Command accompanied by an MI6 liaison officer. There was no one else in the room, and somebody from the US Embassy had yet to turn up.

"Miss Kingdom, we're now off the record. This isn't being filmed or recorded. You understand?" The inspector was in his forties with sunken cheeks and a long nose and ears. He reminded Mike of a giraffe. His name was Wainwright.

"Sure."

"Given whom Terry Bailey worked for and whom you currently work for, is there anything you want to say in private?"

"No, it's like I told the other policeman. I worked with Terry briefly on a project seven years ago and hadn't heard from him since until he made contact ten days ago. We met in The Leather Bottle last Thursday evening for one drink. He told me he was retired. Then, on Saturday, he asked me to call in there again because he had something small to give me. He never said what it was. I reminded him that it needed to be small as I had to carry it on my bike down to Wiltshire ... where I live."

"Can you think of anything he might want to give you?"

"No." She shrugged her shoulders.

"Did you discuss work, old or new, when you met?"

"No, he seemed a bit lonely. I got the impression that he wanted some company and to chat." There was no way Mike was going to mention Henk Visser or that Terry had thought he had seen the man in The Gambia, but she had mentioned the small gift to demonstrate a reason for meeting again so soon.

"Did he say he was worried about anything or anyone? Any threats or enemies?"

"No. Why would he tell me? I work for a different organisation."

"It's all a bit odd, don't you think? Why you?"

"I had the feeling he had been drinking a lot lately. I'm not sure he was thinking completely straight."

"Was he drunk when you met?"

"Not really; he told me himself that he was drinking too much and was still feeling the effects of his stroke, but he was mostly coherent."

"Is there something to do with your last project that he might have wanted to discuss or something relevant he might want to give you?"

"It was seven years ago. We haven't been in contact until ten days ago."

The man from MI6, who was using the name Quilley, said, "I haven't had time to read the files, but that operation didn't end well, did it?"

"No." Mike stared at him with her dark eyes.

"What happened that might be relevant to his murder, if he *was* murdered?"

"Nothing." She was now beginning to tighten up inside.

"Terry Bailey didn't simply ring you out of the blue because he fancied a drink and some company. He had a reason, and the last time you worked together was on the Dutch project ... which didn't end well."

She had to use all her resources to control her emotions, otherwise she would rip off her bandana and rant about the shooting, the crash, Dylan and her own disfigurement. "There was a big US and UK team. It wasn't only Terry and me."

"The project was aborted after your husband was killed and you were injured." It was said as a statement not a question and without any sympathy. He was provoking her.

She said nothing, but she reached down to rub the scar on her left calf.

"It was all Terry's mistake. Did you blame him?" he continued probing.

"For what? Trusting a double agent?"

"It led to the accident." Quilley seemed remarkably well-informed for someone who hadn't read the files.

"It wasn't an accident. My husband was shot" – she was glaring at him with a quiet intensity – "and it was your lot, MI6, who fucked up."

The inspector intervened: "You do see that we have to explore all possibilities, don't you? If Mr Bailey was murdered, you had a motive."

"What motive?"

"Revenge for what Mr Quilley just said happened in Holland."

"What? For something that happened seven years ago?"

"You could have called him to have a drink in the pub, arranged a follow-up meeting and killed him in his flat. You also found the body."

"That's *not* what happened. *He* contacted *me*." She was almost shouting.

"We haven't checked his phone records yet. I'm sure we'll see that you're right."

She bit her lip.

In fact, they wouldn't find a record of a phone call from him as there was none. He had emailed her through the general work system. Although he had written cryptically, this wasn't a message she wanted to explain to anyone. The first phone record would be of her phoning him.

Things weren't looking good, and she may well need to come clean about everything. At the moment, she was the chief suspect in what may well turn out to be a murder inquiry. Mike was feeling overwhelmed; this had crept up on her so quickly from nowhere.

Dealing with the British police, however, wasn't her main fear. If Terry had been murdered, she knew who the prime suspect was: the man whom he had been ninety-nine per cent sure he had seen in The Gambia and who may now, for whatever reason, be after her.

The man Terry had killed in the hotel room was Henk Visser, of that there was no doubt. Nevertheless, it looked as if his real target – Jan the Dutchman – was still at large and had somehow discovered Terry's name. If he had found and killed Terry, why couldn't he find and kill her?

Mike was swiftly debating whether to tell Inspector Wainwright and Quilley from MI6 now or whether to wait and do some investigating herself. What was perhaps the sensible course of action – speaking to Leonard – didn't pass through her mind, or at least it didn't until she thought about where she was going to sleep that night. It was Friday and almost midday. She had to decide whether to ride back to Wiltshire or stay another night at Carol's. This was all presuming that the police released her; she didn't know the British system.

"Are you intending to ride back to Wiltshire after we've finished?" It was as if the inspector had been reading her mind.

"Am I free to go?"

"We've gone over most things we need until we know the cause of death and whether he was murdered. He may have slipped while drunk and bashed his head. We won't hear anything more until next week at the very earliest, I expect. It will probably be very much longer."

"I'll ride home. It'll do me good. I was intending to come back next Wednesday evening and work in the office on Thursday." She had already explained her weekly routine.

"I'm sure it's all been very stressful." Inspector Wainwright was displaying the empathy missing from his co-investigator Quilley. "We have your phone number. As we always say at this time, please don't leave the country or disappear off the radar."

"Thank you, I understand." She was starting to think calmly again.

"You will be careful, won't you, Miss Kingdom?" Quilley managed to make this sound menacing.

Riding a motorbike for two hours to Wiltshire, especially a beautiful Ducati, was exactly what she needed.

The Friday traffic leaving London for the south-west had begun, but she roared past any queues and raced along the numerous stretches of open road. This also gave her the opportunity to lose anybody tailing her.

Although she was distracted by such things as broken-down caravans and cows passing single file across a bridge above her, she always returned to her predicament – or was it two predicaments? How was she to explain away everything without revealing that Terry had shot Henk Visser, and secondly and more importantly, who had killed Terry?

For most of the way to Rodbourne, the one thought that wouldn't leave her head was that if Henk Visser was Jan the Dutchman, he was dead and buried. Who'd care about finding Terry, and possibly finding her, seven years later? It seemed so very unlikely.

By the time she was riding through the chalk downland, with its rolling fields of wheat and barley, this thought had refined itself: Henk wasn't Jan, and this meant Jan was still out there. It began to look as if it really was Jan whom Terry had seen out of the taxi window in The Gambia.

On driving into her village, she had hit a mental block. If she followed her logic, there was a problem because there was no way Terry could have spotted the real Jan in The Gambia; after all, he didn't know what Jan looked like – or his name for that matter. Terry thought Henk was Jan, which was why he had shot the man. So who was in that car in Banjul driving in the opposite direction?

In the main street, Jess the landlady was about to enter The Green Feathers and waved to Mike; there was an hour until opening time.

"See you later," Mike called out, having taken ten years to take this odd British expression on board. For once, it was true; she would definitely need a drink once Wazz was home from work.

The two friendly Muscovy ducks swam away up the ditch that ran along Church Lane as she pushed the bike across the footbridge towards her back gate and then through it. The metallic clunk of the hasp and staple lock closing behind her was strangely reassuring. It meant she was home.

"Howdy, stranger!" Wazz was at the bottom of the vegetable patch, collecting blackcurrants in a bowl.

"Oh, hi. I didn't expect you back yet."

"I finished at 4.00pm. How was London?"

"Well, I wasn't arrested."

He relaxed his arm carrying the bowl, and the berries almost fell out. "Was there a risk of that?" He walked towards her and gave her a kiss.

"Unfortunately, yes."

He opened the back door, as she had the helmet in her hand, had the large rucksack on her back and was carrying a bag from inside one of the paniers.

"Speeding?"

"No, murder."

"Oh, right." He thought that she was joking.

She put down her things and began unzipping her jacket. "That's why I stayed the extra night at Carol's."

"To murder someone?"

"It's a long story."

He put the bowl of berries on the drainer. "Tell me all about it."

The next hour flew by while she filled him in on almost everything that had happened, leaving out anything related to her work and particularly what happened seven years ago. Wazz was a good listener, but even he needed to interject with questions. It was all so unexpected.

Her phone rang, and she jumped up and walked into the lounge. "I need to take this."

"I'll close the door." Wazz knew the rules, but he was severely tempted to listen.

"You're back home?" Leonard began as soon as she had answered the call.

"Please don't ask me to come back up to London. I'm a bit stressed."

"No, not unless the police insist on it. I hear you're the prime suspect?"

"Who told you?"

"Your friend Mr Overton phoned me to gloat. He wanted to know why my agents were killing his agents."

Gordon Overton had severely pissed off Mike on a previous job. Their personalities were about as incompatible as it was possible to imagine. There's no way she could have him as her controller. How the British case officers put up with him, she had no idea. Fortunately, he hadn't been around seven years previously; Terry had been under a different boss.

"What did he actually say?" She presumed that Quilley had updated Overton.

"That the police think you have motive and opportunity and you used his friend to discover the body with you."

"BS. You know better than anyone what happened in Holland."

In fact, she realised, he only knew up to the point that Dylan was shot and she was repatriated to London.

"He also said the cause of death hasn't been determined yet."

"He was a drunk who was messed up in the head by years in our business. I'm sure you've met a few. It looked like he fell over and bashed his head on a table."

"Are you keeping it together? Do you need any help?"

"Yes, and no ... thank you."

"Let the police do their job, and I'll see you next Thursday. Don't get involved and mess things up." He knew that there was zero chance of this not happening.

CHAPTER NINE

Over the weekend, Wazz managed to distract Mike by giving her something to complain about. He draped the lounge furniture and carpets with dustsheets, ready to freshen up the walls and woodwork.

Despite her moaning, she took to the task and found it therapeutic. She wasn't the fastest painter, but she enjoyed undertaking something that had finite limits and a realistic chance of success. He suggested she should apply the emulsion to the walls. This was perhaps a safer bet than the undercoating and glossing of the skirting boards and architraves around the doors.

Wazz was tall enough that he could reach everywhere; therefore, he gave her the small portable step, a tray and a roller. Very little paint ended up on her bandana and old pair of dungarees, although the dust sheets did resemble a work by Brian Morton Rosie.

Music was blaring from the radio, and the time passed quickly. By Sunday evening, they were clearing up and looking forward to a drink after admiring their hard work. They went along to The Green Feathers to be ignored by Jess and to chat to the local Young Farmers.

On Monday morning, after Wazz had gone to work, Mike settled down, reasonably calm and refreshed, to spend three days trying to crack her main work problem: identifying the threat to the microprocessor factory in Arizona.

Over a period of about four hours, she used some of the world's most powerful computer processing to search for twenty-three keywords. These were words such as 'Breda', 'Herefordshire', 'Phoenix', 'airship' and 'factory', which were very likely to appear in various combinations within any messages sent by the group. It was while searching everywhere for these words that Mike had first discovered they were communicating in Spanish. Annoyingly, it didn't give her whole messages and certainly not more than one. The code effectively changed with every message.

Eating an open sandwich for lunch, she had a breakthrough on one element, but although this might have been rewarding at a personal level, she wasn't sure how far it moved her forwards.

The nickname or handle 'Gordon Moore' appeared in a message that contained six of the keywords. This stood out because he had an apparently English name, but the snippets of messages were all in Spanish.

At her laptop, she tapped in 'Gordon Moore', and most references came up with the man who, in 1965, was co-founder of the computer company Intel and became immortalised in Moore's law, in which he suggested the concept that the number of transistors on a microchip would double every two years. He had proved incredibly prescient.

She stopped to digest all of this.

Why choose this nickname or alias? Was the ringleader of the group attempting to slow or reverse the momentum in the world of microchips? The person operating under this pseudonym came across as clever and someone who was comfortable playing around in English. Did that make him – or her – American, British or another nationality entirely? It was unfortunately a long list.

Threatening the construction of a cutting-edge microchip production facility outside Phoenix, and possibly outside Hereford in the UK, would definitely lessen the speed of microchip evolution and of so many branches of life, from communications to medicine.

Where did this get her? As with all her projects, progress was never linear but always bifurcating like a tree. She would make progress up a branch and often to the end of a twig, only to reach a dead end and have to go back to the main trunk and start again.

However, she now had a toehold. She could begin to build up a mental image of a man who perhaps thought using a name like this was clever or possibly it meant something to him – and vanity always comes before a fall.

As with code-deciphering in World War II, it takes the addition of one or two keywords to aid the process enormously. Days of the week, numbers and months were always a good starting point for her. She would ask her superiors for an update on the day the critical machine would leave Breda, the flight schedules, lorry transition times and final delivery date to the factory. These, or some of these, must feature in the messages and exchanges.

By Wednesday, 24th June, Mike had made no more progress on her project before all the messages stopped or the CIA computers' ability to crack the code had suddenly failed for some reason. She wasn't to know that the group had switched from Spanish to English to throw anyone tracking them off the scent. 'Never do anything the same for long' was the spies' mantra.

Repetition provides opportunities for anyone following you to break your codes or routines.

If this wasn't a big enough setback, she had heard nothing about Terry's death.

Mike set off for London as usual and arrived at Carol's house in the evening. The other tenants were in the lounge, having a discussion about quarter days; in the UK, Midsummer Day was apparently one of these quarter days when, traditionally, rents were collected. She gave this conversation a miss and went to her room, glad of the peace and quiet.

Flat out on her bed, she wondered how many more years she could do this weekly trek up to London and back. It was beginning to wear thin and take its toll. Would she do this in her forties? She thought the answer to this was a firm, *No way*. The fact that her fortieth birthday was less than a month away brought it all into sharp focus.

Wazz had asked her to marry him. Her reply of "Are you mad? Why would you want to marry me?" had rather deflated him, but she had eventually said she would think about it and added, "And thank you," as if prodded by an embarrassed parent. A couple of days later, she had said yes, much to his surprise, because he had no idea what she was talking about.

Maybe the planets are aligning, and it's time to close the chapter on one part of my life and start another. This was her last thought as she went to sleep before heading into the office the next morning.

At Security, she was handing in her phone and rucksack when her friend and fellow analyst, Morag, appeared behind her.

"Is that a new bandana? Are those clown fish?" Morag asked.

"I bought it to highlight the threat to the coral reefs. I'm wearing it to show solidarity."

"Really? Right on, sister. More grease to your elbow." Morag was renowned for her gullibility.

They chatted away, only sharing conversational banalities until they had passed through the scanners, and even then, their chinwag was restricted until they were in their room.

"Leonardo wants you to go up at 10.00am," said Chuck, another colleague, using his nickname for their boss, as Mike entered.

"Does he ever go home?" She rolled her eyes.

Chuck shrugged. "He was here when I left last night."

"Leonardo still hasn't finished painting the ceiling?" Morag asked.

"That's Michelangelo," Mike corrected her.

With that, she spent an hour and a half reading everything that had come in overnight and then began processing it all. At least she had some developments to report to him. After collecting her thoughts, she climbed the stairs, smiled at Lana and waited to gain entry to his office. She was soon allowed through.

"Did the Brit police get hold of you this morning?" Leonard asked as soon as she was sitting in front of him.

"No, why?"

"They tried to call you."

"My phone's at Security. What do they want?"

"Terry Bailey died from what the Brits call 'misadventure'."

"What does that mean?"

"He swallowed a bottle of Jack Daniels, fell over and smashed his head on the table. You're not a mass murderer after all."

She let out a long breath as she digested this. "Who told you? Overton?"

"You know I can't reveal my sources, but I suggest you call the investigating officer back. Go to one of the rooms and ring him when we've finished."

"Thanks. It's a weight off my mind."

"What about your project?"

"The good news is that I have the name or nickname of the ringleader, I think. I'm convinced he'll make a mistake soon. The bad news is that the messages have dried up or they've swapped something to lose us. Do you know if there's a date yet? This would really help me in my searches. They must be still messaging and phoning each other."

"The Brits have just told me they intend to fly their machine on July 9th. I also hear that a group from Arizona is in Holland now. I expect we'll get a fixed date and schedule for their shipment within a day. I'll make sure you get it immediately."

"That would be helpful."

"What's your gut feeling about the ringleader?"

"I think he's an American; possibly an American with Spanish connections. That's just a hunch; he could be a Brit."

"If he's a Brit, it throws open who's funding them and makes me think they may be after both Arizona and Hereford."

"I tend to agree. I know the dates will give me another way into their communications. The speed at which they learn the actual date will also tell us if they have anyone on the inside."

"Great. Go phone the nice policeman, and then get back on your project."

Inspector Wainwright was very sympathetic and apologised profusely for having had to press her so hard in the interview. Mike explained that she understood and was relieved.

"I'm surprised he could stand up given the amount of alcohol in his blood as well as some opioids," he stated. "There were no signs of bruising on his body and no signs of a break-in. It was a tragic accident. I'm sorry."

"Where's his body now? I was wondering when the funeral

might be." Mike was thinking to herself that she owed Terry a great deal.

"I believe it's being released to Mr Rosie. He's the name in Mr Bailey's will, I'm told. I'm not sure he had any family."

"I'll ring Brian and find out about the funeral. Thanks, Inspector."

The call ended, and Mike returned to her work. With relief coursing through her veins, she then spent a tedious afternoon using AI to analyse the various messages and comments in an attempt to pin down the nationality or likely background of the ringleader and the rest of the gang.

When she collected her phone at 5.00pm, she sent a WhatsApp message to Wazz. It read "I'm no longer in the frame for murder. I may stay up here tonight. Speak later."

He replied: "Did you plead insanity?"

"Unnecessary."

Mike didn't get straight on her bike but made another phone call. It was to Brian Rosie. "Brian, it's Mike Kingdom."

"Oh, hi. Did you get the news?"

"Yes, death by misadventure, as I understand it. Probably no surprise?"

"Well, I'm glad he wasn't murdered."

"When do you collect his body?"

"I've arranged for a funeral director to collect it tomorrow. There's some paperwork to sort out first. Then I need to organise a house-clearance company to empty the place. He has no close relatives; the nearest is a cousin in Australia or New Zealand he hasn't spoken to in years."

"Brian, can I ask a big favour of you? Would you let me into his place tonight or tomorrow morning? I want to have a quick look for whatever he was intending to give me."

He hesitated, then finally said, "Tonight would be easier. Can you be there in half an hour?"

"That would be perfect. I'll see you at the flat."

Mike didn't bother to call Carol because she hoped she could find whatever it was Terry had for her and ride on down to Wiltshire rather than spending another night in London. She set off through the traffic to Chiswick, reflecting on what had happened.

"Terry, you were tilting at windmills," she said aloud to no one in particular, her words lost in the roar of the motorbike. "Literally, windmills ... Dutch windmills."

Her last two weeks of hell had been all about nothing. Seven years ago, Terry had killed Henk Visser, who was Jan the Dutchman. He didn't see him in The Gambia; he was mistaken. There was no one after him and, consequently, no one after her. Terry wasn't murdered; he got drunk, took some drugs and fell over, bashing his head on a coffee table. That was it. She could erase the last two weeks from her memory and resume her very happy life. OK, she was never really happy, but this was as good as it was going to get.

The rest of the ride was undertaken in a dream as she weaved around the cars and buses.

On reaching Harding Road, she turned into the car park behind Terry's flat, pulled up and waited for Brian. The two young men in the hoodies came down from their upstairs flat. They said something about being very sorry to hear about Terry. They didn't linger but, rather sheepishly, jumped into their car and drove off. Had they supplied the drugs to Terry? For all she knew, it could have been the other way around.

She was standing there in the early evening sunlight, leaning against a wall with her feet crossed at the ankles when Brian drove into the tight car park. He reverse parked, got out and walked over to her. He was wearing a white shirt with a grey-and-brown bow tie.

"So sorry, Mike. Are you ready? I've no idea what state the place is in." He had a forlorn look on his face.

"And I have no idea what I'm looking for, but somehow, I

know Terry wanted me to have something. I spend my life looking for things without knowing where they are or what they are."

They walked down the steps, where there was some discarded 'Police – Do Not Cross' tape on the mossy bricks.

Brian took out his key.

CHAPTER TEN

Strictly speaking, there's only one type of silence – just as there's only one shade of black. However, they can both be interpreted very differently by the senses.

The flat was eerily quiet, as if no noise dared to enter.

It was oppressively dark, and Brian reached to turn on the light. Untouched, on the kitchen table, the bird book lay open, and there was no immediate indication that anyone had recently died here or that the rooms had been searched by the police.

With every step, Mike felt as though she were intruding.

While the all-pervading smell of death remained, it was being supplemented by odours from overripening bananas in a bowl, the unemptied bin on the floor and the dirty plates in the sink. There were flies trying to escape at the window.

At first, she avoided touching anything, but she gradually realised she had no choice if she was to find whatever it was that Terry had felt to be so important. Where to start? At least the flat was compact – there were only four rooms and a small hall – which she hoped would make the task manageable. "Let's go to the bedroom first. He said the item was small, and I believe it's likely to be there." She imagined it to be a piece of jewellery or a framed photograph. They moved through the lounge and into the bedroom, her eyes drawn to the stain on the coffee table as she passed it.

Apart from some personal items on the surfaces in the bedroom, there was nothing odd or of interest to her. She began opening the drawers of the dresser and bedside tables. The feeling that she was intruding worsened as she lifted out piles of sweaters and folded polo shirts. There was nothing in the wardrobe or in the pockets of the jackets.

Brian – looking out of place in his baggy, white shirt and bow tie – was standing in the door with his arms folded, not knowing how to help.

She was struck by the fact no one would know that the man who had died here had lived a secret life – a life of lies and deception. It all looked, perhaps purposely, mundane and boring. There were no photographs, no pictures on the wall, and nothing apart from a pair of binoculars that might indicate his interests or hobbies.

Did spies like Terry spend so long being other people that they forgot who they were?

In this, Mike excluded herself. She never considered herself to be a spy. That term was reserved for the agents, the case officers and all those operatives out in the field at the sharp end. She was very firmly at the stern, although she neatly managed to exclude what she was doing today as being field work.

There was nothing in the bedside cabinets, which she had thought might be a likely location, or on the windowsills. She was moving quickly and not undertaking a thorough search; there was no taking up of floorboards or meticulous cataloguing of all the items.

She pulled out two well-travelled suitcases from under the bed, one of which turned out to be empty and sporting a label from a hotel in The Gambia. The other, when unzipped, revealed a potpourri of random items from his travels. Some were typical tourist tat, and others were such things as authentic carved masks or arrows for hunting monkeys in Indonesia. She rooted around before an incongruous object took her eye: it was an old mobile phone.

There would have been no reason for her to know if this was his intended gift. She took it out and turned it over in her hand. It had a protective cover with an image of a windmill on it; in fact, it was the only thing in the whole flat with a connection to Holland.

"May I take this?" she asked Brian.

"Of course; take what you want."

She put it into her pocket and moved into the lounge, where there was only one place that might be of interest: a long sideboard. Mike took twenty minutes going through the contents, which were mostly his receipts, his bank statements and the usual heaps of paperwork that are saved but never looked at again. She flicked through these quickly, looking particularly for diaries or an address book. There were some keys and an old-fashioned money box full of coins from around the world that were of no significant financial value. The only thing of interest was a notebook with some names and addresses, so she put this in her pocket as well.

The bathroom and kitchen revealed nothing, and she stood with Brian, surveying the scene from the back door.

"I really thought it might be a piece of jewellery; I don't know why, but I didn't see anything. It was a shot in the dark."

"It's all a bit sad."

"Thank you so much, Brian. I know that you're busy, and this can't be easy for you."

"Before the house-clearance people turn up, I need to collect his bank and credit card stuff. I have his wallet already. I'm one of the executors in his will. You agree to these things, but you never think you'll actually have to deal with it all." He shook his head as they walked across the kitchen to the door.

Once they were both outside, Brian locked the door behind him, and they made their way up the stairs to the car park. They both took exaggerated breaths of air in the subconscious hope of removing anything unpleasant that remained in their lungs. Even emerging from a dank basement and surrounded by brick walls covered in sooty grime, London had never looked so attractive.

The gold watch that had belonged to Terry's mother remained wrapped and hidden behind a cushion on the chair in the bedroom. She would never know that this was what he wanted to give her – a decision made in some alcohol-fuelled fit of melancholy and regret.

After her regular long commute home, she and Wazz had eaten and were sitting either side of the kitchen table. It was almost 10.00pm.

"Take a look at these." Mike had taken the old phone and notebook out of her rucksack and placed them in front of him. She had decided they weren't officially work. They were presents from a dead friend. If necessary, she was quite capable of talking herself into any position.

Wazz picked up the phone and twirled it around in his fingers. He paused to look at the case. "Well, it's an iPhone XR, launched in 2018. I know because I had one."

"And?"

"What am I meant to see? Is this work?"

"Yes and no. Let's say no."

"Where did you get it from?"

"It was left to me by a work colleague who died recently."

"Is the PIN in that notebook?"

"Not that I can see from a quick look, but it might be hidden in some of the phone numbers or text. I'll look properly tomorrow."

"So it's useless. If you charge it up and reset the PIN, it will wipe all the data. Unless the CIA has software that the world doesn't know about."

"We don't. That's what's bugging me; why give me a phone whose data I can never access?"

"What's with the windmill?"

"I think it came from Holland; that's quite likely, but I'm not certain."

Wazz picked up the notebook and flicked through it. Nothing took his eye. It was only a quarter used, containing the names and addresses of tradespeople, travel agents, airlines and other useful contacts. There were maybe thirty of these. "There are no personal or work contacts in this notebook."

"Hmm, well spotted. I picked it up just in case it held the PIN or passwords."

"How long will it take you to enter every combination and sequence of numbers in this notebook?"

"Months ... and he might have used simple encryption by adding five to every number or requiring the omission of every third number or ... you get the picture."

"So why give it to you? He must have thought it had some value."

"That's what I was thinking about all the way here."

Wazz thought for a second. "Is this from the man you were suspected of murdering?"

"Yes, actually. He died from natural causes. He fell over and banged his head."

He looked at her cynically. "Really? Well, I'm glad he wasn't struck by lightning while being kicked by a donkey."

"He definitely banged his head, OK? He might have had a glass or two, but it was an accident."

"And you knew him from the past, obviously."

"Yes, but it was over seven years ago. He's not CIA, in case you're wondering."

"Why share all this with me?"

"I want to. It isn't really connected to my current work ... and because you think differently to me, and I can't ask anybody else at the office anyway."

He began to speak, but she cut across him: "Don't ask why." There was no way she was explaining about Terry and Henk Visser.

Mike had got up and was lifting the dishes into the sink when he reached across to a drawer and pulled out a tangled mass of cables before identifying the charger for his iPhone XR. "This should fit."

He was fiddling with the connection when he unclasped the case, which clattered onto the table. A piece of paper the size of a credit card fell out. On it was written what looked like a PIN.

"You're a genius!" she shouted, and she threw her arms around his neck.

Gordon Overton, as the MI6 controller on the microchip project, was in a meeting first thing on Friday morning with some senior military figures and a permanent secretary, who was the only other person not in uniform. His boss, the Secretary of State for Defence, had decided he himself had more important things to do.

The team met every other week, but they had assembled now as they had received the confirmed dates for the transportation of the machine from Breda. They were assessing where and how any terrorist or terrorist group might try to destroy it or use it to gain publicity.

"The good news is the damn thing is being flown door to door; it never touches the ground. The bad news is I can run faster than that airship." This came from someone called Major Phipps.

A senior RAF officer, who was providing the update, continued with his report and answered any questions. "The Dutch will make sure it gets to 7,000 feet over the Channel, then it's down to us. With Commicron, we've identified twelve airfields that could be used in an emergency if the airship needs to be diverted or needs to deposit its load overnight. This, however, is problematic if the weather turns and the airship has to fly back to France or to the safety of a large hangar."

"The machine is boxed and weatherproof, though, isn't it?"

"Yes, it can theoretically stand outside for days if it has to, but you have to remember how sensitive this machine is."

"What's the best prediction of the route?"

"The most likely route is north of London; this takes Gatwick and Heathrow partially out of the equation. It will be at 10,000 feet over the Essex coast. Of course, this messes up both Stanstead and Luton holding patterns and approaches. The fact that it's travelling slowly helps, fortunately. All RAF bases are on standby, and no unnecessary activity will be permitted."

"Are they likely to use drones or conventional missiles?" Phipps chipped in again.

"They've been trying to acquire drones, but it could be either; because we aren't sure who this group is and who's backing them, it's difficult to say. If they're a bunch of amateurs, then drones are more likely. If they're state-backed, they might have small missiles. Remember that this airship is a glorified balloon and can't sustain much damage."

"Can we eliminate any of the potential areas, otherwise we're talking about the whole of south and east England?" The permanent secretary was trying to keep the meeting on the agenda.

The RAF officer continued, "If it were us attacking it, we'd choose a place and time close to the Dutch factory or close to the Hereford end. There are two reasons for this: firstly, the airship is at a lower altitude and probably travelling more slowly; and, secondly, the exact route for the middle part of the journey is in the lap of the gods, but either end is a fixed point. My guess would be that they'd use a drone somewhere along that last fifty-mile stretch, beginning somewhere near Stratford-upon-Avon and over Leominster to Hereford."

"Even if we assumed a ten-mile wide strip that's fifty miles long, that's 500 square miles to search and monitor." Phipps wasn't the most positive voice in the room.

"What about light aircraft?" someone else asked.

"We've contacted twenty-four airfields and asked them for details of all take-offs and landings during the critical period by any aircraft that isn't owned or flown by one of their regular clients. It's a big area." The RAF officer looked across at Gordon Overton, who had a pinkish face from golfing in the sunshine and had yet to say anything meaningful.

As was his wont, Gordon had been saving up his meagre contribution until it would have maximum effect. "There hasn't been any more intel from GCHQ or the Americans, nor any suspicious activity" – he waited for the disappointment to build – "except that we've cracked some of the phone messages and some of the code they're using." He used the word 'we' to suggest him and his team, although everything to date had been discovered by Mike Kingdom. "We've temporarily lost the ability even to crack parts of their messages, so don't get too excited just yet; they must have changed their code or system. They'd been using Castilian Spanish; therefore, it makes me think that they're European, and it's the British machine that's their focus, rather than the US one, but nothing is excluded at this point."

"Gordon, are the transmissions originating in the UK?" another person asked.

"We can't tell at the moment, but we're all working on it. We have a hundred theories why they've changed their communications. I think they're very experienced in that, which limits the field, but that, of course, is only a feeling and subject to change."

"Well, we have thirteen days if the long-range weather forecast is right and the date isn't altered," the major concluded. "Shall we schedule anything that needs to be put in place? We'll meet next week and as necessary until that machine is safely inside its new home in Herefordshire. The Prime Minister and the committee have made our objective very explicit."

"You must be happy, Major? The SAS have never had a job that close to home."

"Don't worry; we'll be ready for anything."

CHAPTER ELEVEN

The smell of waffles and syrup filled the kitchen. Wazz was cooking breakfast while Mike disconnected the phone from the charger. How he had managed to make her leave it alone overnight was beyond him, but he accepted that his Saturday was now likely to be dominated by her playing and searching.

Mike had come to the conclusion that she wanted to include Wazz in this small part of her world. What had happened seven years ago was no longer about a long-forgotten narcotics operation, and it wasn't about the CIA; it was now very personal. It was a moment in time when her life had changed completely: the moment when her husband had been killed.

With Terry dead, the phone she held in her hands was her only contact with that part of her past, and she wanted to share its importance with the person who now filled her life. She rotated it and prepared herself mentally. This wasn't about solving anything; the man she knew as Jan the Dutchman was dead. She had checked this out herself and even knew where he was buried. Instead, this was about gaining closure on one episode before she moved on to the next. In her mind, it was a precursor to leaving the Agency and settling down with Wazz.

She believed that Terry – despite gradually ruining his life with alcohol and drugs – was an inherently good man. The phone he had stolen from the table after shooting Henk Visser had been hidden away for years. Even if it might have proven useful to the team immediately after the killing, he could never admit to having been in that hotel or to what he had done. Instead, he had put it under his bed in a box with other paraphernalia from his many travels. After he had met Mike in The Leather Bottle, perhaps he felt that holding the phone might give her closure. Whatever the reason, it was now in her hands as she drank a coffee.

"What are you expecting to find?" Wazz was concerned for her mental well-being. Would raking over the past really help?

"No idea. None of it will be relevant to today, and as I explained, I can't reveal to anyone where it came from."

"Is it worth it?" he asked as gently as he could.

"We'll find out. There's no way I'm throwing this away without taking a look, but don't get too excited." Her downplaying of expectations was a projection of her own on to Wazz.

He lifted the card from the table and tilted it so she might see the PIN more easily. To Wazz, it was simply a random sequence of numbers. She tapped it in.

The phone flashed into life, but the fact that most of the messages and emails were in Flemish or Dutch made accessing it an anticlimax.

Of even less interest, the wallet was full of expired train tickets and hotel reservations. She flicked through the photographs, but these were almost all of family and friends. Visser appeared to have had a wife and one child, who was perhaps nine back then; he would be seventeen or eighteen now. There were all of the standard family shots: the visits to the play equipment in a park, feeding ducks, birthday parties, holidays and elephants at a zoo. Trips to the UK featured several times, including the tourist spots in London and lots of swans on the

River Avon, according to a sign. Two pairs of grandparents featured frequently, as did two other families – perhaps siblings with their own children.

She stopped on one selfie and zoomed in. So this was the man who had shot Dylan – or at least had organised it – and ruined her life? His face transfixed her for a time, during which Wazz wisely said nothing. Visser looked so harmless, but she knew the cartel in which he had been involved was evil and dangerous. Tracking them had been Mike's whole existence for a year.

It was now time to move on in her life, but a small part of her wondered if Terry had saved the phone for a reason. Was he expecting her to do something with it or any information it contained? If she had a few minutes over the next few days, she might run some of the messages through a translation program.

For the rest of breakfast, she gave Wazz a potted history, leaving out much of the operational information. He was in awe of what she did for a living and what she had been through in Holland, but he still regarded the phone next to her plate as if it were an unexploded bomb.

"Thanks for telling me all that. I prefer to know your past, or at least the part you can tell me. It helps me make sense of you."

"Hmm, good luck on the sense part." She was laughing at herself.

"What next?" he continued.

"We forget about it, I work all day, and tomorrow we go see a white horse."

"What are you talking about?"

"At the weekend, I want to walk across the chalk downs and stand on the eye of a white horse. The one cut into the hillside above Westbury. It's one of my last weekends as a single woman, and I want it to be memorable. Up for it?"

"You're crazy ... but that's a fantastic idea. I'll make a picnic." Wazz was thrilled. He had expected her to spend Saturday and

Sunday playing with Visser's phone, becoming ever more irritated and maudlin.

It was Saturday afternoon, and they were sitting in their kitchen.

"At least the ice creams were good." Wazz was trying to put a positive spin on their visit to the white horse carved into the steep chalk hillside, but now with a concrete surface.

Mike hadn't been impressed and was more taken by the hang gliders and parasailers leaping off the crest of the escarpment. They had eaten the picnic in his van, as the weather hadn't been kind, and then driven back home.

In exactly twelve days' time, they were getting married at Salisbury registry office. They had decided not to invite anyone but to grab two witnesses off the street. While Mike hadn't really been bothered whether her parents or family flew across from Oregon and attended or not, Wazz had been disappointed when his son had said he was playing football that weekend.

He was now more Spanish than British, having lived there for the majority of his life. He and his male friends, who were local boys, played in a well-respected football team. Scouts from Atlético Madrid had already been to watch him play, and there was nothing else he wanted to do. He had wished his father and Mike the very best and looked forward to seeing the photographs on Facebook.

In a way, his decision had made it easy for his father and Mike. Wazz was divorced, and she was widowed. They'd marry locally and without fuss. It was all booked for 10.30am on Thursday, 9th July, followed by a drink with some of the locals in The Green Feathers in the evening. Any honeymoon would have to wait, but it might involve a trip to Portland in Oregon to see her family.

Having had a disappointing trip to Westbury, they decided to go down the pub at 6.00pm to drown their sorrows and confirm the arrangements with Jess, not that these were complicated.

Under grey clouds with beams of midsummer sunlight breaking through, they set off to walk the short distance up Church Lane and into the High Street. The rusted sign outside The Green Feathers was stuck permanently at a jaunty angle, as if in a freeze-frame shot. It was barely legible. They pushed open the studded oak door, and the brass bell tinkled.

There was no bar; instead, Jess would come out from behind a faded tapestry curtain to take any orders. Whether she came out, whether she took your order and whether she returned with a tray of drinks depended on which way the wind was blowing or possibly how many letters there were in your name – there were numerous theories.

About twenty people were sitting at tables; they were mostly dressed in white morris dancers' outfits, their hats removed. They had finished their performance across the street and were in need of refreshment. This would test Jess's patience. With her thinning, white hair and saggy, brown cardigan, she pushed her way through the tables, which rattled with the tambourines and bells. She began to take a large order of drinks.

Wazz asked one of the dancers if he could move an inflated pig's bladder on a stick and his hat from a vacant table. Once clear, he and Mike sat down together, expecting a long wait.

A matter of minutes later, Jess appeared with two pints of beer and a plate of gherkins on a tray. She walked over to Mike and Wazz and put them down on the table. "Evening," she said, then she took payment and retraced her steps, exiting the room via the curtain. Nobody made a note of which way the wind was blowing or how many letters were in Wazz's name. It was Waldemar Wasielewski and nineteen letters, if anybody could be bothered to count.

"Cheers!" Mike offered the toast, lifting her drink. "Here's to our last week of freedom."

“Cheers!” He shook his head while taking a large mouthful.

“I’m not taking your name. No one can spell Wasielewski.”

“Fair enough. I’m bored having to spell it, although it scores a lot of points at Scrabble and gets me served first in here.”

“Huh!” She took a swig while staring at the men in their white outfits, who were busily chattering away. “What’s with these dancers? I think we have them stateside. We’ve taken most of your screwy traditions.”

“No idea, really. They jig about waving handkerchiefs above their heads. Not very hygienic. Probably started in the plague.”

“Probably *started* the plague.”

He shook his head again. “Glad to have you back after the last two weeks; I’ve been worried about you. Now let’s focus on the wedding”

“I’ll drink to that.”

———

Daniel Drinkwater had inherited most of his father’s Mediterranean features, except for his eyes, which were blue like his mother’s. There were lines on his forehead, and his hair was greying at the temples. Overall, he was in good shape. This might, in part, be put down to the gardening and the tennis.

He had been looking in a mirror before sitting down to book a flight to Spain. This journey was something he did very frequently, as he divided his life between Stratford-upon-Avon and a villa just outside Valencia. He had the trip, and particularly the timings, down to a fine art. Birmingham airport was twenty miles away and had direct Ryanair flights to Manises airport in Valencia.

He had never felt that he was Catalan or British or indeed any nationality. When his Spanish father left his English mother for an opera singer, Daniel went off the rails. This wasn’t a rapid descent into drugs, violence and rebellion, but more of a controlled decoupling from his family and society. He was bright and did this all knowingly, if that's possible – like driving a train into a barrier in slow motion.

It led to various conflicts with the authorities, who found him hard to pigeonhole. He was both asocial and anti-social, becoming ever more self-centred and introspective. All this was mostly hidden behind a charming persona and high intellect, except that, every few years, this façade would break down, and he would have to move on from some scam or misdemeanour.

He had tried to analyse his personality himself, only coming to a clear understanding aged seventeen when he had shouted, "*I don't care!*" at someone from Social Services, and this had been his mantra ever since. Daniel Drinkwater didn't care about laws, other people, the environment or the planet. He simply cared about himself and his very small family. It had served him well, and now, at fifty-five, he wasn't going to change.

His world consisted of his mother, his wife and children, and his widowed sister and her son. That was more than enough. He had millions of pounds hidden or invested around the world, and that sum would only increase exponentially.

His business empire was truly global, but nobody had heard of him, and he employed not a single person. Everything was done through half a dozen intermediaries, all of whom knew the consequences of failure. He had spelt this out to each and every one of them. They were extremely well remunerated and knew he never wanted to hear about problems, only solutions. He, for his part, also worked for a very small group of clients who wouldn't tolerate failure.

Over time, this list of clients hadn't grown, but rather it had morphed as they began to appreciate his success rate and to trust him; they began to give him larger and more diverse projects. As a consequence, he got wealthier and wealthier.

While most of his work could be done from his office or garden shed outside Stratford-upon-Avon, some of it required him to be in Spain, hence his need to book his ticket. He would be away for two days. There was no need to travel with anything other than the minimum of hand luggage; he had everything duplicated in both properties. The only things that mattered were his two phones, a passport not in his real name and his wallet.

He was scrupulously private and always taken to the airport by his wife in a car that wasn't registered, taxed or insured in his name. Tracking Daniel's movements around Europe would be difficult, but he was well aware that facial recognition was going to reveal some of his journeys and locations.

Cutting the times to the absolute minimum, he would be on that 5.55am flight tomorrow morning.

CHAPTER TWELVE

It was Monday morning, and the birds outside the window were fighting over the bread she had put out for them. Mike had the house to herself and was looking forward to a solid day of listening to all the phone and internet chatter picked up over the weekend. There was always hope that the terrorist group had made a mistake.

Mike had also been given both of the delivery dates: 9th July for Hereford and 16th July for Phoenix. She had burst out laughing; the gods were playing with her. Thursday, 9th July was to be her wedding day – not that it mattered as this was a problem for the Brits. Her main focus was Phoenix a week later. Perhaps this would make an ideal honeymoon destination? She could see Wazz's face now.

Her phone rang; it was Brian Rosie.

"Hi, Brian."

"Mike, I have the date for the funeral; well, the cremation. It's 8th^{h} July."

"Oh ... that's the day before I get married down here in Salisbury."

"Oh, congratulations. I wanted to let you know. I think it'll just be me accompanying him to the crematorium, unless you know anyone else I should tell?"

She felt awful. "Brian, I'm so sorry. I wish I could have been there, and I'm sorry you might have to do this alone. You're a real buddy to Terry. I don't know anybody else to invite. To be honest, it's a bit crazy in our world when it comes to things like this. It's a lonely existence."

"I wondered about putting something in the paper. Actually, I will do that. I owe him that."

"Great idea. We don't know who he was friendly with locally and who might like to pay their last respects."

"Was that phone useful?"

"No. We couldn't open it, but I'll keep it as reminder of Terry."

They said their goodbyes, knowing they'd likely never speak to each other again.

Reflecting on what Terry Bailey had done for her, she jumped up to make a coffee before resuming her searches, now she had the key dates, which would surely appear in the messages and group chats. For hours, various programs in the background were checking millions and millions of combinations of letters and numbers to no obvious effect. Oddly, this didn't depress her; it made her more determined to find out who these people were and what they intended to do.

There was still time.

In a villa outside Valencia on the east coast of Spain, Daniel Drinkwater was, despite his surname, enjoying a glass of white wine from Asturias; this was his favourite. The villa wasn't owned by him directly; rather, it was owned through a series of offshore companies in a false name. It hadn't been the eight bedrooms that had attracted him or the driveway with its row of Washingtonia palm trees; instead, the villa had the unique advantage that it sat in a large plot on the top of a small hill, thus giving fantastic views without being in any way overlooked. Privacy was paramount. The building and gardens were covered in an array of visible and invisible cameras and sensors. The external doors were ostensibly oak but actually steel-lined. The lower windows were barred with ornate wrought iron.

He was drinking on one of his terraces, having a private meeting with the man who was his friend and fixer; neither of them came from Valencia originally. They were, however, both a mixture of British and Spanish heritage and had met while working together for the first time in France and the Netherlands almost ten years previously. Daniel Drinkwater's guest was called Roger Fortuna, but everyone knew him as Lucky – a nickname that had stuck from a very early age in East London. However Roger tried, he looked like a thug; this was probably due to his thick neck and closely shaved head.

"So what do you think, Lucky?"

"Well, at least we now have the dates, even if we don't have the route for the British machine."

"You have eleven days to get everyone and everything in position."

"The drones are already in the warehouse in North Ockendon." Here, Lucky was describing the only part of London that lay outside the M25 orbital motorway. It was the broad area of Essex in which he had grown up and was now the easternmost part of the capital.

"Ironic, don't you think, that both our places might be right underneath the bloody route?" Daniel wasn't a lover of irony.

"The last thing we want is to draw any attention to our places. Nearer Hereford is safer and more likely to succeed, I think."

"The Americans are a week behind."

"True, and I think the race between them works in our favour. The Yanks are more likely to cut corners and take their eye off the ball." Lucky threw a handful of nuts into his mouth.

"Our new friend in Breda wasn't much help, apart from giving us the date?"

"True, but it was worth a shot."

"He's too low down the pecking order and can't get near to either machine. He's still useful to have inside the factory, though, picking up what's happening."

"It would have been so much easier to take out both machines while they're in the factory, but it's just too well protected."

"I bet the President won't like the British getting their machine first. It steals his thunder." Daniel reached across to take the bottle out of the wine cooler in order to top up their glasses.

"My guys out in the USA have got it easier. That's a long journey from the USAF airbase to the new factory, even if it's heavily escorted. They've picked a place halfway along the route. Any security will have relaxed by then, and they won't be expecting to be hit in the middle of nowhere."

"I'm worried that the Yanks will be on edge when you've blown the British machine out of the air."

"Possibly, but what can they do? I'm not worried about the team in Arizona as the drones are remote controlled, so our guys aren't near. To change the subject, how are we doing with the money? Is it in yet?"

"I can give you $2 million tomorrow." Daniel wasn't going to reveal that the Chinese had already paid the first $5 million into his account. A further $4 million would be transferred once the machines had been destroyed.

"Let's drink to that. I'm looking forward to the final payment."

"Me too, but you do know that we can't fail? They'll chop us up into tiny pieces and feed us to the sharks."

"We've never failed; well, only once. It won't happen again."

"That wasn't a total failure. We dealt with it." Daniel had grown serious at a memory that had cost him so much money and had such a personal impact.

There was a coldness, a detachment, in their voices that showed why these two men were so dangerous and so successful at their respective roles. Daniel had an air of respectability that concealed his ruthlessness, and Lucky only needed to stare at people to get what he wanted.

"Now, perhaps we should talk about the other main item on the agenda before we drink too much."

"When have we ever had an agenda?" Lucky swallowed a large slug of wine, tipping back his shiny head.

"How was the last shipment of dog food. Kosher?"

"Can you get kosher dog food?"

"Yes, if you pay enough. I sell it all over Europe and in the Near East, but it doesn't come from China."

"Oh, I didn't know. Anyway, the container was as agreed. No problems."

Daniel had met Lucky years before when he needed someone to act as his fixer and enforcer. The business had evolved from smuggling South American cocaine to importing illegal bespoke drugs made to order in Chinese laboratories. They had also moved the entry point around Europe; it had been Valencia for four years.

The drugs were manufactured by pharmaceutical companies in Chinese cities such as Shijiazhuang and Wuhan. This was one of the worst-kept secrets in the world. The USA had consistently accused China of openly trafficking illicit synthetic drugs and had said that the production was subsidised and state sponsored, despite Beijing's denials. Daniel didn't care either way. All he knew was that a container turned up every few weeks with thousands of pre-addressed packets hidden in sacks of canine treats made from cereal and bone meal.

It had been Daniel's idea to use dog food. He thought it would confuse the sniffer dogs, which it did to a degree at first. Now there were sophisticated scanners doing the same job, but they thought that they'd continue with their system. If it ain't broke, don't fix it.

He had bought a legitimate pet-food business with an industrial unit and used it as a cover. Inside the warehouse, the small packets were extracted from the sacks and the appropriate courier label added. Inside each package, the illegal drugs were credibly labelled as aspirin or paracetamol. A small lorry from an international courier company turned up every couple of weeks to collect the packages and distribute them across Europe. There was no reason for anyone to question anything, and if any of the packages were opened accidentally, it all looked *bona fide*. All the dog biscuits and other canine chews were collected up and put into new sacks to be sold throughout Spain. Nothing was wasted.

Without any knowledge of the earlier stages, Daniel distributed a wide range of Chinese synthetic pharmaceuticals and illegal drugs that were advertised openly on social media platforms – everything from cannabis to nitazene, an opioid much stronger than fentanyl. A customer anywhere in Europe who had ordered online would receive their bespoke drugs roughly forty-five days later.

Daniel was one of the largest importers from these labs and had a very good working relationship with several of the key Chinese companies. It was through one of these contacts, a man called Qingtao, that he had been asked to become involved in other projects. All this had led to several jobs sabotaging infrastructure and destroying factories. The Chinese enjoyed the benefit of being once removed from any action and could deny all involvement.

It hadn't taken Daniel long to realise that these one-off projects were extremely lucrative. While he enjoyed the planning, Lucky and his network of thugs, mercenaries and low life had provided the execution – sometimes literally.

In this way, he had ended up with the task of destroying the two machines that were soon to be installed in Arizona and Herefordshire. He would be paid a total of $9 million – a miniscule sum for the Chinese, who would have set the domestic microchip industry in the USA and the UK back by at least a year, which equated to billions of dollars for Beijing. Everything from military hardware to communications would be affected.

Daniel Drinkwater and Lucky Fortuna finished off the bottle and turned their attention back to how they were going to discover the route of the airship for the last fifty miles of its journey.

"Will it be on Flightradar24?" Lucky asked what seemed like a stupid question.

"I don't know. They put US nuclear bombers on there, so why not?"

"The airship will need to be made obvious to all other air traffic because it's not 100 per cent controllable. Perhaps they will?"

"Let's have that as the back-up plan." He uncorked another bottle. "Now how are you getting on with plan A?"

"Doug has adjusted it a bit. He's going down in his caravan with his family."

"What?"

"Think about it; it's a clever idea."

"*Lucky!*" Daniel's tone was showing his exasperation.

"What better cover story than an Essex family going on holiday to the Malvern Hills for a few days? Who's going to pull them over? He was going to rent an Airbnb, but he decided they'd leave fingerprints everywhere, and the booking can be traced straight back. This way, he's in control. Everyone takes their fingerprints home."

"What about all of the kit?

"I'm taking it over from Essex in the Range Rover. The rest of the controls fit in the roof box on Doug's car. He's a clever geezer. He'll get it done, don't worry."

Daniel, however, did look worried. "What's he told his wife?"

"Nothing. I don't know ... that he's going to play golf, fly model aircraft off the Malvern Hills ... I don't know. Look, I take the drones, and he takes his electric mountain bike on the back of his caravan. He chucks his kit in a couple of rucksacks and toodles off to a vantage point away from any other twats. He tracks the airship, presses some buttons and drives home. I'll hang around to see the explosion and then do the same. We'll all be back in Essex before you can say, 'Bob's yer uncle.'"

Daniel swallowed a large mouthful of wine, but he was warming to the idea. "Are we sure it has to fly over the Malvern Hills?"

"Yes, they're unavoidable, but even if it's blown off course by a couple of miles north or south, it doesn't matter; we've got it covered."

"There's so much at stake."

"Have I ever let you down? We've thought of everything. I'll have two drones in the car, but it'll only take one. There should be a stunning view from up on those hills."

Daniel calmed down, but he would remain twitchy until the two machines were destroyed. His mind moved on to another concern. "Lucky, I trust you, but please be careful with Gabby. She's a bit too clever-clever; a bit too cocky for my liking."

"I know, I know. Don't worry, she's good at hiding all our conversations. Nobody uses their real names, and we can't be traced. You can relax. Leave her to me."

"Her silly names and jokes are unnecessary. Tell her to keep it businesslike."

A large, black flying beetle angrily zoomed around them, then headed off back into the Spanish sunshine.

Lucky hadn't flinched. "Who's going to understand Gordon Moore? I didn't get the connection."

Daniel didn't bother to explain what he really thought – namely that there were millions of people smarter than Lucky and that was just in Essex. However, Lucky wasn't employed for his brains but to make things happen and happen on time. He was providing the grunt work.

It was Lucky's daughter, Gabby, who did all the communications, much of which was on the dark web. Gabriella, as she had been christened, was a troublesome thirty-two-year-old who refused to leave home; in fact, she mostly refused to leave her room or open the curtains for that matter. Lucky and Gabby had arrived at a working relationship after her mum died, which basically meant that she sorted out the communications and internet searches for him, and in return, he left her alone with her computers.

Gabby had a lot of IT equipment. Lucky had lost track of how many deliveries the various couriers had brought to his house in Ockendon. Her study looked like mission control for a space launch with it having so much computer-related hardware.

However, Gabby was happy in her own world, and Lucky left her to it. She was a very smart girl, but keeping her at school had proved difficult; although he was proud of the A levels she had passed. The four framed certificates on her bedroom wall were testament to that. They were also testament to her ability to forge.

For ten years or more, she had paid her way by dabbling in Bitcoin and other cryptocurrencies. Lucky secretly loved having her at home and tolerated her strange obsessions. At thirty-two, she was still his little girl, albeit that this wasn't an accurate description of a woman who barely moved off her chair and snacked on fast food and fizzy drinks all day and night.

"I have one more thing I'd like you to help me with. Something not on our non-existent agenda." Daniel had a pressing issue that had cropped up recently.

"Always happy to help. Lay it on me."

CHAPTER THIRTEEN

On Monday, Gordon Overton was having a late lunch at his club in Longford Place, St James's, a salubrious area of Central London. Eating here was one of the perks of his position, along with an associate membership of Staunton Grange Golf Club, which he was also allowed to put down as an entertaining expense on his tax return. Although it didn't have the exclusivity or longevity of some, the Commonwealth and Overseas Club was popular, having been established after the dissolution of the East India Company in 1874, and it was frequented by many diplomats and senior FCDO managers and directors.

Gordon looked the archetypal vicar's son who'd been tapped on the shoulder while reading history at Magdalene College and fast-tracked into the secret services, but nothing was further from the truth. He was from the Home Counties and had acted the part for so long that he had become what he always wanted to be, right down to the foppish fringe.

However, despite all his many faults and despite being universally disliked by his junior staff, Gordon was successful – even if his methods weren't always by the book. His nickname in the service was 'Teflon'. He had a thick skin and nothing ever seemed to stick to him.

Today, he was having lunch with one of his counterparts, Leonard de Vries from the CIA in London, with whom he had worked and liaised on many projects. They had met in the club several times before, and in return for a free lunch, Leonard was always prepared to put up with Gordon's dated position that Britain ruled the waves – although he had drawn the line at eating something called 'figgy pudding and custard'. What was wrong with apple pie and ice cream?

They weren't natural bedfellows and couldn't be classed as friends; however, they did share a grudging respect for their opposite number's successes. Every so often, the slightly older, overweight American with the thinning, ginger hair would peg back his host in his grey suit and yellow-and-ivory striped tie; this was done without malice, and Gordon took it in good measure.

On their first visit, Gordon had been busy describing the history of the club and the rules when Leonard casually dropped into the conversation that he was a member of an ancient gentlemen's club established in Maryland in around 1746 – over 130 years before Gordon's club. Leonard's club still only admitted men to the clubhouse on the four pilgrimage days. He had also accepted membership of a prestigious golf and country club in Washington, but he had only viewed the irrigated fairways from the safety of the dining room and bar.

As on every other occasion, they had chosen to meet on a Monday and selected high, red-leather wingback chairs in a quiet corner of a lounge where they could speak relatively freely. Gordon had a Kümmel on ice, not because it was his favourite drink but more to uphold the traditions of the Secret Service. Leonard was drinking a bourbon on the rocks and shovelling handfuls of peanuts into his mouth.

Gordon was the first to bring up work. "At last we have the

dates, or hopefully have the dates, on which all of this should happen, weather permitting."

"We sure do, Gordon, but I don't believe that your one will end up being first. That airship can't fly if a mouse farts. Ours, at least, is in a C-5 Super Galaxy and then on the freeway."

"The intel from your chaps appears to indicate they're going to use drones. I presume that means on the road part of the journey; they'd never get near the plane at the airport, would they?"

Leonard didn't bother to correct Gordon on the gender of his team. "Not a snowball's chance in hell. It's gonna be while it's travelling along the highway, and we've got a couple of trucks carrying anti-drone systems, not to mention a few helicopters patrolling the route. The asphalt is going to be covered in police cars and Fed SUVs, and that's without the Ford Mustangs from the Department of Homeland Security – particularly, the Transportation Security Administration."

"Well, if Commicron is right, it will be us the week before. You'll know what they used to attack our machine on its journey from Breda."

"I'm sure hoping we identify these bozos way before they can get their fingers on the trigger."

"No more leads on whom they are?" Gordon sipped the clear liquid, savouring the flavour of caraway seed, which always seemed to come as a surprise to him. It had been the drink of the aristocracy, and this had transferred to the old Foreign Office. Today, it was known as 'putting mixture' by golfers due to its reputation for calming nerves. Either way, Gordon had bought into the history.

"My team still think they're Europeans, probably Brits or perhaps Brits and Spanish. Their motive escapes me, unless they're eco-nuts or anti-tech."

"You could be right, but they're surely state sponsored by China or Russia, who'd prefer to use intermediaries. I know they usually favour the Balkan gangs or the Eastern Europeans, but maybe a Spanish–British group is more geared up."

"We're trying to pick up on where they're getting the drones or missiles. They can be bought for enough money, I know, but they also come out the back doors of factories or get accidentally lost by soldiers out in the field."

"China or Russia could be sending the equipment themselves. Perhaps the gang or gangs are using what's provided to them."

"Are any of the usual suspects involved?"

"Cheltenham is tracking everyone on the lists, but nothing has turned up yet."

Leonard leant forwards and grabbed some more nuts as shafts of sunlight came in through the tall windows. "They could be using different actors here and over in the US of A? It doesn't have to be one group."

"True, it could be one group or two. Either way, they have to get hold of drones or kit in both our countries."

Leonard was pensive, and he found himself looking at a large, old oil painting of fox hunting in some bucolic English setting. It gave him an idea. "It doesn't help me, because I'm pretty sure they're going to attack somewhere along that 120 miles of highway, but over here, I think it will be very close to Hereford. If I were going foxhunting" – he nodded towards the painting – "I wouldn't prance about on a horse with a load of dogs in the middle of a field. I'd go and stand near the foxhole with a gun."

Gordon shuddered at this thought and that such heresy had been uttered in the walls of his club. "They're called hounds."

"I don't care if they're the hounds of hell; I'd still stand a few yards away from the foxhole with a gun – preferably an AK47." Leonard knew what he was saying and was enjoying the reaction from the man leaning back into the corner of his chair.

Gordon, however, let the abhorrent idea of shooting foxes with AK47s dissipate and instead concentrated on the interesting thought at the heart of the suggestion. "We've been concentrating on the last fifty miles, but what you're saying is that there's more certainty right next to the factory in Herefordshire."

"You got it. I don't mean stand outside the gates – that would be loopy – but how about a couple of miles away? Why not choose a spot the airship has to pass over whichever route it takes or is forced to take by the winds?"

"Mmm." Gordon pondered this for a moment, but he was already sold on the idea. He turned the thought around. "It's presumably the opposite for you. Why attack near the airbase or near the factory where everyone will be on high alert and have back-up nearby? It would make better sense to do it out in the open after an hour or two when everyone's dropped their guard. Are there any obvious places to hide? I don't know that route."

"It's a long piece of asphalt with too many possible places from which to attack, but we've had people flying and driving the route thinking exactly along those lines."

Daniel had just been to the kitchen in the villa and returned with two bottles of ice-cold water. "Out of the blue, someone I know in Rotterdam – Piet van der Veen – called me. I've now put him on the payroll, by the way."

"What did he want?" Lucky asked.

"He had met someone new who'd told him something interesting. His new best friend is in Dutch intelligence and had recently been called by a woman about Henk's death."

Lucky kept quiet, knowing this was a very sensitive subject.

Daniel breathed in before continuing. "Piet discovered that this woman who rang works for the CIA in London. It was her husband who you shot. Obviously, Piet knows nothing about this; he was reporting what he had heard."

"Jesus Christ!"

"Don't worry, she isn't reopening the case; she wanted to know if our operation had ever been busted. The guy in intelligence told her it had been shut down immediately and there was no further activity."

Lucky looked surprised, but he kept absolutely silent.

"The thing is that I bet she knows who shot Henk." Daniel let this hang in the air. He had never forgiven himself over the death of his brother-in-law. Henk wasn't originally meant to stay in that hotel room; it was a set of boring and mundane events that had led to him spending the evening there. It was a simple case of being in the wrong place at the wrong time.

Henk wasn't connected to Daniel's drug-smuggling activities in any way and knew nothing about it. He wouldn't have been suspicious when his killer had knocked on the door of his room and would have opened it in all innocence, only to be shot and his body left sprawled across the sofa.

Daniel had immediately closed down the Dutch operation and transferred it to Spain; this was annoying, but he was used to moving dates and destinations at short notice. For months afterwards, he had tried to find out who had killed his brother-in-law. He had given his word to Ana, his sister who now lived in England, that he would find out and bring them to justice, but without explaining what form such justice would take. He felt he owed this much to her and her son, Theo. Yet despite calling in every favour and offering substantial sums as bribes, he could find nothing. Nobody in the authorities or in the criminal world seemed to know anything. Daniel refused to believe that this was a random killing or robbery gone wrong; it must be connected to his drug-smuggling activities.

Over the years, the guilt had gnawed away at him. Despite his wealth and criminal contacts, he couldn't discover one relevant lead, and he had been frustrated for seven long years. He was unaware that his lack of success wasn't surprising given that

Terry Bailey had acted alone and had only told one person on earth: Mike Kingdom.

Daniel had helped his sister in every way possible, but she remained traumatised and introverted. Money couldn't replace Henk. Theo, their son, was doing well at a good private school in Surrey, funded by his uncle. He had been nine when his father died.

"Can you find out about this woman?" Lucky asked.

Daniel lifted his eyes. "No, but you can, ably assisted by Gabby or whatever she's called this week."

"I'm afraid you can't change these geeks. They're a breed apart."

"I don't think they should be allowed to breed."

"That's harsh. She's just a bit different."

"If she finds this woman, I'll be eternally grateful and will happily accept her stupid jokes."

"I'm guessing you want this, like, yesterday?"

"Of course, how effing difficult will it be to find her? Ignoring cleaners, secretaries and chauffeurs, how many females work as agents or managers at the CIA in London? I'm guessing twenty, forty ... fifty max. And how many were widowed seven years ago?"

"OK, I'll get her on to it pronto." Lucky pressed the ice-cold bottle of water covered in condensation against the back of his neck. Good job it was a big bottle.

Meanwhile, Daniel's thoughts were running ahead.

"We know she has been around for at least seven or eight years, and her husband was killed in that effing pickup. Gabby knows all about the background to Holland, and I'm guessing it shouldn't take her long."

"I'm sure it won't. Leave it with me. I'll call her on the secure network as soon as I get back to my place." Lucky had known Daniel long enough to realise that finding this woman was pretty much at the top of his list of priorities.

"Good, but I don't suppose the bloody CIA publish a list of its employees."

"I'll get her on to it." Lucky was thinking back to events in Holland. "They never put anything about the shooting or the crash in the papers, did they? It was like nothing happened. Gabby checked for weeks."

"That doesn't surprise me. I'm sure the CIA jumped on the story and killed it. They wouldn't want the fact that an agent was killed to get out; it's bad for business, as well as the fact that they didn't catch us. Now we've had a bit of unexpected luck. We have the lead I've been waiting for."

"Do you want to meet this woman?"

"I don't care. Just find out from her who shot Henk – that's what I want the most. Check out the bastard properly, make him suffer and then kill him."

"What about her?"

"I don't want her sniffing around and getting back to you and me. Get rid of that sodding woman as well."

CHAPTER FOURTEEN

The next day – Tuesday, 30th June – 'that sodding woman' was walking around Rodbourne, trying to clear her head and find inspiration. She often did this when she hit a brick wall, and it was good for her to stretch her damaged leg every few hours. Searching could be so frustrating and yet so rewarding. She was passing the beautiful front garden that belonged to Vic, the local character who acted as the village Neighbourhood Watch scheme all by himself. He had his own chair in The Green Feathers, which he occupied most nights from opening time onwards.

Vic was watering his hanging baskets; these were a delightful mix of red geraniums, blue lobelia and peach-coloured petunias. "Morning, Mike; fancy a squirt?"

"Not today, thank you."

Vic enjoyed using his hosepipe to spray children and adults alike. "Thee coming down the Feathers tonight with Wazz?" His very broad West Country dialect was always tough for Mike to follow.

"Wasn't planning to."

"It's 'arvest festival."

"Vic, it's June ... well, almost July. Where does all the fruit and veg come from?"

"I dunno, Waitrose probably. The vicar'll be there."

"What ... in a supermarket?"

"No, in the Feathers; 'e blesses the produce before it's auctioned off. Jess always makes a curry."

"What?" Mike was having difficulty trying to understand Wiltshire village life. "You know that she only does a ploughman's lunch in five different ways."

"No, it's the same every year. On 30th June, she makes a girt big curry, an' damn 'ot it is too."

"Why?"

"It's 'er late uncle's birthday. The one who worked in India. All the proceeds go to charity."

"Oh ... right. Well, I'll talk to Wazz."

With that, she sauntered back to her house, wondering how the British had conquered so much of the world.

After opening her white front door, she stepped into her tiny lounge and made for the kitchen, where her computer was set up on the table. While she had been out, the Agency system had been checking another list of words and dates. Mike logged in and waited for the results to filter through.

"*Geronimo!*" she shouted.

There, on her screen, was an intercepted message that had been written in English. It had been sent not on the dark web but between two burner phones in the USA. The two individuals must have felt confident that their short message was unlikely to be picked up. They hadn't used any names, and both cell phones were moving during the call. It meant Mike and her colleagues at Langley couldn't fix either address, only where on the road they were at the specific moment of the call. CCTV footage would be checked, and if they were very lucky, they might identify one of the vehicles – but this was a long shot. Mike didn't mind; she was getting ever closer.

The text of the message described the arrangements for two individuals to meet at an unspecified ranch at a specified time. She couldn't wait to call Leonard, who'd be relieved and able to get the President off his back.

There was no time like the present, so she called his cell phone. This was something Mike took for granted as very few people had either of his two main numbers.

"I need some good news," he answered immediately.

"You got it. I have a date, a time and that they're meeting at a ranch somewhere near Phoenix."

"Hey, that's great. No names, I'm guessing?"

"No, zip on the names front, but we're getting closer. I'm sure I'll crack the whole thing soon."

"Have you found the location?"

"I've been looking for possibilities along the highway. I've identified several farmhouses. One seems the most likely as it looks abandoned on the aerial shots."

"Send me what I need to know. I'll call Langley. They can monitor these locations and take over the problem. They should be able to catch them when the terrorists turn up for their meeting and nip this potential threat in the bud."

"I'll keep searching."

"You do that, but I have a feeling you've cracked it. On Thursday, I'll give you another job that's super important."

"I haven't finished this one yet. What about the Brits?"

"Don't worry about the Brits; they're working on it too. With any luck, we can tell them the names of the group once we've arrested the US end."

"Oh ... OK."

"You've done a great job and given HQ enough to work on. See you Thursday."

The call ended, and she set about sending Leonard the key text, location and aerial photographs.

A few minutes earlier, Keith Herring had landed at Paris-Le Bourget airport at the north-eastern edge of the city. The flight in the Gulfstream had been uneventful, and he had begun to nod off – or perhaps simply had his eyes shut – as the plane had begun its descent. Although the private jet terminal was only seven miles from the centre of the capital, he was being driven thirty miles in the opposite direction out past Charles de Gaulle airport towards a state-of-the-art industrial facility.

It was a piece of good fortune that the airship factory and hangars were only 200 miles from Breda, to the north-east in the Netherlands. It would take them three hours to fly it up to collect his machine before the complicated flight across the English Channel and west across southern England, or perhaps the Midlands if the winds picked up. The latter prediction came from Keith's son, who was pressing hard to be allowed on the airship as one of the passengers, together with the pilot, co-pilot and two security guards who'd secure the machine if they were diverted to an overnight stop.

Keith had made up his mind that he didn't want to add the worry of having his only son on the airship as well as the machine. He didn't want to lose either of them – together or separately.

On walking into the vast, high space of the manufacturing hangar, the sight was impressive. Three of the dirigibles, each 200 yards long and 50 yards high, were under construction or finished.

The *directeur general*, Pascal, escorted Keith across to one of them. At the bottom of a flight of steps, he turned to his guest. "Shall we?"

"I can't wait, Pascal." This wasn't entirely true as he suffered from vertigo and would under no circumstances be flying in the cabin – or gondola – slung beneath the huge, white, gas-filled envelope, which looked more rigid close up. Even the word 'gondola' gave him the jitters. He wasn't entirely content on private jets and never looked out of the windows.

The gondola had a dozen seats and was very light and airy, even in the hangar. Pascal took him up to the cockpit, and passing down the aisles, he pointed out – in a well-rehearsed routine – the emergency exits. "The life jackets are under the seats," he said, smiling and doing his best impersonation of a cabin-crew member.

Keith didn't want to think about the airship coming down with his precious load hanging beneath it. He made his way back through the gondola and down the stairs, pausing only to look at the ridiculously small wheels – all that was needed for a vehicle that took off vertically. The two engines, mounted either side of the cabin, would provide the power to fly the airship at a speed of about sixty miles per hour, despite the resistance from its bulky shape.

Once back on the concrete floor, Pascal took him around to see the array of steel ropes and hooks that were ready to connect to the platform on which the machine in Breda was now sitting. Everything looked so perfect in the echoing hangar, but Keith couldn't shake off a deep unease. He knew the steel cables were strong enough, and he knew the gas inside was non-flammable, but the photograph of the passenger airship *Hindenburg* in flames as it tried to land at Lakehurst, New Jersey, in 1937 was seared into his mind. The cover of the second Led Zeppelin album had been one of his favourites.

As he walked back across to the office, Keith tried to reassure himself that he would be having kittens whether the damn machine was transported by land, sea or air. All he could do was count down the days until it was safely installed in its brand-new factory deep in the Herefordshire countryside.

He had been concentrating so hard on the journey from

Breda to Hereford that he hadn't bothered to ask Pascal about the security arrangements at the facility in which he was standing. He hadn't seen much evidence of security on-site, and if the airship were sabotaged, he couldn't exactly order up another in five minutes like an Uber.

On enquiry, Pascal's answers didn't fill him with any confidence, and Keith suggested that he himself would be happy to pay for some private security firm to patrol the facility twenty-four seven until the airship left for Breda.

There were, unfortunately, too many ways and places where terrorists could stymie his plans. The hangar he was standing in looked like an easy target.

Gabby Fortuna was talking to her two closest friends: Carmen and Lola.

They were a pair of scarlet macaws, with stunning red chest feathers and multicoloured wings, who lived in a conservatory on the end of the massive mansion in Essex she shared with her father. Effectively, she had taken over the 'West Wing', as she called it, which comprised a bedroom, kitchenette, lounge, study and shower room. Outside the study, the long steel-and-glass conservatory had its roof painted white to block out the direct sunlight. Instead of having rattan furniture, potted palms and soft, flowery cushions, it was home to substantial trunks and branches of apple trees, which were now stripped of all bark, and a hard plastic paddling pool full of water. It gave the macaws about thirty feet of space in which to fly. On the floor was a selection of wooden toys and puzzles to challenge and occupy these inquisitive and intelligent birds.

The two macaws were sitting next to each other nodding and sneezing as Gabby sprayed them with a mist of water droplets from a diffuser. They squawked and chattered away, occasionally saying something in Spanish or English in their nasal dialects.

They provided Gabby with company and a distraction from her computer, at which she spent most of her day before listening to audiobooks on her sofa.

While Carmen and Lola preened their plumage and enjoyed the cooling effect of the spray on a hot day, Gabby returned through the connecting door to her study. She had been given a new project by her father, and this time it was different. Lucky had asked her to find people before, but on every previous occasion, he had given her a name, an address or perhaps a telephone number. Now he was asking her to search with the bare minimum of information.

Sitting in front of her array of computer equipment while drinking a can of ice-cold Coke, she wondered where to start. All she knew was that a woman, presumably American, who worked for the CIA in London had called someone in Holland asking about Henk Visser's death and the smuggling operation back seven or eight years ago. Where should she start? Phoning the CIA was out of the question, and they didn't make the names of their employees available. Of course, this woman might also be using an alias. Her father had told her that she was the wife of the man he had shot while driving along the embankment, but this death had never been made public, and there was absolutely no mention of it in the media or online.

She knew about the Dutch fiasco and the need to transfer the cocaine-smuggling operation from Rotterdam to Málaga and then to Valencia. She had started to work with Daniel and her father about a year before these events. Back then, she had developed a role helping Daniel and Lucky communicate with their Colombian suppliers and the shippers. Gabby and her father didn't have many secrets; they were an odd couple, with just the two of them sharing the house and making money from a series of illicit enterprises. Somehow, this relationship worked.

She had her two macaws, and he lived alone at the other end of the house, never seeming to bring any women home – or at least Gabby had never heard anyone.

"*This is impossible,*" she shouted out to the person chatting away in the background on Capital Radio and to the macaws, all of whom ignored her. "*How am I meant to find a CIA agent?*"

She slammed her podgy hands onto the arms of the chair while pushing back with her short legs. What could anyone do? Stand outside the US Embassy in London, record the whole scene, photograph every female employee and then use facial recognition? Apart from being arrested, then what was meant to happen? Which person in all these photographs was in Holland seven years ago? It was all impossible. Gabby took a deep breath and thought that what she had been asked to discover by Daniel and her father was crazy.

It wasn't as if she had nothing else to do. She was effectively their office manager, communications director, security expert, data archivist and all-round bottle washer. The dog-food operation took hours and hours of her time each day as she had to use special software to catalogue and enter into a massive database all the names and addresses on the labels already applied in China. This had been her idea. "Why not keep all this personal data for possible future use?" she had asked Daniel. "It's a free list of drug addicts and pushers all over Europe who have enough money to pay the Chinese." Daniel had been impressed. Sometimes, she felt as if she were actually the managing director of this outfit.

She mused some more about her problem and settled on buying the information. On the dark web, her activities would be well hidden. Gabby checked if there were lists of CIA names, but to no avail; however, it was worth the effort as you could buy everything from bundles of credit card numbers to the addresses of the rich and famous. Using one of her aliases (Gabby needed to use pseudonyms online), she asked if anyone had the names and job titles of London-based CIA staff of all ranks.

By the next morning, the replies would have rolled in, and if they were available, she would negotiate the price and pay using Bitcoin. She moved on to her next task.

CHAPTER FIFTEEN

It was Wednesday, 1st July, and the sun was peeping over the tops of the poplar trees at the bottom of the large garden surrounding the Fortuna mansion in Essex.

"Pinch, punch, first of the month." Gabby was scratching Carmen under her chin.

The macaw was fully concentrating on cracking a nut in her powerful beak while holding another in a claw. Lola, meanwhile, was on the floor and preoccupied with a child's toy, putting brightly coloured cubes into a wooden tray. With both birds content in the conservatory, Gabby returned to her study to check the overnight responses.

In 2008, when she was fifteen and having a breakdown following her mother's death, she had discovered the dark web and been fascinated by it. She was now more than adept at using it, having tried all the systems and developments since. When she discovered the onion routing project, or TOR, which had come out years before in 2002, she began to understand its potential for communicating in a secure way – and she couldn't believe it was legal.

She had quickly grasped the advantages of the TOR system,

based as it is on the multiple layers of an onion, where each message passes through three random routers. She loved how, at each stage, no one could follow her encrypted messages back to the previous stage. It was all anonymous, and there was no indication of where in the world the message originated. None of the security agencies in the world had been able to crack the system, and they had been reduced to searching for the length and timing of each message transfer, which was a laborious and not entirely fruitful pursuit.

The overnight responses in her inbox were pretty disappointing – mostly scams or selling porn or drugs. However, she did make a note of a money-laundering scheme that she might pursue later. In addition, there was – she was pleased to note – one interesting reply that might be useful.

Someone identified as 'Assange the Third' purported to have lists of all overseas US government employees in the CIA and all embassy staffers over many years. He wanted $100,000 in Bitcoin for any 1,000 names, with details such as position and division included. He was happy for Gabby to specify which embassies or CIA divisions she was interested in, meaning she could choose where any 1,000 names came from. Interestingly, he offered an alternative whereby for a much smaller sum he would search for a specific name that she provided. He, of course, didn't know Gabby's real name or why she required the information.

She asked him how much he would charge for the lists of CIA and other embassy members in the Netherlands over the period in which she was interested. This, she told him, was 2018 to 2019. In addition, she asked about the current staff at the London embassy, it having occurred to her that this sodding woman, as she was now known, would appear on both lists, and this could make identification easier.

Assange the Third sent her two pages of names from a different country at no cost as a taster, and it worked. Gabby transferred a few thousand dollars as a first step and awaited the next tranche of names. Four pages came back relatively quickly, and she began to check through the names and positions.

Half an hour later, she had spotted one woman's name whose position was assistant to Her Excellency Prudence Bushnell. Two minutes afterwards, Gabby had checked that Prudence Bushnell had never been the US ambassador in the Netherlands or indeed anywhere in Europe. It looked like she had held this post in Guatemala in 1999 before working in Africa. Gabby searched further and found that Debra Winger had played her part in the film *Sometime in April* about the Rwandan genocide. This was all very interesting but not in any way relevant.

Wherever the list of names came from, it wasn't what Gabby was looking for. She found one other incontrovertible anomaly and called out her new contact online. There were a series of excuses and prevarications, but after going back and forth, she decided this man was a chancer who had a few out-of-date pages from somewhere and was hoping to con her into sending him a pile of Bitcoin. It had been worth the try, but it looked like this avenue on the web was dead.

A line had been reached, and she decided not to waste any more time searching for this CIA woman. Gabby was very confident in her computer skills, but finding the name and address of a CIA operative was beyond her capability. She would suggest to Daniel that he went back to his new contact, Piet van der Veen, in Holland to ask him to find out this woman's name from his own contacts in Dutch intelligence.

She walked across to the fridge in the corner and took out a can of Coke. Many years previously, she had given up trekking all the way along the corridors to the main kitchen. This wasn't just laziness; Gabby had complete control of the West Wing, knowing to a fraction of an inch the location of everything.

This made her life easier – Gabby was blind.

Twenty miles away on that Wednesday evening, Mike had arrived at Carol's house in London. For an hour, she chatted with the other housemates to relax her after the journey up from Wiltshire, then she headed upstairs. There, she had to remove piles of cardboard boxes from the single bed in the corner; Carol had obviously been busy on Amazon.

The next morning, she went into the office, excited that progress had been made on the location of the terrorist's base in Arizona for the attack and that she was to be given a new job to work on. Frankly, the relevance to her skills had evaporated once the group had changed from Spanish to English in some of their direct communications. Hopefully, the next project would be about her main interest: the trade in narcotics from South and Central America into Europe and the USA.

The body-scanning machine had broken down, which meant there was a queue to be searched manually as she entered the building. It seemed an age before she was able to walk up the stairs to the office she shared with five other analysts.

"Good morning one and all," she said as she sat down at her desk.

"Good morning, good morning, good morning," Morag replied in a faux Irish accent. She was of Scottish ancestry and came from Maryland.

"You sound happy, Morag."

"Leonardo has given me a new job. I'm on top of the moon." Everyone knew what she meant, but her co-workers had learnt that it was better not to correct her unique take on the English language.

Mike organised her workspace and logged in. There was little new of relevance, but she wasn't expecting it now Langley had the intel and had taken over her part of the project.

Her phone buzzed, and she was called up to Leonard's office.

A few minutes later, she was chatting to Lana, Leonard's PA, outside his large, sound-proofed door. The green light above it illuminated, and she walked across the carpeted hall and entered.

He interlocked his hands on the desk before him and asked her to take a seat, which she did.

"Great job," he congratulated her, having been impressed with her persistence on the microprocessor factory project. "Your intel on the ranch in Arizona was perfect."

"You can always rely on the troops to break the rules and use a phone. Have they found anything?"

"They identified the farmstead from your intercepts and staked it out. They removed four drones from inside and bugged the whole place. Once the terrorists return, they'll grab them. Job done."

"I'll keep listening ... and watching." She was relaxing slightly.

"It was an abandoned ranch with centre-pivot irrigation all rusted up and rotting in the desert sun. They thought they were safe using it as a launch pad."

"It looks like there are only a few farms in the area, and they're well spread out. Should be easy to monitor from above."

"And you might have saved the asses of a bunch of guys from Langley, d'you know that?"

She looked confused.

He continued, "Since our friends from the Department of Government Efficiency threatened to stick their nose in, Langley set up its own internal group. Obviously, they couldn't let those DOGE assholes near our data. Making progress on one of the President's pet projects scored lots of points. That means no redundancies in that division."

Mike had no idea why her boss was telling her all this, so she kept quiet, which in itself was unusual.

"That leads me on to the new project I'm giving you. It's fentanyl made in Chinese labs and sent to the US of A and Europe."

"I know South America and Europe, not China."

"Fentanyl is the President's other pet irritation. He wants it sorted, whether it comes from Canada or China, and that's important for you and me."

"Why?"

"Because all of you here, including me, are being assessed. At the moment, they're talking about a ten per cent reduction of staff in overseas stations. If we're all working on the President's pet projects, we might be safe ... well, that's what I've argued."

She had always wondered what he did all day in his office, apart from eat, but now she realised that he defended his team from attacks from the echelons above. It hurt her to admit that he was a good boss, if irritating at times.

"Morag's going to work on it as well, so you can speak freely about it. She'll show you the intel we've got. It's right up your street."

In the lounge of the villa outside Valencia, Daniel Drinkwater was *not* happy. He was pacing up and down while staring at his friend, who was sitting on a large sofa wearing a white tee shirt and dark-blue shorts.

"Lucky, the Chinese will chop us into little pieces. How the fuck did the Americans find out about that farmhouse?"

"It might have been luck. They must be checking the route and possible attack points."

"Whatever the reason, they now know someone is intending to target the machine when it's on the transporter. They now know we intended to use drones."

"Daniel, it'll be OK. They haven't contacted our guys out there or picked them up. They were using burner phones. I've given them a bollocking and have described what will happen if they break the rules again."

"How did they find out that the Feds or CIA or whoever had discovered the cache?"

"They aren't complete numpties; they left cameras monitoring the roof access in the farmhouse. They could see the raid taking place. They aren't going back or anywhere near there."

"So what's the back-up plan? We have about ten days."

"I've asked them for their ideas. Gabby's just sent it over to them through TOR. I'm waiting for their reply."

Daniel looked skywards and began to speak, but Lucky cut across him: "My thinking is that attacking it along that highway is now a waste of time. They'll double the protection and double the searching beforehand. Let's see if our guys come up with anything brilliant that I haven't thought of, but I'm not expecting miracles. I think that we should attack the US machine in Holland."

"What?"

"Think about it. The Americans are busy searching Arizona now they think they know what we're going to do. They'll find nothing. On 9th, we'll blow the British machine out of the sky. They'll be expecting us to do the same to their transporter in Arizona a week later. Instead, I'll go to Breda myself with a couple of mates and make sure it never makes it out of Dutch airspace on that C-5 Super Galaxy plane."

Daniel paused to digest all of this. "Isn't Breda going to be more protected than Arizona, especially after we've blown up the one over the Malvern Hills?"

"Now the Yanks have discovered the drones at the farmhouse, I think Holland will be easier. Not easy but easier."

"Will you use drones in Breda?"

"I'm working on it."

"What does that mean?"

"I have this idea that the factory will be too well protected – it already has a no-fly zone overhead. I don't think we should try to blow it up in Breda. The thing about the Lockheed C-5

Super Galaxy is that it needs 2,500 yards of runway to take off."

"And?"

"Breda's runway is 830 yards long; Rotterdam's is 2,200 yards. Eindhoven is the nearest at 3,000 yards."

"How far away is Eindhoven from the factory? Fifty miles?"

"Forty miles through Tilburg."

Daniel walked across to a brown leather chair and sat down, now deep in thought. "So are you thinking along the route or after take-off? The airport will probably be too protected, I would think."

"I'm working up two ideas. Along the route seems the easiest by far and the frontrunner in my mind. Shooting the largest US cargo plane out of the air would be pretty spectacular, but we'd need some serious drones or rockets."

"While it's on that transporter from Breda to Eindhoven sounds much better. The lorry is probably only moving at 40 miles per hour or less, depending on where you choose."

"I think I should go there tomorrow and suss out possible locations. I don't know that road very well."

"Good idea."

"I'll stay over there tomorrow night and get back to Essex over the weekend. Then it's four days 'til my trip to the Malvern Hills."

"I feel better that you're going to be present at both operations. I didn't like leaving it to some hired hands we hardly know out in Arizona."

"I'll book my tickets; there's a Ryanair flight tomorrow direct from Valencia to Eindhoven, leaving at 7.00am."

"And I must get back to Stratford. Get Gabby to send me what you find out using the usual system. No bloody mobile phones."

CHAPTER SIXTEEN

In Herefordshire, a milky sun was shining through high cirrus clouds. The surrounding wooded landscape was at its most verdant.

It was Thursday, 2nd July, and down in the new factory, it was the first time some of the military and defence personnel had met Keith Herring. They were in the newly furnished reception area, where the building was ninety nine per cent complete. All construction that involved dust or vibration had been finished. There were only seven days until the machine was flown from the Netherlands, and unusually, the main contractor and subcontractors were ahead of schedule; this was unsurprising given the eye-watering penalties and damages in the contract should the project overrun even by one minute.

There was a group of eight visitors standing together as the final introductions were made. Keith Herring welcomed everyone and took them into the large general office behind reception; all the furniture was in place, but with no staff, there was an eerie emptiness.

The meeting had hastily been rearranged once the information had come through from the USA that drones had been found hidden in the farmhouse roof. This would be the last such gathering, and the military personnel present were refining their thoughts on how to defend the factory in the long term and the machine from imminent attack during its journey from the Netherlands. The intel from across the Atlantic meant the threats were no longer imagined or theoretical but real.

Major Phipps, the coordinator, was firmly of the view that the attack *modus operandi* would be the same in the UK as in the USA. The terrorists would use drones along the route, and in the UK, this meant bringing down the airship. He and most of the group became convinced that the attack would be at the factory or very close to it, perhaps a mile away. At that moment, the airship would be low – just a few hundred feet above the ground – and moving very slowly. It would be a sitting duck, as the major put it.

There was already provision to locate anti-drone and anti-missile defences permanently at a site nearby, but this was meant to protect the factory from threats from a hostile power once the factory was operational, not on the day the machine arrived. These defences weren't yet in place, and talk now moved on to whether this should be brought forwards to complement a mobile system that was needed along the general route the airship would most likely follow.

The helicopter accompanying the machine all the way across England would have a special forces' contingent on board in case the airship was forced to land, but they'd also act as extra eyes and ears in the sky. They'd be able to direct the ground units to the terrorists, should drones or rockets be launched. A reconnaissance unit had already driven and walked the general area, checking out abandoned or unused farm buildings. Nothing had been found.

The amount of military and government staff involved in preventing an attack was wholly disproportional to the threat in most people's eyes, but this is what happens when the US President and the British Prime Minister designate something to be a flagship project and attach their names to it. If the production of microchips on their respective home soils had achieved an unwarrantedly high status, it had been increased further with the gradual strangulation of Taiwan by the Chinese, where sixty per cent of the current production was based around Taipei. This figure rose to ninety per cent if one was talking about the latest advanced chips, similar to those to be produced in Herefordshire and Arizona.

The meeting at the factory drew to a close with confident handshakes and a feeling that the matter was under control. Major Phipps said his goodbyes and explained that he would be based at the SAS base at Credenhill from Tuesday.

They all stepped outside into the sunshine, which had perhaps lulled them into a false sense of security about the weather and the impacts should the force and direction of the wind change on the critical day.

Daniel Drinkwater landed at Stansted airport, having flown in from Valencia, hired a grey Audi and immediately drove the thirty miles to Lucky's house, where he wanted to speak with Gabby to avoid any electronic means of communication.

He rang ahead to Agata, the housekeeper, who cooked, cleaned and generally ran the Fortuna household. She opened the ornate, black gates in readiness and waited on the steps for him to drive in across the gravel. He soon arrived, parked up and got out of the vehicle.

"Good afternoon, Agata." He jogged up the steps.

"New car?" she asked.

"Hire car. I had a change of plans, and mine is at Birmingham airport. I take it Gabby is in residence?"

Agata, who had seen Gabby in all her moods over ten years,

raised her eyes heavenwards. "She's waiting for you. Would you like a cup of tea? I'll bring it down before you get down to business."

"Perfect, thanks."

He made his way down a long corridor and knocked on the door to the West Wing.

"Come on in," a voice called out.

Daniel opened the door and walked across to the woman sitting at her work desk. She swivelled around, and he reached for her hand, bending down to kiss her on the cheek.

"How are you?" Gabby shuffled her considerable bulk to make herself more comfortable while he pulled up a chair to be close to her.

"Hot, but not as hot and sweaty as in Spain. How are the birds?" Asking after the macaws was a prerequisite before engaging in any business. They were family to Gabby.

"Carmen is moulting a bit."

Daniel didn't bother to probe further as to how she knew this. "Good." He wasn't sure if it was good or bad, but the conversation moved on: "Agata's bringing me a tea, then we can run through a few things."

They chatted about nothing until there was a knock on the door, and the tea arrived.

"Thanks, Agata." Daniel took the cup and saucer from her.

"Gabby, do you want anything?" Agata asked.

"No thanks, I'm good. Actually, if you could bring down some more milk later, that would be great."

With that, Agata left and shut the door.

Daniel wasted no time. "You saw that the idiots in Arizona have blown the plan?"

"It might have been bad luck, and the Feds stumbled on the drones in the farmhouse, but I expect they used phones to talk to each other."

"Have they been caught yet? That could be curtains for us."

"Not that I've heard, and I'm following all the newsfeeds."

"Your dad and I have agreed to ditch the plan in the USA and attack the convoy in Holland between Breda and Eindhoven. He's flown there from Spain to check out the route himself."

"If you want something doing well, do it yourself, eh?"

"Exactly," he replied, although this was from a man who always paid someone else to do the work in order that he might have one degree of detachment.

Gabby was staring past him towards the sounds coming from the conservatory, where the macaws had appeared at a set of French windows and were trying to peer in at Daniel. "Do you want me to tell the guys in the USA to abort it all?"

"Yes, please. We'll pay them ten per cent to keep them quiet, but I can't trust them, and the various Feds and police will be all over that area now, if they weren't before. Tell them to disappear and lie low for a while."

"Dad will need money to buy some drones or whatever in Holland, won't he? Do you know how much? I'll need to sell some Bitcoin."

"He'll tell you tomorrow when he gets back ... but do whatever it takes. We're in too deep, and there's shedloads of money ... but we cannot fail." He lifted his cup from the saucer and took a sip. He stared at the blue-and-white pattern of a Dutch landscape on the cup.

"Fine."

"Have you found that CIA woman?"

"No, it's impossible. I've tried every avenue open to me and paid out a bit of money, but getting a CIA agent's name is beyond my skills."

"OK, thanks for trying; it's not our priority for the next couple of weeks until both those machines are blown off the road or out of the sky."

"I did wonder if you could ask your new informer to get her

name from his contact in Dutch intelligence. All I need is the name, and then I reckon I'll find her."

"I'll ask Piet to try to get the name, but I have no idea what his relationship is with this Dutch agent."

"Everything good in Valencia?" She was listening to him sip his tea, which smelt awful to her. Coffee and Coke were her drinks of choice.

"All good. The next ship docks in two days, as planned. I'll get you the photos of the address labels to scan. We must have 3,000 now, don't we?"

She turned towards her monitor and, not using the keyboard, barked out her instructions. A voice immediately gave the number as 3,105. Gabby didn't need to add anything, and Daniel looked at her with admiration and some disbelief at what she was able to achieve. He could barely type an email.

"That list of names and addresses will make us even more money over the next few years if the Chinese mess us about or disappear."

"I'll drink to that." She felt along the desk to find her can of Coke.

Twenty miles to the west in Central London, Mike was reading up on the latest reports about the Chinese laboratories manufacturing drugs fifty times more powerful than heroin, with the latest one, nitazine, fifty times more powerful than that. All of these were marketed openly on the internet as well as on the dark web.

She was trying to imagine someone in their bedroom in Seattle or Sheffield using their phone or laptop to answer such an advertisement by emailing or calling. The Chinese salesforce at the other end would take down their requirements – which may be bespoke – and their address, and then take payment in

Bitcoin or with their credit card. A few days later, the small packet of powder or handful of tablets would be packaged to look like bottles of paracetamol or aspirin. Once the address label was affixed to the outside of the padded bag, they were ready to ...

Here, Mike stopped and leant back. What did they do with these hundreds and thousands of small packages and parcels? How did they get to Seattle or Sheffield?

Meanwhile, upstairs, Leonard de Vries had just finished a call from his boss on the seventh floor in Langley, Virginia.

Even though the air conditioning was on full in his room, he was sweating and having to wipe the thinning strands of ginger hair from his brow. After a long period of contemplation, he pressed the button on his desk and asked Lana to call Mike Kingdom up to his room immediately. He continued to marshal his thoughts, weighing up what to do.

Before long, he heard the knock on the door and called her in. She looked apprehensive and was fiddling with her bandana.

"Take a seat; you'll need it."

"What have I done now?" She couldn't think of anything that had happened since she was sitting in the same chair a few hours earlier, but she always assumed she was guilty of something.

"Nothing to my knowledge."

"I'm still reading all the background on the China narcotics project."

"Good, and keep at it. We need a result. Your job is to find out where it comes into Europe, probably Spain. It's not about that end of the route I wanted to speak to you about; it's something that's crossed my desk in the last hour. Relax and listen. I still haven't decided what to do." He paused and moved a pen on his desk for no apparent reason. "Our guys in Langley and China have discovered something interesting about your new project. They've been monitoring conversations from many of the labs suspected of producing nitazine and fentanyl. They've now identified several of the girls who call themselves 'shipping agents' and who take the internet orders from the USA and Europe. Their phones are being tracked, but this only leads to users and buyers abroad, not to Mr Big."

Mike wondered where this conversation was going and what it had to do with her, but she kept on listening.

"They've had a breakthrough from hacking into the phone records of one of the lab managers or head scientists; I don't know who exactly. This individual is in charge of sending the pre-addressed packages to a central point for hiding in something legitimate, which is shipped all over the world. He has been a bit indiscreet in his phone calls and has mentioned someone we think is the individual at the European end—"

"That's great," Mike interrupted, genuinely thinking that this would give her the toehold she needed at the European end.

"His codename is Jan the Dutchman." He waited for her to digest this and react, but she simply sat there staring at him while making shapes with her open mouth but emitting no noise.

"Mike, I'm sorry; I should think long and hard about this, but we don't have time. I'm not sure if you're the right person to work on this project, and I get it if you want me to give you something else to do."

It had been Leonard who had sent her to Holland with Dylan all those years ago. It was Leonard who had to deal with the aftermath of Dylan's death and getting Mike back from a military hospital in Germany to the UK. All this had to be done without a word reaching the press. He had achieved it with the help of powerful people back in Washington and Europe, but he had to watch the cartel instantly shut up shop and move the operation to Spain or France.

She still hadn't spoken, so he filled in the silence. "Mike, whatever happens, I don't want you going to Holland. That's a no-no, d'ya hear me?"

She nodded, but deep down she knew that she would have to do whatever was necessary. "But Jan the Dutchman is dead. He's dead," is all she said.

PART TWO

CHAPTER SEVENTEEN

Mike was staring at an old wooden dresser that had been left by the previous owner. Having no plates to put on display, the shelves were piled up with books, files and assorted bits with nowhere else to go in such a small cottage. She was sitting on the sofa with her laptop on her knees, deep in thought.

She couldn't help but have a terrible feeling of *déjà vu*.

Searching for Jan the Dutchman again after all these years wasn't what she expected to be doing, especially on the Friday before her wedding. She would have preferred to be listening to the phone conversations of terrorists intent on destroying some state-of-the-art machines or smuggling narcotics into Europe, not stressing over a man she thought was dead.

She tried to think calmly and logically. There was the possibility that Jan the Dutchman may be the generic name that this drug cartel or gang had been using for their group over many years. It might not refer to an individual but instead to any of the current senior members. She so wanted this to be true, but however hard she tried, couldn't completely fool herself for one minute.

The alternative meant that Jan the Dutchman was still alive;

this frightened her, and such a shiver went up her spine that she needed to pull back both her shoulder blades to remove the feeling. It would, of course, mean he was still active in the narcotics-smuggling business, having moved to suppliers from China, but this wasn't the real problem. It brought Terry's death back into focus.

How had he found out Terry's name, followed him to The Gambia, tracked him down to his flat and killed him?

Mike had absolutely no idea, but she needed to figure this out quickly as she must surely be the next target on his list. She had immediately decided that she needed to tell Wazz her life was in danger, even if she couldn't go into too many details. He deserved to know and could perhaps play a part in protecting them both.

It had been a difficult conversation the previous evening at around 10.30pm, after the ride down from London.

"There's been a leak," was how she had begun. "Various lists of names have been stolen. My name might be on one of the lists."

"Jesus! What's the Agency doing about it?"

"They're on the case, trust me, but so am I. My priority at work is to track down who has these lists. By the way, there's no guarantee I'm on these lists, but I could be." She had come up with this cover story so Wazz might understand why she was on edge all the time and why she might be looking over her shoulder.

"Is your life threatened by this? I mean, are people after you and the others?"

"Possibly."

"Do you want me to stop work for a week or two and stay at home with you?"

"No need, but I wanted you to know."

"I'll pay a bit more attention to unknown people in the village. Jesus."

"We're a long way from Washington and London, so don't get too excited." She wasn't in any way convincing him, but it was a good try.

Wazz was letting his own mind wander. "Was that man you didn't murder on these lists?"

"Well ... um, yes, probably, but he died from natural causes."

"Yeah, right, and I'm a Dutchman."

Mike had never heard this expression, and it caught her off guard. She tried to control her facial expression, which had morphed into a rictus. "Let's go to bed and wake up fresh in the morning."

"Mike, it's time for you to quit the Agency for good. You've given fifteen years' good service ... well, actually, you've gone way beyond what anyone could expect. From this coming weekend, let's start a new life away from the threats that come with your past."

"I wish it were that easy. Firstly, let me catch whoever has stolen these lists." She was having to concentrate to maintain the pretence she had created. She hated lying, and she especially hated lying to Wazz.

He walked across to her and held her in his arms. She felt safe for a few seconds while he kissed the top of her head, but she knew it wouldn't last.

"Wazz, I'm so sorry you're being dragged into this. You didn't sign up for any of it."

"That's not the problem; I can defend myself. It's protecting you that's bothering me."

They checked that all the doors were locked and turned off the lights. The bedroom beckoned.

In the morning, she would begin looking for Jan the Dutchman all over again.

Piet, Daniel's new informer in Amsterdam, had given him the real name of his contact in Dutch intelligence – it was Jakob. Daniel had made it clear that he wanted this agent's real name and home address; he didn't want codenames. Finding where he lived had taken Piet several hours longer as he had only ever met this Jakob in a bar.

Armed with this information, Lucky had arrived in the Netherlands with two pressing tasks: firstly, to recce the route from Breda to the airport at Eindhoven; and, secondly, to arrange a meeting with Jakob. Two of Lucky's long-time friends from Amsterdam were waiting outside the airport to meet him. If it were possible, they were even bigger and more menacing than him. They hugged and patted each other on the back before jumping into a dirty, black Ford Ranger Double Cab four-by-four.

On the way to a safe house, Lucky filled his mates in on the plan of action regarding Jakob. They'd be doing all the work as it was important he kept a relatively low profile, given his return in two weeks to sabotage the machine on its way from the factory in Breda along the A58 to the airport. Finding the killer of Daniel's brother-in-law was important, but it was of lower priority. Lucky made himself at home in the safe house while his friends set off to grab Jakob.

Having been well briefed, they arrived outside a modern building set back on a pleasant tree-lined road and drove past slowly, taking in the lie of the land. There was no obvious activity, and there were no cars on the driveway. Piet had told Daniel he believed their target usually arrived home at about 6.00pm, but there could be no guarantee. Apparently, he lived there with his wife and two children.

Lucky was hoping Jakob wouldn't prove to be stupid and would freely give up the name and contact details of this female CIA agent who might lead him and Daniel to the man who shot Henk. If he didn't play ball, it could get very messy for him as

Lucky had decided it was better not to leave any witnesses once Jakob had seen their faces.

Jakob never knew what hit him. He had driven his car up his driveway towards his garage. As he opened the door and stepped out, one of the thugs stepped out from behind a tree and grabbed him around the neck. He couldn't scream, remonstrate or, most importantly, breathe. The Ford reversed part of the way up towards Jakob's car, and he was bundled into the backseat. There was no roaring of engines or spinning of wheels. No one in the neighbourhood saw what was happening.

It was a thirty-minute drive to the safe house, which was located in the countryside away from other dwellings. At the back was a large shed into which the terrified Jakob was pushed. Lucky came out of the back door of the old farmhouse, walked across the yard and followed them inside the wooden building. He was greeted by the sight of his prisoner being tied to a chair in the middle of the floor, which was covered in a sheet of heavy-duty polythene; similar sheets were hanging from the walls.

"Jakob, welcome. You speak English, I understand."

There was no response, merely a nod.

"I'm sure you want to get back to your family and live happily ever after, so I'm going to make it easy for you. This is what's going to happen. Either you answer my questions fully without forgetting anything, and we leave you alone or, stupidly, you refuse to answer, and we hurt you beyond your worst nightmares until you do answer, then we leave whatever is left of you on the floor here. Either way, we're going to check your answers, and if they aren't right we'll bring your family here and hurt them in front of you until you do answer. Do you understand? It's very simple." This was all said in a quiet voice that merely added to the menace.

"What do you want to know?" Jakob could hardly speak.

"I want a name, address and phone number ... that's all. So

let's start with who was the CIA woman who called you to check up on Henk Visser's death?"

Jakob took this in and tried to work out what was happening. This was a mistake.

The largest of his kidnappers picked up an axe from a workbench and brought it over towards where Jakob was sitting. In Dutch, he said, "Would you like to answer the question or lose the fingers on your right hand?"

Jakob screamed and began sobbing. He stared at Lucky and said, "Mike Kingdom."

"That's a man's name; I said I wanted the woman's name."

"She's known as Mike. Her name is Michaela Kingdom."

"Where does she work?"

"For the CIA in London. She's an analyst working on narcotics."

"Where does she live in London?"

"I don't know." His voice wavered. "How would I know? I don't know where any CIA staff live."

"That's not a very helpful answer, Jakob."

"If I don't know it, what can I say? I want to tell you anything, everything, but ... I don't know it."

"What about her phone number or email address?"

"She has only phoned my office from the CIA number in London" – in this Jakob wasn't being entirely accurate – "We don't give out private phone numbers to colleagues in my business."

Lucky paused and walked a few paces back and forth, stroking his chin.

Jakob, in a pleading voice, filled the silence: "I might be able to ring her from my office and get her address and number."

"Nice try, Jakob."

Lucky reached forwards to one of his friends and asked for Jakob's phone, which had been taken away from him.

"I'll tell you anything I know," Jakob pleaded.

"You're right; you will tell me. I'm going to get this name checked. If you're lying, we'll go and get your kids, understand?"

"*It is her name. It was Mike Kingdom who phoned me,*" he screamed.

"I'll go and check. What's the PIN for your phone?"

Jakob gave it to him, and Lucky typed it into his own phone as a record.

"Please," Jakob begged.

"I'm going to have the name checked. I hope for your health that it's right. I'll leave you in my friends' capable hands. They'll help you remember everything about this Mike Kingdom."

He pulled back a sheet of polythene and left, having seen a message on his phone that another old acquaintance was waiting for him in a Land Rover Discovery at the front of the farmhouse.

Three hundred and fifty miles to the west, Mike – who was refreshed and alone at her workstation – began a systematic search for Jan.

It was tempting to start with the recent intel on the phone call from the Chinese lab, but in truth, there was little she could realistically do that wasn't currently being undertaken by the NSA, MI6 and GCHQ. If there were more indiscreet telephone conversations, they'd pick them up, and she would be informed. It was unlikely there was a direct link back to Jan in Europe, if that's where he was based; there would be cut-outs to protect him.

Instead, she took the opposite approach and rewound almost eight years to revisit what had happened and any new intel that had been added in the interim.

She now had access to virtually all the files on the ill-fated operation in Holland from the Brits, the Dutch and her own agency. Some of it she recognised and was her own input, much she had never seen before, and some had been added after the accident.

Mike began at the point when the Dutch had partially identified the drug-smuggling operation and she herself had come at it from the Colombian end, discovering the use of false floors in the shipping containers under thousands of cardboard boxes of green bananas.

She flicked or scrolled through so many reports and transcripts, often pausing only when she saw her own or Dylan's name. Keeping the emotion out of the process proved difficult. She didn't expect to find anything new or valuable until she reached the point where GCHQ had traced Jan the Dutchman's phone from an intercepted call in 2018. This had been passed on to Terry, who was undercover in Rotterdam and befriending drug pushers and dealers.

It didn't look like he had made any progress in the seedy bars and brothels as he tried to buy decent-enough amounts of cocaine to interest the Dutch importers and the cartel behind them. So what did he do once he had been given the name 'Jan the Dutchman'? Did he try to meet the man? Turn him?

Mike could find nothing.

Terry's last inputs appeared to be a short report on the latest rumour about the arrival date of a container ship into Rotterdam and a note that he had gone to ground for a few days after the attack on Dylan and Mike. He cited fears for his own safety and that his cover must be blown. He reappeared in London six days later.

Mike guessed he had used these days after the attack to attempt to track down Jan and kill him. Terry must have gone under the radar, but he continued to check the latest intel from London, in which he had discovered that Jan had reserved a hotel room for a few days. Before MI6 or the Dutch authorities could monitor the room or arrest Jan, Terry had struck out of guilt at what had happened to Dylan and Mike – all this no doubt fuelled by an unhealthy dose of alcohol and drugs.

None of what she had read helped Mike in any way. Jan hadn't been identified, wasn't in that hotel room when Terry shot its occupant, and had disappeared to Spain or France, taking the operation with him.

It was all as Terry had told her or implied. He had innocently betrayed the covert operation to the cartel and felt guilty at Dylan's death and the impact on her. He had gone underground, shooting the person he thought was Jan the Dutchman.

Mike had reached a dead end – again. Should she go to the funeral and talk to Terry's coffin? Otherwise, she wasn't sure how she could crack this problem.

CHAPTER EIGHTEEN

Lucky had been picked up outside the safe house in a Land Rover Discovery driven by an old mate, who'd take him to look at potential launch sites for the drones. With a broad smile on his face, the driver turned off the radio as Lucky jumped in, and they shook hands across the central console.

They had been briefed by a man called Doug, who was tech-savvy and going to be the drone operator; he would actually launch the attack in thirteen days' time.

For a few hours, Lucky was able to forget about Jakob while he concentrated on the main task in hand: checking out the best location from which to attack the US-destined machine.

His trip to Holland was going well, and he was happy with the revised plan, which removed the need to attempt to destroy the machine going to Phoenix while it was travelling on US soil. Acquiring attack drones had been surprisingly easy in England and Holland, but it was more difficult in the USA. They'd take out the British machine over the Malvern Hills and the Dutch one en route to Eindhoven airport. He would now be present at both operations.

They had driven to the town of Tilburg, midway between the

Breda factory and the airfield. Lucky knew the city from the days when he had used the industrial warehouses as part of the drug-smuggling route into Europe. That system had worked so well for three years.

Now he was concentrating on a totally different problem: the route from the factory in Breda. He had already worked out that the convoy, including the sixteen-axle transporter, would have to travel east along the A58 past the city and towards Eindhoven.

He was driven through a totally flat landscape with woods and lakes that could only truly be appreciated from the air. A safari park along the way provided the only distraction from a quintessentially Dutch scene.

They had pulled into a rest area on the westbound carriageway, where they sat for fifteen minutes, picking the best spot to leave a farm vehicle with the drones inside. It would have a camera positioned in the cab to show the explosion when it happened. The plan was to drive this lorry laden with strawbales covered by a tarpaulin and park it strategically so another one of Lucky's team could get there ten minutes before the convoy would pass by on the other carriageway. He would remove the tarpaulin, enabling the two drones nestled among a grid of bales to fly across and strike the machine. By the time the attack happened, the man would have driven back to Tilburg and disappeared.

Doug, the drone operator who lived in Essex, had undertaken a virtual search online and chosen a location that would enable him personally to be 500 yards away on a parallel minor road, with clear sight of the straw lorry and the convoy. His position would be hidden by trees from above. There was no quick road connection from the eastbound carriageway to his chosen vantage point. Once he had destroyed the machine, using a laptop to control the drones, he would pack it away in his rucksack and roar off on his motorbike, along the straight lane first and then across two farm tracks to bring him out on another road, which would lead him to where he had parked his van away from prying eyes. The motorbike would be pushed inside it, and he would drive north, away from the pall of black smoke. This was the plan.

At least, Lucky reassured himself, there were two drones in case one failed to work or was shot down by some sharp-eyed member of the accompanying security contingent. He also had insisted that a tarpaulin was used to conceal the drones from any helicopter or overhead surveillance until the last moment. The security forces' focus would almost certainly be on their own eastern carriageway, junctions and slip roads.

Lucky was feeling confident. At the moment the machine exploded, he would be sitting in Eindhoven airport, drinking a cold beer and waiting to catch the 11.05am direct Ryanair flight to Stansted in Essex. It would land there at 1.15pm, and if he couldn't make it because the convoy was delayed, he had the 9.15pm flight as a fallback position.

Once settled in the airport, he would be able to find a quiet corner in which he could watch the live footage through the windscreen of the lorry, confirming that the machine had been blown to pieces. All this had to work; there was no alternative.

Doug would make his own way back to London on the ferry from Hook of Holland to Harwich. They had agreed not to travel together.

Everything being prepared wouldn't take place for almost two weeks; before then, Lucky had to get back to the UK and concentrate on what had to happen in Herefordshire.

It was while he was sitting at the departure gate at Eindhoven airport, waiting for the evening flight, that he received a call from his two friends who had abducted Jakob and continued to interrogate him. Using WhatsApp, they confirmed the name 'Michaela Kingdom', but could add nothing that Lucky hadn't heard himself. It seemed that Jakob really didn't know anything more of value. Lucky had thanked them and asked them to

continue and send an address or phone number if possible. He knew how difficult it would be for Gabby without this information.

The reply came back: "Not possible."

This was frustrating, and it wouldn't be until many hours later that he would learn the reason why. Unfortunately, there hadn't been time to get the address from Jakob. His heart had given out from the violent beating and the application of power tools not wholly in accordance with the manufacturer's instructions.

Gabby was sitting outside, leaning back with the sun on her face. She was surrounded by the buzz of insects and was concentrating on the new noise of a farmer with a tractor, far off in the distance. *He can't be trimming hedges in July,* she thought to herself, but very quickly, she could smell the dust and pollen as he cut the rye crop. She didn't suffer badly from hay fever, but it did irritate her eyes enough that she limited her time in the garden.

With her break over, it was time to go back inside, much to the delight of the two macaws; their attention had been drawn to her every move since she began sitting on the bench outside the conservatory. There was a sad irony that these were two of the most beautiful and colourful birds on earth, and yet she couldn't see them, but what mattered to Gabby was that they were very tactile, friendly and spoke to her. Macaws are intelligent, and this pair seemed to be aware of her blindness, always placing things in her hands or chattering away if they wanted her attention.

Her phone buzzed, and she answered it.

"Gabby, darling, I'm sending you the name. Get to work."

"Dad, when are you back?"

"Very late tonight. I need to see someone on the way home

from Stansted. I'm only back for a few days. You know where I'm going then. Bye."

It was the briefest of telephone conversations, but it communicated everything that was necessary.

Once back at her desk, she fired up her system and leant back in her chair, waiting for the name to arrive in an encrypted form. Her computer's AI-generated voice, something resembling Stephen Fry, informed her that a message had come in and then read the message: "Michaela Kingdom ... known as Mike."

"Perfect, we don't want a common name such as 'Sue Smith' or 'Liz Jones', eh, girls?"

The macaws were bobbing their heads-up and down outside the window and squawking to each other.

She had been hoping for an address or phone number, but this was clearly not available. Looking for a person without these or further information was new to Gabby, but she had decided on a strategy. Mike Kingdom most likely worked in Central London, and therefore she would need to commute every day so she wasn't likely to live in Scotland. As a CIA agent, she wouldn't be on social media and would be keeping a low profile. Gabby also had come to the conclusion that Mike Kingdom might not be American. She could be another nationality, even British, and on the CIA payroll.

How many Michaela 'Mike' Kingdoms were there in the UK? She used AI and was very unhelpfully informed that: "There are no publicly available records or government databases in the UK that track the exact number of individuals named Michaela Kingdom, making it impossible to give a precise count. The availability of such specific demographic data, including unique names, isn't generally shared due to privacy reasons."

"Great," she said under her breath, but she wasn't really expecting anything different, and so she began the thankless task of checking the electoral registers, beginning in Central London and gradually radiating out into Essex, Kent, Surrey,

Buckinghamshire, Berkshire and Hertfordshire. Gabby was well aware that Mike Kingdom may have opted out of being on the electoral roll, even if she were British. In fact, this would be probable, but she needed to exhaust this line of enquiry.

Many hours later, she was beginning to get frustrated. Persisting wasn't a problem if she knew for sure that this sodding woman's name was definitely in the system somewhere. On reaching Oxfordshire to the west, she gave up, swearing at everything in hearing range. The macaws beat a hasty retreat down the polished branches and out of sight, not that Gabby was aware of this.

Nor was she aware that, even if she had continued to the next county of Wiltshire, it wouldn't have mattered. Mike may have bought a house in Rodbourne, but she wasn't on the electoral roll.

After rolling her head back and rubbing her temples, she slapped her forehead. "You aren't playing the percentages. You know she's probably American, you twat! That means she can't vote." Gabby had come to the realisation that she would also probably not buy a house in the UK but would have staff accommodation or was perhaps renting a flat. None of this was good news.

It was early evening, and she had got nowhere.

She took out of the fridge a macaroni cheese that Agata had prepared, put it into the microwave and set it going. This gave her time to adjust her plan. While spooning the hot and comforting food into her mouth a few minutes later, she settled on putting the names 'Michaela', 'Mike' and 'Kingdom' into the main social media platforms in various combinations just to see what came up.

Although it was fascinating, she wasn't sure how useful her initial searches were. They threw up five Michaela Kingdoms, all of whom could be eliminated by consulting other publicly available information. They were either too old, too young or, every few hours, posting pictures of their pets, family and houses.

The grandfather clock in the corner of the room – which had indeed been left to her by her grandfather – chimed, telling her it was 7.45pm. She had hoped to have an address before her dad got back much later.

She decided on a new tack.

It was Saturday morning, and Mike and Wazz were shopping in Salisbury. It was only five days until the wedding. He had stopped outside a fancy-dress hire shop.

She had said, "Don't tempt me," before walking on down the street. They were meant to be buying their outfits.

"What's wrong with a 'vicars and tarts' themed wedding?" He was trying to wind her up.

"There's just the two of us, and we're unlikely to be able to drag two witnesses off the street dressed like that."

"And that's your only reason for not wearing it?"

"I could buy a new wig?"

He smiled, but this question changed the tone of the conversation from flippant to serious. "You come however you want. I don't care what you wear as long as you're happy." He knew this was probably a difficult decision for her to make.

"Well, if I turn up bald as a coot, we definitely won't be able to get the witnesses off the street."

"You mean they might not have seen a bald vicar?"

It took her two seconds to catch up, and then she burst out laughing at the thought of Wazz dressed as a tart.

"I wore the whole 'white frock and veil' combo last time in Las Vegas, so this time I'm going to wear the black wig. There, decision made. I'll try not to make it too goth."

They walked along the pavement towards a men's outfitters,

where Wazz stopped to look in the bow window. Mike continued walking while looking at a very old carved-stone gateway and watching a flock of pigeons explode into the air above the old, tiled roofs. Wazz turned to see three men walking towards her. Years of escorting rich wives around Marbella or Marrakech meant he switched seamlessly into protection mode.

"*Mike!*" he shouted, and then he closed the gap between them in half a dozen paces. He grabbed her and lifted her into a doorway. She was completely disorientated as he placed himself between the three men and her.

"Easy ... easy," one of the men slurred while staggering slightly.

His mates pulled him past Wazz as they continued to stare at him.

"What the ...?" Mike was rubbing her elbow from its contact with the doorframe.

"Sorry, sorry; I didn't like the look of those guys. Sorry. Guess I'm on edge since you told me that you were on that list."

"I'm fine. Nothing is going to happen to me walking down a street in Salisbury, OK?"

Wazz looked embarrassed, and they began walking again. Mike was thinking that the Skripals were probably thinking the same thing as they walked around Salisbury before being poisoned with Novichok.

She kept this thought to herself.

CHAPTER NINETEEN

Gabby had made no progress and had abandoned the search for Mike Kingdom while she dealt with other pressing matters, mainly her Bitcoin trading and paying 'subcontractors' for Daniel and her father. She also was the accountant to the pet-food business, ensuring everything was sanitised and in order before the books went off to the well-paid real accountants and to be audited afterwards.

When Gabby had reached a suitable juncture, she went back to her search; this was more because she needed a distraction from the pet-food business – a world of doggy chews and cans of rabbit meat. It was as she was exploring new avenues that she accidentally instructed her system to enter Michaela Kingdom's name into search engines she didn't usually use. This often happened in her life and were her equivalent of a typo. It was a random mistake, but these sometimes led to a new thread or an opportunity. It always took her a few seconds to correct things by having to select the right verbal instructions.

While choosing her words, she listened as the details of an art sale were described – an obvious dead end. She was about to tell the system to cancel the search when she heard the name 'Michaela Kingdom' and the word 'American'.

It concerned the sale of a Giacometti sculpture entitled *The Running Man*, which Gabby learnt was one of many created by the sculptor. They were tall, thin and almost-black stick men. Gabby couldn't see what was on the screen, but she guessed it wouldn't be to her taste. She had never heard of Alberto Giacometti, but that didn't matter.

It transpired that the word 'American' hadn't been attached to Mike Kingdom but to a benefactor who had purchased the sculpture and donated it to an art gallery and museum in Washington, DC. The search contained details of the London auction house and the provenance of the artwork. It had sold for £850,000.

The seller was Michaela Kingdom, and this stunned Gabby. This couldn't be the London-based CIA analyst whom she was after, surely?

The bill of sale gave her address as number 3 Church Lane, Rodbourne, near Salisbury, Wiltshire. It had been sold on Friday, 11th August 2023. She was clearly not whom Gabby was looking for; the house was too far from Central London, and there was no way an analyst would be able to afford a piece of artwork like this one. Gabby wasn't to know that Mike had been given it by the Murchison brothers as a very big thank you; they were indebted to her after she had played such an important role after the death of their father. She had sold it to avoid having a mortgage on her new cottage.

There was no logical reason why Gabby didn't cancel this search, but she had a feeling deep down. *Odd,* she thought to herself, *why this woman named Michaela Kingdom might have one of these sculptures.* It couldn't be the woman she was looking for – the idea was ridiculous – but like so many crazy ideas, it was actually true.

Most people would have moved on and pursued a new line of interest, but not Gabby. She remained doggedly holding on to the thread, not knowing where it could lead. Something inside told her that there weren't many Michaela Kingdoms in the UK, and she should persevere – there was a very small number to check, and one of them must be her target.

She instructed the computer to put in the name and address, hoping to find out a bit more about this Michaela, even if this meant she could be eliminated from the search.

The voice on her computer began to read out the authority to marry from the superintendent registrar in Salisbury and revealed the time and venue as 11.30am on 9th July at Salisbury registry office. Her partner was listed as Waldemar Wasielewski, a name that tested the AI-generated voice. He was down as divorced and British but, she thought, clearly of Polish extraction. Michaela Anne Kingdom was listed as widowed and American.

Gabby was excited; she had at last found an American Michaela Kingdom living in the UK, if a bit far from London. She got up and walked to the freezer compartment of her fridge, where she took out a tub of chocolate ice cream as a treat and reward for making real progress.

At that moment, there was a tap on the door, and Agata walked in. "That reminds me; I must order some more of those ice creams. OK if I dust around a bit and hoover?"

"Oh, hi. Yes. I was just taking a break."

Agata walked across the room, carrying her cleaning equipment and materials in a yellow plastic box with a handle. While making her way past the screens, her eye fell on the name of a fellow Pole, Waldemar Wasielewski. She said nothing and began her tasks, starting with the large mantlepiece.

Dusting and wiping here always gave her strange feelings. In pride of place was a porcelain urn in a distinctive cobalt-blue-

and-white pattern. According to Gabby, it had been made by Delft, which had been producing this pattern in South Holland since 1653. Agata moved the urn, wiping it gently and trying to concentrate on the sailing ships and windmills while ignoring the fact that it contained the ashes of Gabby's beloved mother.

Lucky drove over to his sister's house for lunch. Rita lived twenty minutes away in a new estate of mostly four-bedroomed houses, where the struggling saplings and shrubs did nothing to hide the fact that the buildings were crammed in. He had bought the property for her and her husband when Daniel had paid him a bonus for dealing with a drugs warehouse manager who thought he could build up a parallel business himself, which in a way he did. He was part of the foundations of the extension to the warehouse in Spain.

It wasn't his sister whom he had really come to see; it was his twenty-eight-year-old nephew, Smiler – a tall, thin strip of a man with floppy hair who, in his pale-green sweatshirt, looked like a stick of celery.

Rita chose not to know any of the gory details about Lucky's activities, but she had worked out he was involved in drug smuggling in some capacity. She had met Daniel a few times and knew he must also be involved and was probably the brains behind the business.

All she asked of her brother was that he didn't involve her son in anything illegal. Smiler was smart but lazy and had never settled in a job. Occasionally, he had acted as a chauffeur for Lucky, picking him up from airports or had carried messages or packages.

"Smiler, do you want to earn £250 in cash, plus a bit for petrol?" Lucky asked.

"What's it involve?"

"Driving to Wiltshire, finding out if someone lives at a house and driving home ... tomorrow."

"Can't you ring them up and find out?"

"I don't have their phone number, you muppet. That's why I need to send you. I have a lot on this week."

"Who's is it?"

"She's an American who owes me a lot of money. I just want to know where she lives and when she's going to be at home. I want to have a chat with her." Here, Lucky was diverging substantially from the definition of 'chat' in the Oxford English Dictionary.

"How do I find out? Who shall I say I am?"

"Watch the house for a while. Knock on the door and ask for Brian Jones. See who answers."

"Who's Brian Jones?"

"He was in the Rolling Stones, but it doesn't matter. Pick any name. If she answers the door, check if she's American. If someone else answers the door, apologise and say you must have the wrong house."

"What if no one answers?"

"Walk around the village and chat to anyone you meet, or go into the pub or village shop, if they have one. Ask around. Make up any story, but don't ever mention your name or mine."

"Do you know what she looks like or how old she is?"

"I don't have a photograph, unfortunately, but she must be in her thirties or early forties. Oh, and she's getting married on Thursday in Salisbury to a bloke with a stupid, long Polish name beginning with W. I don't know anything else about her. Reckon you can do it?"

"Sounds easy."

"Don't get cocky and don't stick out. Dress like a normal person and blend into the background." Lucky was staring at the green sweatshirt and white jogging bottoms.

"When do I get paid?"

"I'll give £300 to your mother now, and when you tell me what you've found, I'll tell her to give it to you. Ring me tomorrow evening on WhatsApp as soon as you get home. Don't write anything down, know what I mean?" Lucky, or Uncle Roger as he was today, tapped the side of his nose.

"Where's this house?"

"In a village called Rodbourne in Wiltshire, somewhere in the Wylye valley near Salisbury. I think she lives at number 3 Church Lane. She bought it just over a year ago."

"How long will it take to drive there?"

"Two and a half hours around the M25 and down the A303. I should set off about 9.00am – if you can get out of bed by then."

Lucky left after lunch and drove home. The traffic was flowing, and he made it back in half an hour. There was a lot happening over the next week or two, and he was preoccupied for the whole journey. He parked and walked to the far end of the house.

He tapped on Gabby's door, which was always kept closed – not just for privacy but also so she could more easily hear people enter.

"Hello, my angel. Anything happened since I left?" He bent down and kissed her.

"Nothing apart from some communications from China, and I can't find anything more on this Mike Kingdom. Will Smiler go down there to check her out?"

"Tomorrow. Even he should be able to find out if she's still there. I'm not sure when I can go down there myself. I might drive down on Tuesday. On Wednesday, I'm intending to load up the Range Rover with the drones, and early on Thursday, I'll be driving to Malvern."

It was Monday, 6th July, and Mike was in London, having stayed overnight at Carol's house. She had changed her routine so she could be back very late evening and could look forward to a week and a half before having to go to the office again. The wedding on Thursday was her priority; it was the day her new life would begin.

Leonard had called her into his office, knowing he wouldn't see her again for a few weeks. "I feel like I should've gotten you a present."

"There's no need, thank you. It'll be a quiet wedding ... just the two of us."

"That explains why I never got an invitation."

Mike wondered about his marriage with his wife and married daughter living in Montgomery, Alabama. "Nobody's invited. We'll grab two witnesses off the street."

"Well, if you want to take a couple of extra days, just put your time down to the China project. I'll sign it off."

"That's kind, but we're not going on honeymoon."

"Too bad. Well, you've taken the microprocessor machine off the job list. No one stateside thinks they're mad enough to try again. The route is crawling with Feds."

"Have they caught whoever cached the drones?"

"Nope, but don't worry – they will."

"I expect they've gone to ground."

"I don't think they'll hang around. It's all too hot." He paused and let out a long sigh. "I sure would like you to crack the China lab project. Remember that I'm trying to keep all our jobs."

"I've gone back to the beginning seven or eight years ago in Holland. It's a bit odd seeing your own work again. There's no more information on Jan the Dutchman." Mike was carefully trying to avoid any mention of Terry Bailey.

"Have you made up your mind on whether it's an individual or an organisation?"

"No, still open on that."

"Shame Terry Bailey died. He might have had some new ideas."

Mike held his stare and wondered, not for the first time, whether her boss was psychic, lucky or just very experienced. "Yeah." She waited a second and then changed the subject: "Did you see that the Brits have picked up another message from that lab guy in China?"

"No. Any good?"

"It looks like a list of about 100 users with addresses all over Europe. Something appears to have gone wrong with their labelling of the packages."

"What are the Brits doing with the names?"

"I believe they're arranging a series of raids, but they don't want to tip off China that they've busted their system."

"Those names'll mostly be sad users and bottom feeders. It's probably not much use unless they kept the packaging ... that would show us whether it's Holland or Spain where the drugs come into Europe."

"The Brits are working with the main courier companies, monitoring all packages to a few of the addresses. They'll intercept and see where they came from."

"Mmm ..." Leonard was thinking. "Couldn't the couriers check back in their records and see where they came from? I'm guessing these saddos don't receive that many Amazon parcels."

Mike looked at him with a mixture of awe and incomprehension. She hadn't thought of that idea. "Could you suggest that to Overton? It's above my paygrade, but it's an excellent idea."

"Will do. I'm seeing him at lunchtime in his club."

"Yes, I remember that club." It had featured heavily in a recent exploit when Mike was searching for a missing operative.

"Club's pretty lousy, but the food's good."

Mike left him running through the menu in his mind. She had managed not to mention that one of the thirty UK addresses on the Chinese list was in Warminster, not twenty miles from her house.

Why did the Fates always tempt her?

CHAPTER TWENTY

Smiler was playing Capital Radio very loud in his VW Passat as he drove clockwise around the M25. There was no need to concentrate on the route as it was essentially two motorways and the A303. On this Monday morning at 10.00am, the motorways were busy, especially near the junction leading south towards Gatwick airport.

At Cobham services, he filled the car with petrol, cursing that he should have done this before leaving Essex. Still, not to worry, his uncle had given the money to his mum.

The journey dragged, but he made it into Wiltshire before he stopped to stretch his legs and have a vape – blueberry sour raspberry, his favourite. He leant on the car, hypnotised by the swoosh of the cars and lorries hammering downhill on the A303. Before getting back in, he checked on his phone the route for the last few miles along some country roads. It wasn't difficult to memorise. He loved the jobs for his uncle Roger; they were easy money.

Lucky, for his part, knew his nephew wasn't as daft as he looked and would quite easily establish if the right Mike Kingdom, an American, still lived there. After that, he could pick his moment to pay her a visit and extract the information he needed. He assumed she worked all week in London but would go down to Rodbourne at the weekend. Lucky wasn't to know that, ironically, she was in London on that Monday, but this wasn't her usual routine.

Smiler drove slowly into Rodbourne, spotting a pub but no village shop. He turned into Church Lane and parked at the end, next to the lychgate with its flint pillars and slate roof. The birds were singing, and the sky was a faded blue. There were only a dozen houses in the lane before the junction with the main road through the village. Wearing a grey, checked shirt and black jeans – his attempt at not standing out – he walked unhurriedly back the way he had come.

His long legs, lanky frame and lolloping gait meant he arrived at number three in a matter of minutes. Separating him from the front door was a small ditch, across which was a wooden footbridge. He decided to continue on to the main road and return later. He could neither see nor hear any activity inside. Two Muscovy ducks began swimming towards him, expecting some bread. They were disappointed and glared at him with their dark eyes surrounded by bare, red skin. He didn't like the look of them.

At the junction, he paused. There was no traffic and no activity, but on looking right, he spotted an overweight man in brown corduroy trousers and a cap enter The Green Feathers. It was a couple of minutes past midday, and the pub had just opened. Vic, who lived diagonally opposite, was never late and always ready to take up his favoured seat in the corner next to the fireplace.

While Smiler was staring down the road and deciding what to do, a van with a trailer carrying a ride-on mower turned into Church Lane and parked outside the main row of thatched cottages. A very solid-looking man with a thick neck and biceps that tested the fabric of his black tee shirt got out, walked across the little bridge and ducked into the tunnel between numbers three and four. Any confidence Smiler had immediately evaporated. This man resembled his uncle in so many ways – most importantly, in the way he would be able to snap you in two. Perhaps he was a gardener or, even better, going to number four.

Smiler decided to go to the pub and ask; it would be simpler and safer. If he was unsuccessful there, he may need go back and knock on the door, but he hoped he wouldn't need to. He lurched along with his hands in his pockets trying not to look furtive.

A brass bell tinkled as the large, studded oak door opened. He was confronted by a lounge bar that lacked only one obvious feature: a bar. There was only one customer, who was sitting in the corner with no drink in front of him yet.

"Marning." The man was obviously glad of company.

"Morning. Where's the bar?" Smiler was spoilt for choice of chairs, but he sat down at the next table to Vic.

"Jess'll be out in a minute."

Smiler looked around just as a white-haired woman in a long, brown cardigan emerged from behind a heavy curtain made from a piece of tapestry and red velvet. She was carrying a pint of beer.

"Here y'are, Vic," she said, and she placed it on the table in front of him. "What d' you want?" she asked, looking at Smiler with her washed-out blue eyes. It wasn't the warmest of welcomes, but Jess treated everyone as an inconvenience.

"I'll have a pint as well, please."

Jess said nothing, but she turned and disappeared back behind the curtain, watched only by a stuffed green woodpecker in a domed glass case on an incongruous games machine, which was obviously not plugged in.

"What brings you to sunny Rodbourne?" Vic's accent was thick.

"I'm looking up an old friend ... Brian Jones who lives here, I believe."

Vic rubbed his stubble and gave this some thought, "No one 'ere by that name ... an' I know everybody. I've lived 'ere all me life. They call me the local Neighbourhood Watch. I'm Vic, by the way."

They shook hands, and Vic took a cheek-filling swig of cloudy beer.

"I'm Darren," Smiler replied, trying to hide his nervousness.

"Brian Jones – he were in the Rolling Stones. He's buried in Cheltenham."

"Different Brian Jones, then, I expect. It's a common name." But Smiler was regretting listening to his uncle in case this conversation went further.

"Where'd this Brian Jones say he lived?"

At that moment, Jess came out of the back room, carrying a pint and a dish of chopped gherkins. Smiler wasn't sure what they were and looked at them strangely before he recognised them as something he thought came from a Big Mac. She thrust a card machine out in front of her, and he scrambled to remove his phone from his pocket to pay for the drink.

"Would you like another pint?" Smiler asked Vic, hoping his new drinking buddy might save him the pain of tapping on the door of number three.

"Don't mind if I do." Vic quickly finished his drink and placed the empty glass onto the tray, the froth still sliding down the inside of the glass.

"You want another one?" Jess nodded at Smiler's full glass.

"No; no, thanks. I'm driving."

Jess added Vic's second drink to the bill and pushed it in front of her young customer again, who offered his phone without checking the amount. If it was for thousands, his uncle Roger would come down and torch the place.

"Where'd you say this bloke lived?" Vic was pressing on. "And ta for the pint. Ask me anything about the village; I'm at your disposal all lunchtime."

"In Church Lane. I thought he said number three, but I might be wrong."

Vic and Jess looked at each other.

"'e don't live at number three, that's—"

"—someone else," Jess cut in.

"My mate, Brian – his wife's American, by the way – told me he had moved here a year ago." Smiler was better at improvising on the hoof. He was wasted playing computer games in his bedroom.

"Wazz's lady friend's American; she's called Mike, which is a bit confusing, but 'er partner definitely ain't called Brian Jones."

Jess turned towards the curtain again, wondering about her most regular customer – and not for the first time.

"Not to worry. I was passing through on my way back to London, and it was worth a shot. Cheers."

"This Mike, she goes to London every Wednesday evening and comes back Thursday evening, otherwise she's round here. Bloody long drive every week."

Smiler lifted his beer and took a good mouthful while Vic reached automatically for his non-existent second pint, yet to be delivered. Uncle Roger would be very happy. Perhaps brains did run in the Fortuna family.

"Glad to see you've still got a job, Leonard." Gordon Overton was sitting in a red leather armchair at one of their irregular Monday lunches at the Commonwealth and Overseas Club.

Leonard could take the gentle ribbing from most of the secret squirrel community, but somehow taking it from Gordon was different. The man had that ability to put everyone's backs up. "I'm fine, but how about your job? It's time your government had a reshuffle. Your Prime Minister is under pressure."

"Very likely, but unlike your government's efficiency drive, we never sack anyone; we just nudge them sideways into another job."

"Well, my team is working on two of the President's pet projects, so no need to apply for my job just yet."

"Glad to hear it. Glad to hear it. Let's drink to that." Gordon raised his Kümmel on ice and took a sip as Leonard took a larger mouthful of his bourbon on the rocks.

"What's in that drink?"

"It's made from caraway seeds. It was first brewed in Holland in 1575."

Leonard flinched at the word 'Holland', which was recurring too often in his life – and never with a happy ending.

A man with a small head, small feet and a substantial middle that poked out through his open jacket walked across and apologised for interrupting: "Hello. Sorry, Gordon, just wanted to say I was sorry to see your boss in *The Times*' obituaries today. Sad news. I'll leave you to it."

"I haven't seen *The Times* yet today, but I don't read the obituaries in case I'm in it." Gordon was talking to the retreating wide back making its way across the lounge towards the dining room.

"Who's died?" Leonard asked.

"Oh, I don't know; someone in the Bank of England or the Treasury. Almost everyone here thinks I work there. Wish I did some days."

"How's the project in Hereford? Any progress?"

"Not as much as you've made. You've removed the threat before the machine has left Holland."

"True, but we're still no nearer to identifying who's behind it all."

"I hope that you having discovered their *modus operandi* in the USA will help us find their drones over here before they get chance to launch them ... or I'll be out on my ear with no hope of a sideways shuffle."

"Are you checking every farmhouse?"

"Unfortunately, we're talking about half of southern England. I dread to think how many farms, barns and sheds there are. No, we're concentrating on the last few miles. I think we need a spot of luck or a breakthrough by GCHQ."

"Speaking of which, you're doing well on the China labs. The new list is a great set of leads."

The normally effusive Gordon Overton appeared to downplay the list with a shrug of his shoulders. "I'm not sure; they're all users and perhaps the odd middleman, but we won't know where the stuff comes into Europe."

"You're intercepting some of the next batch of packages, aren't you?"

Someone walked into the other side of the lounge to pick up a newspaper, leading Gordon to lower his voice even more. "We are, but that may take time. We only received the list yesterday."

"Have you thought of getting the couriers to tell you where the last batch of packages were despatched from?"

"We're on the case. I'll let you know."

"It must be simple for the courier companies to check their computer systems?"

"True, but if not, I'll get Cheltenham to hack in and find the address in Europe where the Chinese are shipping before redistribution. My guess is somewhere in the Netherlands, given that name on the first message."

"Jan the Dutchman?"

Mike felt strange being in the office on a Monday afternoon, but there were only two hours before she began her long commute to Rodbourne; she wouldn't be back in London for almost a couple of weeks. For no earthly reason, she was cleaning her keyboard using an air spray. There was an end-of-term feel.

She had the list of users, but there was nothing more she could do with them – the users weren't going anywhere, and the British police were organising a series of raids over the next few weeks. She was slightly frustrated that they hadn't gone straight in and tried to find the packaging, its source or even fingerprints. She needed to leave that to others and to use her last hour on finding the elusive Dutchman.

For an hour, she read Terry's records and reports in the MI6 archive. It confirmed what she suspected: he had never met Jan. It looked like any communication had been by email and WhatsApp, but these addresses and numbers were long discontinued. She wondered about Terry. Did he realise Jan was the lead drug smuggler, or did he think he was dealing directly with someone who was working, or wanting to work, for British intelligence?

Unhelpfully, there were time gaps, especially covering the days when he killed Henk Visser. There was absolutely no information on where he was staying or his movements. It was recorded that he had lost his phone and had a new number. Mike could see that he wouldn't want his phone tracked or his contacts viewed. This was another dead end.

It was while she was staring at the word 'phone' on her screen that another thought began to form. If Henk Visser was using the hotel room booked by Jan, they must be close business acquaintances or friends. What was their relationship? The Brits and Dutch could find nothing in Henk Visser's past to connect him with the narcotic smuggling or distribution. This made Mike think that perhaps they were friends outside the criminal activities. How might they know each other?

Henk could not have been a more typical family man; if anything, his life was grey. So why was he friends with an international narcotics Mr Big?

She looked across the office at Morag and Chuck, wondering about relationships and why we spend so much time with people with whom we share little in common. Would she let Morag and

Chuck use her hotel room? Then it dawned on her. The people we're forced to interact with are family and in-laws.

Perhaps Jan was related to Henk Visser in some way. Was he in one of the family photographs on Henk's phone?

As usual, there were too many questions, but this is what Mike loved about her job. As she logged out of her system, she couldn't wait to ride home and look at the phone again.

CHAPTER TWENTY-ONE

The Green Feathers was very busy, despite it being a Monday evening. All the other pubs for miles around were closed, and serious drinkers were grateful that Jess kept such odd opening times. She would open solidly for three weeks and then randomly shut for two days midweek. What she did on those two days was a mystery because she was never seen leaving the village. There was no reason for her to go anywhere as all the beer was delivered in kegs that were tipped off a lorry onto a sack full of straw before being rolled down a ramp into the cellar. The wines and other supplies were also delivered on Mondays and Thursdays.

It was early evening when Wazz entered the pub in need of a drink after a hard day weeding flowerbeds – a back-breaking job and his least favourite. Mike was on her way back from London, and he would be home in time to meet her.

There was no chatting at the bar with the other regulars, the pub not having one, but instead, the locals sat or stood around tables, putting the world to rights. Food wasn't the priority on Mondays, if it ever was, but rather the consumption of much beer and cider.

Sitting in his corner seat, Vic called Wazz over to him. "'Ere, Wazz, I've zummat to tell 'ee."

"What's up, Vic?"

"Did you see thic' young bloke who was 'ere at dinnertime?"

"Where?"

"In 'ere 'avin' a beer. Said 'is name was Darren. Looked as if 'e'd snap in two in the breeze."

"No. Sorry, Vic, I didn't. Why do you mention him?"

"'E was askin' about who lives at number three down your lane. 'E was lookin' for a friend called Brian Jones, but I said there were no Brian Jones in the village."

"Really? What else did he say?"

"'E said this Brian Jones 'ad an American wife. I told 'im you 'ad an American wife but you weren't called Brian."

"Anything else?" Wazz was beginning to feel uneasy about this. He was already worried about Mike's name being on this leaked or hacked list.

"No, 'e said 'e was on 'is way through on 'is way back to London."

"Thanks for telling me. I'm always suspicious of people like that. Want another pint?"

"Don't mind if I do, ta."

Wazz stood up to grab Jess's attention the next time she came out from behind the curtain. He fared better than most in this endeavour, towering over most of the other drinkers as he did.

With a pint ordered for Vic, he swallowed the remains of his own beer and bade everyone goodnight. On the short walk home, he paid extra attention to his surroundings, but he saw absolutely no sign of human life. When he got home and opened the front door, he switched on the lights and checked both upstairs and downstairs. He had a decision to make: should he tell Mike or not when she arrived later?

He turned on the TV and watched a football match to

occupy himself until she arrived. He must have dozed off because the sound of her bike outside woke him up as she pushed it over the bridge and down the tunnel. He jumped up and went into the kitchen, turning on the rear outside light. He had opened the back door before she had put the bike up on its stand.

"Hi, good journey?" He stepped out onto the small patio.

"An accident on the M25 near Heathrow, but otherwise the usual. Glad I don't have to do it for a couple of weeks."

She removed her helmet, and they kissed.

"You smell of beer. How was The Green Feathers?" she asked.

"Pretty busy. I didn't stay long. I came back to watch the football." He had decided not to mention what Vic had told him. It would only make her more stressed, and he wanted her to relax after the bike ride.

They carried her helmet, black rucksack and a bag from one of the paniers into the kitchen, and then sat at the table. He took bottles of beer out of the fridge for both of them and a plate of chicken salad for Mike.

After quenching her thirst, she bit into a piece of cold breast. Once swallowed, she leant back. "I can't tell you how happy I am not to be working for ten days. Leonard says I only need to keep a watching brief."

"Perfect."

They clinked beer bottles.

"And only forty-eight hours until we get married. It's suddenly around the corner." He drank a mouthful of his beer, having only opened one for himself in order to keep her company.

"There's nothing left to do, is there?"

"I hope not. We just have to turn up."

Wazz was hoping nothing happened in the intervening time to mess up their plans. He had an ominous feeling after his chat with Vic down at The Green Feathers. "Made any progress on finding who was behind the leak of that list?" He tried to keep it as casual as possible.

"No, the team are still searching, but don't worry; I'm a long way down the list and even further from the centre of the action." She didn't sound entirely convincing. Lying wasn't in her nature, and she loathed having to do it.

"You will be careful, though, won't you?"

"Of course; threats come with the territory. We're used to it. I know it's not your world."

"My world is now a twenty-mile radius from this house, thank goodness, and I can't tell you how good that feels."

"We're getting there, we're getting there." She repeated the words in part to convince herself. "By the way, how far away is Warminster?"

The following morning, Wazz had already left to pick up some fencing panels from a garden centre on the outskirts of Salisbury when Mike sat down at her kitchen table, eager to reopen Henk's phone. She left it on charge while opening his cache of photographs in anticipation of testing her theory that Henk, while not involved in the narcotics smuggling, was a friend or relative of the mysterious Jan.

When she lived in her cabin in the woods, Mike would clarify her thoughts or seek inspiration by staring at the grain pattern or knotholes of the pine boarding in her shower. Since moving, this process had been transferred to the bike journey to and from London, on which she would allow the random shapes in the landscape to generate thoughts.

Yesterday evening, somewhere along the A303 as she stared at the verges illuminated by the headlights, she had convinced herself that her theory was sound. Henk's phone could hold the answer. Perhaps Terry had known this all along and was subtly trying to point her in that direction. In this, she was wildly mistaken. He never intended for the phone to be found and had put it in the old suitcase when he got back from Holland and had never looked at it since.

Not being able to tell anyone that she had the phone was going to limit her. She couldn't officially ask for any support from the Agency or its partners. If she discovered anything relevant, she would have to think of how she would introduce this information to the Agency system. That, however, was a problem for the future. All her professional life, she had needed to tell herself to fight today's battles, not tomorrow's wars.

She copied the eighty or so photographs across to a file on her laptop and examined them one by one. Half of them were of local landscapes or sporting events, with no people in the foreground, so these could be dismissed, but many were of the Visser family unit: father, mother and son. In total, there were eighteen people with recognisable faces who appeared, often multiple times.

She created new files for each of the individuals who appeared, cropping and zooming into the images. Each of the eighteen subjects was given a letter, Henk was A, his wife B, the son C and so on until she reached the letter R.

With a cup of coffee next to her, she began with D and E, who often appeared together. She ran their faces through facial-recognition software and sifted through the results. There was little doubt that these were the CEO of a fair trade banana grower and exporter from Tanzania and his Dutch shipping agent. They were photographed with Henk at two award ceremonies, where there was no attempt to hide their relationship or avoid the public gaze. These two individuals appeared to be innocent, but Mike had a natural suspicion of any fruit exporters – whether in Colombia, Mexico or East Africa. They were natural bedfellows with the narcotic cartels, who were attracted to the mass use of shipping containers into the USA and Europe.

She had searched and dismissed some other characters before she refilled her coffee cup, by which time the man tagged as J became her next target. He had been captured on film with the family, feeding swans on a river. He also appeared together with another man and woman, in several wedding photographs with many other guests who weren't really identifiable. Mike fed the images into the facial-recognition software and waited.

There were several possibilities, but the best match was to a man named Daniel Drinkwater – a Brit.

She felt a wave of disappointment as she had been hoping for a match with a known suspect on the CIA or other agency databases, particularly someone operating in Holland or nearby at the time of Henk's death. It was lunchtime, and a need to stretch her legs drove her from her searches. Normally, she would walk around the village for fifteen minutes, but Wazz had begged her to stay in the house with the doors locked until she was told that she wasn't being threatened. He had no idea whether she would listen to his advice. Actually, he did, but he chose to ignore this thought.

Outside, it was a lovely day with a blue sky streaked with daubs of milky white from dissipating contrails. It was too inviting, so she half-listened to him and unlocked the back door and stepped into the garden, but she didn't make her way through the tunnel and out into Church Lane. From the end of her garden, near the fruit bushes and compost heap, she turned around to look at the back of the terrace. It still fascinated her that old houses like these had been built in brick with panels made up of lumps of napped flint. The builders were, she supposed, only using the materials found locally in the chalk hills or clay valleys. Above the walls, a faded thatched roof sat heavily, like a winter duvet. Only the brick chimneys and a pheasant made of straw provided any visual relief.

To the sound of chirping sparrows, frustrated by the fine chicken wire stretched across the thatch, she meandered back to her kitchen as slowly as possible. The sun was warm on her face. She was tempted to stay outside longer, but finding out more about Daniel Drinkwater and the other people in Henk Visser's photographs was too tempting. She locked the back door behind her and thought of Wazz and his warnings.

Once back at her computer, it wasn't long before she was feeling frustrated. "You're the most boring Brit I've ever investigated, Mr Drinkwater."

In this, she was sadly way off the mark, but it wasn't a surprising conclusion given the lengths to which he had gone to hide his real life. She did find that he was on the electoral roll and lived in Warwickshire, which she found was known as 'Shakespeare's county'. His house was located on its own along a road leading to the village of Foxley. This wasn't where she expected Jan the Dutchman to live, if this were him.

Further delving revealed he was the owner and managing director of pet-food shops in the towns around Birmingham and was a member of the local golf course. Nothing else caught her eye. He didn't look that promising.

But what was his relationship to Henk Visser? she wondered, *Why was he prominent in the wedding photographs?* He must be a close friend or relative. Going through Henk's phone directory, she found a number listed as Dan. This would be checked later with any others she uncovered or suspected. Parking her searches on Daniel Drinkwater, she moved on to the next possible person – the one she had tagged with the letter K.

Lucky had just finished a workout in his gym at home. He had showered and was dressing in his bedroom. After a quick check in the floor-to-ceiling mirrors, he went to his lounge to make a call. He chose WhatsApp and a few seconds later was talking to Daniel and updating him. "Smiler went down to Wiltshire, and he's reported back. He tells me that the woman is American and is the one whom Gabby identified from the info I picked up in Holland."

"Oh, good. I know she's not our main priority, but you know how much it means to me."

"Don't worry about the two big jobs; they're under control, but I don't have time to go to Wiltshire. I'm sending a couple of friends down there tomorrow. They'll interview her, if you know what I mean? I've got to prepare for Malvern on Thursday. Everyone and everything needs to be in place by mid-afternoon. After that, it's a matter of waiting and watching which way the wind blows."

"Great. Let me know if she gives you the man's name."

"Don't worry, she will; she will."

"And tomorrow, I'll be watching the news feeds all day. I'm sure they'll cover the journey across the UK."

"I'll send you an emoji once it's all over and we can move on to the second half of the job."

"I'll be thinking of nothing else; we can't afford any cock-ups, or you and me are toast."

With that, the call ended, and Lucky made his way through the house, past the kitchen and the dining room (which was hardly used), and on down towards the West Wing. He knocked on the door and entered.

"Hello, baby, how are you?"

"Fuming." Gabby didn't sound happy.

"What's wrong?"

"The Chinese have told me they've cocked up the labelling again on a few hundred of the packets. I've got Juan to keep them in the warehouse and not give them to the courier."

"Oh great! What do the Chinese want us to do? Are they sending new labels or what?"

"They're thinking about it. We'd have to open every package, check the contents and put them in new packages with new addresses. It's a fucking nightmare."

"It's their fault not ours. Let them sort it out ... and well done in getting Juan to stop the despatch."

"I'm not just a pretty face."

"You aren't just a pretty face; you're as sharp as a tack."

She was smiling. "We're an amazing team, you and me. I'm sharp, and you're blunt – a perfect combination."

CHAPTER TWENTY-TWO

Wazz had long given up trying to tell Mike what to do, as her inner stubbornness would lead her to ignore even the wisest advice or argument. He did, however, continue to voice his opinions for no other reason than to keep his own sanity. He would never forgive himself if anything happened to her and he hadn't tried to dissuade her from her more extreme suggestions.

"Really? You want to go for a ride on the bike? What's so special about this Wednesday morning?"

"I do. I need to get out of this house. It's my last day of freedom."

"I thought that you were searching for whoever leaked or hacked this list with your name on it?"

She had temporarily forgotten that this was what she had said she was doing. Going through Henk's phone in detail hadn't been mentioned. Going to Warminster to see where a user or dealer on the list from China lived had most definitely not been mentioned.

"I've made some progress, but I need a break. I'll get back on it this afternoon."

"Please, please be careful. We're getting married tomorrow, and I'd prefer you to be in one piece. I need to go to work; grass cutting beckons." He pecked her on the cheek.

"OK, I'll be careful, but no one's going to follow me on a motorbike. They'll stick out a mile. I promise I'll be back about lunchtime."

Wazz left by the back door, and before he was out into Church Lane, Mike was back at her laptop, where she continued her filing and searching of Henk's photographs. At 10.00am, she had reached a natural break and put her equipment into the concealed safe, which had been a requirement before Leonard agreed to allow her all her freedoms.

The previous day, more to give herself a mental break from Henk's photographs, she had googled the address in Warminster. It was the one nearest to her on the list from China, and this had proved too tempting. Twenty-three Chalk Road was where she was headed, and it should only take her about half an hour.

Having checked that the house was tidy and all secure, she put on her bike leathers and helmet and stepped out into her back garden. It was warm but not hot, and there was no wind or rain. It was the perfect day for a ride. She set off.

Two or three times as she travelled along the Wylye valley, she stopped or slowed right down to check she wasn't being followed. Wazz would have been pleased that his advice was having some effect. In the middle of Warminster, she turned left at the main traffic lights and made her way up and down a steep hill until she found Chalk Road.

It had buildings on one side and a long, grassy recreation area on the other. She counted off the houses until she reached an old warehouse or mill that had been converted into flats. Number twenty-three wasn't in the main building but down the side, through an arch from which weeds sprouted. She locked up the bike out on the road and approached the front door down a narrow passageway partially blocked with bins. She was tempted to look inside them, but she wanted to establish whether anyone was at home first. Everywhere was grubby and smelt dank. It reminded her of Terry's basement.

She had prepared for several scenarios with various cover stories, but none of these were necessary as it turned out. She knocked on the door, and it was opened after a long time by a sallow-faced woman who was still wearing a dirty nightdress. She could barely focus or indeed speak. Her eyes kept closing, and she was licking her lips, revealing a wide selection of teeth in urgent need of dentistry.

"... need a signature?" She had started a sentence halfway through.

"What? No, no thank you." Mike realised the woman had mistaken her for a courier.

"No package?"

"No, not today." Mike paused. "Not like last week."

"That's right." The woman, who was no older than forty, closed her eyes and staggered back two paces before regaining control. She didn't elaborate on what was 'right'.

Mike stepped inside while saying, "Do you have the parcel from last week? I'm collecting the old packaging?"

"What?" The woman screwed up her face, trying to make sense of anything.

Mike scanned the front room quickly, but it was a tip. There was rubbish everywhere and few places to walk, apart from a route on the threadbare carpet through to what she assumed was the kitchen. She spotted a brown cardboard packet on top of a yellow padded envelope. There was no time to think, so she picked them up.

"Ah, here they are. Thank you." Mike turned to leave. "No need to make a cup of tea. See you next week."

"Eh?" The woman reached for a doorframe to steady herself, but before she opened her eyes again, her visitor was outside, and the front door had been closed.

Mike was alone in the alley, carrying her helmet in one hand and the two opened packages in the other. Turning over the first, she saw it was from a kitchen shop and clearly labelled from Leeds with a return address, and the second was from a building-supplies company, also dispatched from a UK depot. They weren't what she had been looking for. She was very conscious that she was in a dead end where she could easily be trapped. What was she thinking?

While passing the bins on her way back to her bike, she opened their lids, but instantly regretted it; they were stinking and full of rotting food, none in bin bags. She threw the two pieces of packaging inside and closed them before making her way out to the road, concentrating in case anyone had followed her.

She couldn't wait to get back to the safety of her own house. It had been a truly stupid idea coming to Warminster.

While Mike was riding back to Rodbourne, a hearse was parked at Mortlake Crematorium in the London Borough of Richmond upon Thames. A coffin was being lifted onto the shoulders of the funeral directors as they prepared to carry it on its last journey. 'Samba Pa Ti' by Santana was playing over the sound system as Brian Rosie turned around to see the coffin enter and be placed on the platform in front of the deep-maroon curtains. Ironically, he had been cutting up a similar pair the night before.

Brian had chosen the music based on what he knew Terry liked, not that he would be hearing it. The whole place and the whole process felt surreal. He felt rather emotionless sitting on the pale ash bench; the only mourner. Even more so as the song faded out before the next began.

He had already told the funeral directors that he wouldn't be reading or saying anything. It would be very odd talking to empty rows of chairs, and neither he nor Terry were religious. The funeral director had offered to read some standard humanist verses before the curtains opened and Terry disappeared for good. Brian had agreed to this, and as the banal words floated around the echoing room, he wondered why he had paid for a wreath of flowers on top of the wicker coffin; Terry had suffered from hay fever.

Brian wasn't concentrating, but he heard something about Terry coming from the earth and returning to it. Apparently, he'd had a life well lived, and it wasn't important that he had died, but that he had existed. These words made Brian wonder what Terry's life had actually been like. He was obviously a spy out in the field; no one would put up with him in an office for two days running. It was in bars that Terry was at home – the rougher, the better – but however drunk he got, he had never let his guard down. Whatever secrets he had held would go with him into the furnace.

Unnoticed, the verses ended, and to Brian's relief, the coffin began to move out of sight on the rollers. There was a mechanical whirring, which even the gifted Carlos Santana couldn't block out.

Brian waited a minute or so out of respect, with his head bowed, before standing up and walking slowly to the door and out into the living world.

He thanked the funeral director, who asked him if he would like to write a few words in the book of remembrance. For a second, Brian was tempted to put something about a life well spent spying for his country, but he decided against it. Instead he simply wrote "To a dear friend, you'll be deeply missed", ending it with a flamboyant signature.

Having ensured that Terry had been given a respectful send off, he walked past a group of mourners from another funeral, who were chatting near the entrance to the garden of remembrance, showing the relief on their faces that the worst part was over.

Fresh air beckoned, and Brian headed outside, unaware that someone known as Quilley was watching to see who turned up for the cremation.

The grey Audi had turned around before parking in Church Lane, just along from the terrace of thatched cottages. Two men got out of the car and walked the short distance to number three before knocking on the door; they could have been selling double glazing. They waited before knocking again, but there was no response.

The taller of the two, who had small eyes and thin lips, stayed outside the door while his friend made his way down the tunnel to the back gate. Away from prying eyes, he tried the catch and found the gate to be unlocked. He entered a small garden, staying close to the rear of the house in case anyone in the terrace was looking out from their bedroom windows. He peered in through the glass panels of the door, but he could see no one in the kitchen.

In a series of simple moves, he put on leather gloves, took out a foot-long, blue jemmy from a shoulder bag and levered the door open. No glass shattered, and the noise was minimal.

He went inside and made his way quickly through the kitchen and lounge, but the woman they were after wasn't there. He opened the front door to let his friend enter; as he did so, he had to duck under the frame. Nobody saw them.

"Liam, check out the note on the kitchen table. I'll go upstairs and look around."

Liam was putting on gloves he had taken from his jacket pocket as they separated to perform their respective tasks. Harry moved upstairs surprisingly quickly and quietly for a big man. He peered in the two bedrooms and bathroom, but all was clear.

They met back up in the kitchen.

"Says here that she'll be back at midday. It's 11.40am now. Let's wait." Liam pulled out a chair and sat on the edge.

"Will she come in the front or the back?" Harry asked.

"Front, I'd guess. D'you want to stand in the lounge by that door curtain? I'll wait here. You didn't lock the gate, did you?"

Liam was rewarded with a frown. "No, I'm not that stupid."

Liam took out his knife from a pocket and rotated it in his hand. The wait for Mike to return had begun. They didn't intend to pussyfoot around; they needed to find out the name of the man who shot Henk Visser and where he lived. After that, she was a burden to be removed. Dead, she wouldn't be able to identify them.

Mike was enjoying her ride along the chalk valleys and greensand ridges that led up onto the downs above. Here, there were few hedges, and the fields rolled away to the horizon, broken only by hangars of beech trees and the occasional farm building or telegraph pole. She began to think about her wedding tomorrow and felt so lucky to have found Wazz.

When Dylan had been killed, it had felt as if her life had ended, and there was no way she could conceive of meeting someone and marrying them. She knew her failings – her impetuosity, her stubbornness and her intolerance to just about anything she saw as wrong – but he took all this in his stride. His calm nature was the perfect counterpoint.

Her obsession with her work and the long hours she spent staring at computer screens would put off most men, but not Wazz. As she approached Rodbourne, she vowed to herself that she would leave her projects behind for a few days and enjoy becoming a married woman again. She wanted to make sure Wazz enjoyed the wedding; he had his own troubled past, which he wanted to put firmly behind him. Tomorrow would be equally important to both of them.

The Muscovy ducks were at the far end of the ditch as she pushed her bike across the slats of the bridge. The cool and dark of the tunnel beckoned. She undid the wooden gate, wheeled her Ducati into the garden and put it on its stand. Her scalp was sweating, and it felt wonderful to rub it once her helmet was off.

The back door was ajar. She felt elated; this meant that Wazz was home early for lunch or a late coffee. For him, no two days were the same.

Her note was still on the kitchen table.

"Honey, I'm home," she called out to wherever he was in the house.

There was no reply.

On walking into the lounge, the colour drained from her face, and she screamed. "*Wazz!*"

His body was slumped against the front door, and a streak of blood ran from near the handle where he had been trying to get out before collapsing against the white wood and passing out.

She ran over and felt an enormous sense of relief when she realised he was still breathing. This was short-lived as he was losing a lot of blood. She pulled out her phone and rang the emergency services.

It was while she was giving the details to the woman on the line that it dawned on her he had been stabbed. It didn't take her long to work out what had happened and who had done it. Of course, she was the target, not Wazz, and she turned around nervously wondering if Jan the Dutchman was still in the house.

With the ambulance on its way, she was faced with the dilemma of staying with Wazz or checking out upstairs. She decided to stay but open the lounge windows so she could speak to the medics when they arrived. Moving Wazz away from the door wasn't possible, and she had been told not to do this but to try to staunch the flow of blood until the ambulance turned up.

For what seemed like an eternity, she sat next to him, holding a clean tea towel against his stomach while caressing his head. Tears were streaming down her face.

CHAPTER TWENTY-THREE

Mike was still in tears when the ambulance arrived.

She leant out of the window and told the medics to come through the alley as Wazz's head was against the front door, where he had been bleeding into the brown coir welcome mat beneath him. There was no way she would attempt to move him, even if she could.

Mike couldn't care less about her own safety, but she decided that Jan wouldn't have hung around the village anyway after the fight she presumed had occurred. Whether this happened or not was mixed up in a mental fog. Her thoughts were all over the place.

A few minutes earlier, she had gone into the kitchen and out to the garden in order to leave the door and gate ajar. It was only as she pushed the back door wide open that she saw it had been forced.

There was the sound of people running. The medics hurried down the tunnel and came through the kitchen and into the lounge, carrying their bags. They knelt next to Wazz.

"We're getting married tomorrow," Mike was speaking incoherently and continuing a conversation in her head.

"Let's get your husband-to-be sorted out, then, shall we?"

"He's not going to die, is he?"

"Are you Mike who dialled 999? I'm Julia. You try to relax now we're here. We'll get him to hospital as quickly as possible."

Julia's colleague was pulling up Wazz's tee shirt to see where he had been shot or stabbed.

Mike looked away. "We're not getting married tomorrow, are we?"

"We'll do our best, but let's get him to hospital so they can patch him up."

The paramedics' job was to keep the plates spinning until the hospital, with all its facilities, performed its function.

Mike was distracted as a police car with blue lights flashing and sirens blaring pulled up outside. She walked to the window and directed them down the tunnel while her mind went into overdrive. It was only three weeks ago that she had been interviewed by the police in London. What was she going to say? She was savvy enough to realise she needed to get a grip.

She couldn't mention her job or how she knew who had done this to Wazz and that, more than likely, she would be next. She would have to play the innocent party who came home to find every woman's nightmare.

"Hi, Julia," the policeman said, recognising the paramedic. Turning to the woman shaking near the window, he asked, "Are you Mike?"

She nodded.

"Why don't we go into the kitchen and let Julia and John do their stuff? Come on." He beckoned to her and encouraged her away from the distressing scene.

She walked meekly out of the lounge.

"You're Mike, Michaela Kingdom, who rang 999?"

"Yes."

"Sit here and tell us what happened." The younger policeman

pulled out a chair from under the kitchen table. The radio crackled on his black stab vest.

Mike slumped into the chair and was suddenly at a loss, her mind went blank.

"What happened this morning?"

"I ... I went to Warminster ... on my bike, motorbike, and when I came back, I found Wazz like that up against the front door."

"Who's Wazz?"

"My ... fiancé. We're getting married tomorrow ... in Salisbury."

"I know this is difficult, but please try to help us; we have to ask these questions. Are you aware of anyone who might want to do this to Wazz?"

"What? No, no."

"Has anything been stolen that you can see?"

"No, no; I haven't looked, but I can't see anything missing. I don't know about Wazz's phone or billfold. I didn't want to move him."

The policeman made a calculated guess that she was talking about his wallet. "No problem. You didn't see anyone suspicious around the area over the last few days?"

"Nobody. It's a very small village, and Church Lane is a cul-de-sac. We don't get many visitors."

"Do you have anything worth stealing in the house?"

"Nothing ... as you can see." She turned her head, indicating the lack of anything of value.

"Where do you both work?"

Mike lifted her eyes to both police constables; *Here we go,* she thought to herself.

"Wazz is a landscape gardener and handyman around here. I work in London." She had kept it as vague as possible.

"Does he have any enemies? Anyone who might do this?"

"No. No one. We've only lived here a year."

"The back door was forced. It looks more like a burglary that went wrong. Perhaps he came back and disturbed them?"

"Quite likely. He wasn't meant to be back until 12.30pm or 1.00pm."

A noise in the lounge meant that the front door had been opened. The policemen asked a couple more questions and asked her not to touch anything until the SOCOs arrived.

She stepped into the front room to see Wazz being pushed out on a trolley.

"We're taking Wazz to Salisbury District Hospital," Julia said, and they began to cross the footbridge.

"Can I come as well?"

"Do you have your own means of transport? That might be easier."

"I have a motorbike. I'll leave as soon as the police have finished."

They had arrived at the back doors of the ambulance. There was no response from Wazz to any of the movements or conversation.

Mike touched his hand and turned back to the house.

In the Malvern Hills, it was an overcast day.

A man called Doug had ridden his electric bike two miles down a track, having left his family in the caravan. It had been a long drive from Essex, and the children were fractious. Later, his wife would take them in the car to a farm park, where they could annoy the sheep and geese.

He cycled to a wood on the lower slopes of the hills, which were seventeen miles from Hereford with the Welsh border beyond. His purpose was to find a place to meet Lucky Fortuna tomorrow when he would be handed the two drones.

Finding a well-hidden spot, he sent the exact location to

Lucky using What3Words; one of the three words was 'catastrophe'. Lucky had replied immediately, asking him to choose the spot three feet to the left as he didn't like that word. He was very superstitious. They agreed a rough time to meet up.

Doug had been in the army, in which he had been sent to Germany and Kenya, principally learning how to blow things up. When he had left, he worked in quarries up and down the UK, again blowing things up – in this case, the benches of limestone or granite that supplied the construction industry.

When working at a cement works in the Peak Park, not far from Sheffield, he had been fascinated by the new technology for mapping the faces of the quarry after each blast using drones. This allowed the exact amount of rock to be calculated and helped the geotechnical experts to spot dangerous crevices or fissures that might lead to uncontrolled collapses.

Doug ended up working for a company specialising in this new technology, and he had worked not just at home but in Croatia, the United Arab Emirates and Spain. Over a period of fifteen years, he became an expert in all things connected with drones.

He had met Lucky in a bar when working in Valencia and had assumed that Lucky had a military background. It was while talking about the past that they had bonded immediately, and Lucky had become interested in the idea of stealing explosives from the magazines in quarries, but this hadn't led anywhere. In time, he asked Doug to undertake some surveillance for him of a competitor in the drugs business in Essex and across the North Sea in Holland. This had been very useful, and over a lot of beer in the corner of a pub, he had handed over a wad of notes to Doug. The conversation had meandered on to the subject of taking out the warehouse in Essex. Doug combined his two areas of expertise and asked Lucky if he could get a specific military drone on the black market. Two weeks later, he had been given one, and a week after that, the warehouse was blown to pieces.

Since then, Doug had been Lucky's go-to man for such work. It was no surprise, therefore, that he had turned to Doug when the possibility of blowing up the airship in mid-flight had been first mooted. Lucky had also asked him to step in when the American guys cocked up and the need to take out the other machine on the road in Holland became an urgent matter.

Standing in the small wood, with a panoramic view over the valley below, Doug had used all his skills to select the best spot to remain concealed, down the airship and make their escape. He would cycle back to the family caravan, and Lucky would roar off in his Range Rover.

Doug rode around for half an hour, familiarising himself with the immediate area. Once satisfied, he headed back to the caravan to charge up his bike ready for tomorrow. His family would be back soon, and he had promised the children that they could have a barbecue with sausages and burgers.

There was nothing else he could do before mid-afternoon tomorrow – Thursday.

The surgeon had told Mike that Wazz would have to stay in hospital for a while, but he wouldn't be drawn on any prognosis, which was possibly worse than actually speculating on some recovery date. Knowing that Wazz might regain consciousness and not die was all she wanted to hear. They were preparing him for emergency surgery, and the nursing sister suggested to Mike that, although she was welcome to stay, going home and getting some rest might be for the better.

"I'll send you a message the minute he's out of surgery and has come round." The nurse was at her most encouraging. "If I were you, I'd come in tomorrow morning after 10.00am."

"Thanks, I'm guessing I'm not getting married tomorrow."

"Mike, I'm sorry. You'll have to rearrange that. Have you got someone to stay with you tonight?

"What? Uh ... no." Mike felt an enormous feeling of loneliness, aware that Wazz was her only true friend on earth. She had added unconvincingly, "I'll be OK."

The bike ride home passed in a blur while a range of emotions fought to outdo each other; anger appeared to be winning. Even pulling into Rodbourne gave her no relief and no feeling of being home. The house that had been such a happy place was now full of bad memories. If Wazz died, she would sell it immediately.

She had more pressing problems. The back door wasn't closing properly.

If Jan came back tonight, he could walk in with little effort. She knew that, even if she fixed the door somehow, he had levered it open once and could do it again. Standing inside and using some washing line cord, she tied the door to some copper pipes running down the corner of her kitchen. It took her two seconds before it dawned on her that this was a really stupid idea. She undid it and stretched it across the kitchen, tying it to a more solid anchor.

She was shaking, mostly from fear, when she moved her vegetable rack against the back door and placed plates and pots on it. This, at least, would make a noise if he tried to get in. She would be sleeping – or, rather, wide awake – in the bedroom immediately above.

Sleeping with her trusty baseball bat might give her some comfort; although if Wazz couldn't deal with him, what could she hope to do?

There were other practical matters to deal with, but it was too late to phone the registry office; this was now a task for the morning. She had missed lunch and was starving. It was time to eat and settle her nerves with a bottle of beer. Her hunger was satisfied quickly, but her nerves stubbornly refused to calm down.

Searching on her computer always distracted her, so after putting the plates in the dishwasher, she set up the equipment. As the screen flashed into life, she was more determined than ever to find Jan, given what he had done to Wazz and before he came back to get her.

She returned to the photographs on Henk's phone and put more of her collated images through the facial-recognition software. The first person she tried was a thickset man with a shaved head who looked slightly out of place in the wedding group. In several photographs, he was holding the arm of a young woman who was evidently blind as she was clutching a long, white stick. Mike opened another bottle while she waited for the results.

She put the bottle down, fascinated by what she saw. The man's name was Roger Fortuna, and he had a prison record for aggravated assault. He was British, not Dutch, but he looked much more likely to be involved in the narcotics business than the people in her previous searches.

After taking a sip, she wiped her lips before exploring various databases.

He was of Spanish heritage on his father's side and lived near Ockendon in Essex on the edge of London; several sources mentioned his wife had been murdered fifteen years previously. There was one daughter, Gabriella, who was blind. This solved the mystery of the large woman in the red, yellow and green dress, who was on his arm.

But so what? Was he Jan? He certainly looked a thug and had previous, as they say in England.

She wanted to discuss all this with Leonard, but this was out of the question without telling him about Terry and how she came to acquire Henk's phone.

Having forgotten about her fears for an hour or two, her

hands began trembling again. Would Wazz regain consciousness? Would Jan return tonight? The last question triggered a desperate thought: *What if I'm killed and Leonard never learns what I've found out?*

She typed up a page to explain the key points – including Terry shooting Henk, the phone and her main discoveries – and put it on a memory stick. Then she opened her concealed wall safe and put everything away. If she died, the Agency would come down to collect all her equipment, knowing where it was stored.

Oddly reassured, she double-checked the improvised security measures she had put in place and made her way upstairs. Alone in an old, creaking house that no longer felt so safe, she went to bed, placing her baseball bat on the side of it normally occupied by Wazz.

CHAPTER TWENTY-FOUR

She woke with a start and automatically grabbed the bat. There was a shriek that chilled the blood.

On sitting up, there was another scream, and she leapt out of bed. Torn between pulling on her jeans and getting out of the house, she tried to do both, but she failed dismally. By the time she had on a sweatshirt, jeans and sneakers, she had worked out that this wasn't a mad axeman from Holland but another nemesis of hers: the peacock.

Unbeknown to Mike, it had moved its roosting spot further along Church Lane and had spent most of the night on the thatched ridge above her bedroom. It was now heralding the dawn – and if it continued, it could well be its last.

She sat back on the bed and tried to calm herself, but only when she had checked her phone. There were no messages from the hospital.

After resting back against her pillows, she turned off her bedside lamp and tried to fall back to sleep. This would be slow in coming and wasn't aided by the scratching and snuffling of mice deep in the thatch. Who thought covering a house with a rotting haystack was a great idea?

Eventually, she did fall asleep until she turned over – at which point the baseball bat rolled off the bed and clattered onto the wooden floorboards.

With her nerves frayed, she gave up and went downstairs, relieved to see everything as she had left it. The peacock was staring at its reflection in the glass of her back door, not knowing how lucky it was that the knotted washing line would take too long to untie.

A short time later, while holding a coffee in both hands, she remembered it should have been her wedding day. She tried not to think about it. In an hour, she would call the registry office to rearrange a date before changing not into her wedding outfit but into her black motorbike leathers. A return trip to Salisbury District Hospital beckoned.

She left by the front door, looking quickly in both directions before walking back through the tunnel to collect her bike. It was with some relief that she started it once she had it out in the lane and set off, soon leaving the village behind. Nobody followed her or was waiting in a layby, and the fresh air in her face was refreshing; it blew away the terrors of the night, imagined or otherwise.

Knowing in which ward to find Wazz, she pulled up in a small car park nearby, left the bike on its stand and entered the hospital. The blood was pumping in her ears, and the apprehensions of the night had been replaced by those regarding what she would find inside. Had Wazz even regained consciousness?

She turned from the corridor towards the ward sister's office and tapped on the half-opened door.

The sister looked up at her. "Hi, you got my message; great."

"What message?" Mike's heart sank.

"To say that Wazz had regained consciousness, having been in intensive care overnight. He came around and is talking."

"No, no ... I didn't, but that's fantastic. Can I see him?"

"Let me check when he's coming out onto the ward. Give me a minute. Take a seat."

Mike sat down and stared at the walls of the office, taking nothing in as she clutched her black helmet. She zoned back in to hear that he would be transferred in the next hour.

"Why don't you go and get a coffee and come back later?"

"I will, thank you. Thank you."

She left the ward, and a short distance down the central corridor, she found Hedgerows café. After grabbing a snack, she sat in a corner, where she ate a panini and drank an americano while catching up with world events on her phone. Even seeing that crowds had gathered in Breda in anticipation of watching the microchip machine set off for the UK didn't really register. It was of low importance to her and a problem for the Brits. She was faced with a more immediate dilemma: whether to drink the coffee while it was hot and have nothing to do afterwards or to drag it out and let it go cold. Three coffees later, she had come to a compromise. Even so, the time passed very slowly.

On re-entering the ward, she could see Wazz in the third bed, being attended to by a nurse. It took all her effort not to run to him. She had tears in her eyes, which she was ever more aware was becoming a frequent occurrence.

He looked up at her and forced a smile.

She beamed back, having no idea if she was allowed to kiss or touch him.

"How are you?" he asked in a croaky voice.

"I've only just finished wiping the blood off the front door," wasn't what she was intending to say, but her brain wasn't geared like most other people's.

The nurse looked at Mike and said, "He's very tired and has

lost a lot of blood. He shouldn't be stressed. I'll come back in a few minutes."

Wazz watched the nurse leave and turned back to Mike. "Hi."

"Hi." She felt awkward standing there in her leathers, holding her helmet.

"Glad I came back first." He was speaking quietly and slowly.

"Huh." She was looking at his pale but beautiful face.

"Please don't sleep at home until I've been let out."

It sounded as if he had been consciously, or perhaps subconsciously, thinking this over for some time. The words took some effort to say, and he tried to salivate, swallowing immediately afterwards.

"Where am I meant to sleep?"

"The pub?"

"Really? I'll die of food poisoning instead."

"Please?"

"OK, I'll sleep at The Green Feathers." She was trying to act the sensible and concerned partner, but whether she would actually follow through on this agreement was a subject for debate.

He closed his eyes for a few seconds. "Good. Good."

"Are you going to make it to the wedding?" She didn't know what to say. Their silly banter was what came readily to her mind.

"I'll try, but I might not be able to carry you over the threshold." He smiled at her.

"You'd probably slip on all the blood."

He smiled again, but he didn't want to laugh or move.

"Did you see who did this?" She needed to know.

"A tall, thin guy and a big lad ... both in their thirties. They both had knives."

"Did they say anything?"

"No, the big guy jumped me, and the thin one stabbed me. I remember trying to get to the door. Nothing else."

They had only been chatting for five minutes when the ward sister walked over to gently encourage Mike to leave and perhaps come back later in the afternoon. Wazz needed a few days' rest, although the police were also on their way to ask him a few questions about the attack. When Mike heard this, she thought it was better to skedaddle and avoid any further questions. Wazz knew nothing relevant about Jan and could therefore give nothing away to the police.

She rode back to Rodbourne with not the slightest intention of sleeping in the room above the lounge at The Green Feathers and her thoughts focused on who the two men were. Was Jan the thin or the fat one?

"Got the name?"

"Sorry, boss." Liam was calling Lucky on WhatsApp. "We 'ad a bit of a problem."

"I was wondering why you hadn't phoned. What happened? Don't tell me that sodding woman's got a black belt in karate."

"She wasn't there. We got in the 'ouse and waited for 'er. There was even a note on the table saying she'd be back at midday. Only it weren't 'er who turned up. It was 'er boyfriend who's a bit of a bruiser."

"Jesus, Liam! There were two of you."

"He nearly took us both out. I 'ad to stick 'im."

"How bad?"

"We left 'im on the floor, but 'e weren't moving."

"Didn't you wait for the woman?"

"'Arry was in a bad way, and the bloke 'ad nearly knocked me for six. We 'ad to get outta there ... fast."

"Jesus."

"I only just managed to get 'Arry in the motor. 'E's in a bad way. Dunno what 'e'll tell 'is missus."

"Nobody saw you?" Lucky wasn't interested in their health, only in covering his own back.

"No, there weren't nobody around."

"All right. Forget all about it. Leave it to me. I'll deal with her myself."

Lucky was seething with anger. He would get down to Wiltshire very soon. At least he now knew where she lived and that her boyfriend was out of the picture.

He finished the call and went back to the task in hand, which was lifting the second drone into the back of the Range Rover that had been reversed into the small warehouse he rented nearby. He covered them both over with a tartan blanket and did one final check that he had everything with him.

The two drones had cost him over £100,000. They were modified commercial models Gabby had found on the dark web. There was nothing illegal in this; she was simply hiding her tracks. It had been Doug who had specified the type and range. They came without explosives, which Doug had acquired from someone in his past and fitted himself in Lucky's warehouse. They were now, of course, highly illegal.

Although Doug had a flyer ID from the Civil Aviation Authority (CAA), what he was about to do fell way outside the standard Open Category rules. He was flying beyond visual line of sight (BVLOS), not to mention that they were carrying explosives. He would, in this instance, not be obtaining a Specific Category Operational Authorisation from the CAA.

He would be breaking the rules by flying the drone or drones much higher than the usual limit of 120 yards. The exact height at which the airship would fly over or near the Malvern Hills was unknown, as was the distance away from him. However, this type of commercial drone had a limit of almost ten miles. He felt very confident that the airship would need to enter this zone if it was to land satisfactorily at the new microchip factory in the plain beneath him.

Doug had flown this make of drone before, using them to carry a heavy camera, but never with explosives; this was the only part of the plan that was untested.

Lucky had every faith in Doug and was paying him extremely well. He would deliver the drones to him and stand alongside him until the airship crashed. Doug had explained that this wasn't going to be like the *Hindenburg*; there would be no fireball caused by 7.06 million cubic feet of hydrogen igniting. Modern airships were filled with non-flammable gases. Instead, he would direct the drone to hit the gondola underneath or even the machine slung underneath. He reckoned that he could easily hit something the size of two large coaches.

With the warehouse locked up, Lucky jumped back into the Range Rover. It would take him three and a half hours to drive to the Malvern Hills sticking to the speed limits and not drawing attention to himself. He would stop for a leisurely lunch in a layby to eat the picnic lunch Agata had prepared for him and then arrive early afternoon with plenty of time to meet Doug at the agreed spot next to a patch of woodland.

Before he set off, he checked the weather forecast on his phone and saw that, for most of the route, it was clear and sunny, but with a band of cloud and light rain later in the day along the Welsh borders. The winds were predicted as light but stiffening as the day wore on. He shrugged; there was nothing he could do about it and nor could the airship company. No conditions would ever be perfect.

There had been a big crowd outside the factory in Breda to see the airship arrive from outside Paris. It had been helped in its journey by light westerly winds, and it came into view at a few minutes before 9.00am.

The onlookers had been pressing against the fence to get a

view of the largest current airship in Europe and the largest seen in Holland since World War II. Its pilot lowered it gently onto the tarmac apron to applause and cheers.

As predicted, it took half an hour to attach the cables to the eyelets of the net in which the machine nicknamed Nelly was sitting on its bespoke platform. Everything had been triple-checked. A Dutch military helicopter was a constant presence in the sky, as it would be in a week's time for transporting the second machine to Eindhoven airport. The company had arranged for a drone to hover at a discreet distance away from the action to film what was an historic day.

By 9.30am, the excited crowd had grown and were surrounding the TV crews filming the event.

The morning sun glistened on the rigid plastic facets of the dirigible as it began to ascend, absorbing the tension in the cables. This tension was almost matched by that felt by the company directors standing with the workforce outside the huge factory doors. There was cheering and waving to the men in the gondola as the cargo left the ground, revealing daylight beneath.

The airship turned a few degrees very slowly as it rose on the same spot, and at some seemingly arbitrary moment, it began to fly off north-westwards – a gentle giant making very little noise. The whirling thump, thump, thump of the helicopter, however, grew louder as it circled overhead to take up its position to the rear of the machine's starboard side.

Almost all the workforce were holding their phones – recording videos or taking selfies with the airship in the background. One man wearing white company overalls also had his phone in his hand and had taken a picture of the lift-off, but this wasn't a casual photograph. He sent it via WhatsApp to a number in Essex with a thumbs-up emoji.

In the West Wing of the Fortuna mansion, Gabby received the message with a smile. Immediately, she passed it on to her father, who was beginning his journey to the Malvern Hills.

Nelly – or perhaps it should be renamed Dumbo? – was flying on its way to England.

CHAPTER TWENTY-FIVE

For the first half of the bike ride back home from the hospital, Mike was elated and relieved that Wazz had regained consciousness and the surgery had apparently been successful. She had already telephoned the registry office earlier to explain the situation and asked for the first free date or, even better, any cancellation. Not getting married today didn't bother her at all, she kept telling herself. There were no guests to worry about, and she wasn't even taking his name. Frankly, any day would do.

It's true that she had other things on her mind. These came to the fore as she approached Rodbourne, where another night or two in the house on her own were in prospect.

After arriving in Church Lane, she parked the bike by the footbridge and walked quickly through the tunnel. The back gate opened, and the tiny piece of paper she had put in place fluttered to the ground; no one had been in her garden. She tried the back door, which was still tightly tied up with the washing line. It was as she had left it.

Mike brought the bike into the back garden and put it on its stand. She made her way to the front door after again trapping the piece of paper as she closed the gate.

The house was thankfully empty, and she went upstairs to change out of her bike leathers and put on some casual clothes, once she had washed her face and scalp. She skipped down the stairs to get herself a bottle of water, the three coffees in the café at the hospital having left her mouth dry. Her mood lightened considerably.

As she got her equipment from the hidden safe, she saw her memory stick explaining about Terry and Henk Visser. She left it inside. It may still be needed if anything happened to her. On imagining this scenario, she realised how much she wanted to crack this problem, identify Jan and have him arrested.

As always when she was focused on a specific task without being interrupted, time flew by. It was lunchtime before she looked up, trying to remember if she had eaten breakfast. Either way, the kitchen was calling, and she took all the leftovers from the fridge and concocted a plate unlikely to feature in any Michelin-starred restaurant.

All morning, her preoccupation had been with the remaining people in Henk Visser's photographs. She had identified two more, but she'd failed on the others. Undeterred, she took stock and went back to the beginning, assessing what had been discovered.

Many of the pictures had been from Henk's wedding, but Mike still couldn't begin to make sense of the relationships. For a start, why was Daniel Drinkwater in so many shots with Ana Visser, and why were the Vissers with Daniel in Stratford-upon-Avon?

Mike looked up Henk and Ana's marriage certificate from Holland and had one of those rare rewarding moments among hours and days of lack of progress. She stood up and shouted, "*Yes!*" at no one in particular. Ana Visser was Ana Drinkwater before she married – she was Daniel's sister.

Suddenly, the motive for Jan the Dutchman's attacks on Terry and his attempt to kill her made sense: Daniel was out for revenge for his brother-in-law's murder. He must have been so frustrated that, despite his standing in the seedy underworld of Rotterdam, he couldn't find out anything about what happened to his brother-in-law. No amount of money or clout would get him this information because only Terry knew what had happened and he had told absolutely no one other than her.

Sitting back in the chair, chewing the last mouthful of food, she wondered how Daniel had found out about Terry and her. It was confusing, and she couldn't immediately think of any way this could be possible.

The next big problem was emerging: how was she going to let Leonard know any of this without mentioning Terry? It was time for a celebratory cigarette. She took out the packet and her lighter as she made her way across the kitchen, lost in thought. It was only when she reached for the handle of the back door that she remembered it was tied up with the washing line. Instead, she ended up standing outside the front door, smoking with her right hand supporting her left elbow. She felt like a tart in Amsterdam's De Wallen red-light district touting for trade. She immediately ditched this thought; anything connected with the Dutch wasn't what she needed at that moment. Trying not to look provocative, she looked casually up and down Church Lane, where nothing was moving – not even the Muscovy ducks.

With a sort of decision made about Leonard, she stepped onto the footbridge and flicked the cigarette stub into the water, watching it being carried away towards the High Street, where it went into a culvert and then to where? She had no idea; probably Holland, knowing her luck.

A couple of minutes later, once back at her laptop, she double-checked a few of the things she had discovered and ran the story over in her head for the tenth time. There was no avoiding what needed to be done. She picked up her phone to ring Leonard.

The tyres of the Range Rover crunched over the loose stones of the track. There was a gentle breeze rustling the leaves of the overhanging trees, and most critically, there was no one about. Lucky turned the car around between the fences with some difficulty and parked it in a hidden spot ready for his getaway.

By the time he had stepped down onto the grassy verge, a man was emerging from the dense trees, where he had been watching from a vantage point behind the trunk of an oak. He didn't climb over the wooden fence on the hedge bank marking the edge of the wood; instead, he leant on it like some cartoon farmer with a straw between his teeth.

"How was the journey?" Doug was wearing a black tee shirt and green denim jeans.

"Easy. I wish they were all like that, but I wasn't racing with that much explosive in the back."

"It's completely safe."

"I trust you. Let's get them out of the car before any nosey parker walks by."

Lucky lifted each drone separately, leaning back to counter the weight. He handed them across the fence to Doug, who took them twenty paces away and out of sight, deep in the darkness of the wood. There were three trips for the drones and the control systems before Lucky locked the Range Rover and climbed over the fence himself, cursing the bramble that jagged his shirt.

They decided to move the drones even further away from the track, so they made several trips through the wood to the far side, carrying the drones and the controls. In what Doug described as the perfect spot, they leant against hefty fence posts and contemplated the view before them.

They were high enough up the lower slopes of the hill to be

able to see some distance towards the Welsh mountains. They couldn't make out Hereford, but this didn't matter. There were cows and sheep in the various fields in front of them, and the branches of an oak tree gave them immediate cover from above.

Lucky took a vape out of his trouser pocket, but he put it back when he saw Doug's face. It was best to be extra cautious.

"Let's check where it is and estimate its likely ETA." Doug wanted to maintain a disciplined, military approach.

Lucky bent over to look at Doug's phone, where he was on Flightradar24.

"There we are ... it's currently over the M11, north of London ... I bet Luton airport is pissed off."

"When will it arrive here?" Lucky was street smart, but maths wasn't his strong suit.

Doug did some mental gymnastics and replied, "In three and a half hours, although I notice the breeze is building and veering. It's pushing the airship a bit further north."

Lucky looked at the chunky watch on his tattooed arm. "So ... 5.30pm?"

"That's my best guess."

"We've got a lot of time to kill." He was fidgety and not used to having to wait around.

Doug smiled and reached across to his rucksack, which was hanging from a hawthorn tree. He unzipped it, took out some chocolate and removed the wrapper, which he put back in the rucksack. "Here, this will keep you occupied."

"Thanks, I meant to bring some chewing gum."

"We don't use chewing gum." Doug was still using the present tense when referring to his army days. "Never leave anything that might provide them with your DNA."

"Chewing gum?"

"Yeah, and if you need to shit, do it in a bag or walk 500 yards over there." He nodded towards the densest part of the wood.

"Thanks for picking this place; I won't be leaving a review on Tripadvisor, but the chocolate is tasty."

Doug began moving the drones to a flat area; once he had them in place, he turned on the controls – some of which he had brought with him – to test the connections. He tried the rotors and then switched them off quickly. Everything was prepared, apart from priming the explosives.

A herd of dark-red cows of a short-legged breed, which had originally been a long way off across a large field, were nervously approaching the two men and snorting inquisitively, their yellow ear tags shining in the sunlight.

"Fuck off." Lucky wasn't a man of the wide open spaces, having grown up in the backstreets of East London.

The cows took absolutely no notice and continued chewing.

"God, they stink ... Fuck off, will you? And take these damn flies with you!"

"Easy, they're useful." Doug wasn't used to being accompanied on a clandestine job by someone with no military experience. "We always like them because they confuse thermal imaging cameras. It makes it more difficult to spot you and me."

"Oh, right. This isn't my usual type of job." Here, Lucky was failing to mention that he was being paid several million pounds to destroy this machine, and if he had to sit in cow muck for a day, so be it.

Something bleeped near Doug's rucksack. "Ssh!" he hissed.

Lucky frowned and looked around, but he could see nothing.

Doug tapped a password into another phone and checked the screen. "Panic over; it's a deer."

"What's that?" Lucky nodded at the phone.

"I put a mini camera at the start of the track in case anyone came after us. That's how I knew you were arriving."

"You're a smart cookie." Lucky made a mental note to use Doug on a lot more of his projects; he really was a step up from the usual knobheads Lucky employed.

Twelve miles to the west as the carrion crow flies, Keith Herring had arrived at the factory. He had been driven up from his home in Somerset and was standing in an office with a group of people, two of whom were monitoring the airship's progress. "Where is it now?"

"Um ... it's over Whipsnade Zoo," one of them confirmed.

"That should scare the zebras." Major Phipps appeared relaxed, having been at the site all day to ensure the various security measures were fully in place and operational.

Keith, however, had picked up on the slight hesitation in the voice of the young man tracking progress. "Is Whipsnade on course?"

"It's a bit further north than expected, and the wind speed's increasing and veering. It's pushing the airship even more to the north. The captain is on full power keeping it on track."

"What if the wind increases a lot more?" Keith was already nervous. He had travelled up with his son, whom he had finally talked out of flying on the damn airship. He had enough to worry about.

"Um ... the captain has used more power than he expected, but in his last call, he said he's confident he can make it an hour behind schedule if the wind doesn't increase."

Keith had, of course, heard all the contingency plans many times, but now it looked like one of them may need to be put in place. "And if it does increase?"

Major Phipps was about to speak when the senior RAF officer chipped in: "We have two RAF bases in the general zone into which the captain may be pushed; both are on alert. We've checked the latest weather forecast, and tomorrow looks benign if the machine needs to be flown the last stretch down to here."

"Oh, great."

All this was being absorbed by a middle-ranking civil servant with an unfortunate haircut that made him look like a schoolboy. He was attending solely to keep the Cabinet Office up to date. It had been suggested that a minister or even the Prime Minister might come down for the airship's arrival, but it had been decided it was too unpredictable and too embarrassing if the machine was somehow damaged or worse. If that happened, it wouldn't be the positive photo opportunity required, especially as the airship had turned into a very popular spectacle, with people on the route posting videos on social media and the main news channels covering it extensively.

"If we end up at one of the two airbases, either the one in Warwickshire or the one in Shropshire, the special unit and the helicopter will stay there overnight where they can refuel," the RAF officer added.

"And we have two mobile units out in Herefordshire, which we'll send to the airfield to provide additional security." Major Phipps didn't appear concerned.

Keith shook his head in some sort of resignation as to what might happen. "Given the media interest, everyone will know where the machine is overnight."

"Keith, it's safer on an RAF base than anywhere else. Let's not get pessimistic; it will probably still arrive here tonight, if an hour or so late."

"Time for a cup of tea, I think." Keith turned and nodded to his PA, who walked out of the room to sort out drinks and biscuits.

"Imagine the poor bastards – sorry for my French – in Arizona facing a 150-mile road journey."

"But at least they don't have to worry about being blown off course."

The time dragged, and there was nothing the assembled team could do except wait. The tea and biscuits brought by the

PA were quickly consumed; however, the airship had only flown six miles while they had been drinking and eating.

It would be a long afternoon.

CHAPTER TWENTY-SIX

"Weren't you meant to be getting married? What happened?" Leonard had taken the call from Mike in his office.

"Yes, it's a pain in the butt."

"That's marriage for you."

"I'm ringing to tell you that Wazz is in hospital, so the wedding has been cancelled. Don't worry; he'll be OK, and we'll do it at a later date."

"Oh, sorry to hear that; send him my best wishes." And without missing a beat, he asked, "Are you calling to tell me you've cracked the Chinese narcotic lab network?"

They were dancing around each other. Mike had decided not to mention that it was probably Jan the Dutchman with a buddy who had broken into her house and stabbed Wazz. Leonard, for his part, had decided not to mention he was fighting tooth and nail with Langley to keep her job and those of her colleagues. Times were tough in the Agency, with interdepartmental rivalry and a general fight over a rotting carcass that couldn't feed everyone.

"Yes and no; the good news is that I think I've identified Jan the Dutchman, so I hope we can make progress on the Chinese job soon."

"Wow! Wasn't expecting that." Leonard had just been given all the ammunition he needed to fend off the hyenas. "Who is he?"

"I suspect his name's Daniel Drinkwater, and he lives here in the UK – in the Midlands."

"Really?" The surprises were coming thick and fast.

Mike had thought long and hard about how to explain how she had found Daniel without mentioning Terry Bailey, the shooting seven years ago or how she had acquired Henk Visser's phone.

"When you asked me to find Jan, I went right back to the beginning, when I was involved with Dylan. Everyone thought Jan had been killed in that hotel room outside Amsterdam, but we now know he's still active and distributing for these Chinese labs. In all this, I've presumed we were looking for one man, but I know I could have been wrong."

"Very thorough."

"After the shooting, the Agency, the Dutch and the Brits were thrilled Jan had finally been killed. They checked out this dead man, but no connections to any known trafficker or criminal were made. The case was closed."

Leonard was fascinated to see where this was going, but he kept quiet.

"The Dutch had assumed Jan wasn't shot in that room and the victim was an innocent man in the wrong place at the wrong time, but I wasn't convinced. They knew Jan had booked the room via a tip-off and were poised to arrest him, so who had Jan allowed to use that room? This made me think the man who was shot in that hotel must be connected to Jan somehow, but not necessarily through any criminal activity. It was the Dutch who checked him out. His name is probably in the files somewhere, but I checked the local papers anyway and found both his name and where he was buried. His name was Henk Visser."

"Who was he?"

"Well" – and here she massaged the truth – "I checked out him and his wife. She's British and was Ana Drinkwater before she married. I checked out her wedding photographs; her brother is Daniel Drinkwater. I believe Daniel let his brother-in-law use that hotel room when someone, persons unknown, showed up and shot him ... perhaps a rival gang."

"Where's this Daniel now?" Leonard's mind was racing ahead.

"I've sent the address to you. It's near Stratford-upon-Avon ... you know, William Shakespeare and all that."

"Wow, and wasn't Hamlet Dutch?"

"Danish, I think." Sometimes, Mike didn't know whether Leonard was joking or not. She tended to underestimate him.

He continued, "What makes you think that this Daniel guy is Jan?"

"He's the owner of a pet-food business. He owns shops around Birmingham."

"And?"

"He imports and distributes pet food from China. I haven't found out anything else yet, but I have a gut feeling that it's him."

"Do you have any other leads to follow?"

"I'm meant to be getting married. I'm not actually supposed to be working, remember?"

"While you're waiting for your fiancé to get well, why not see how and where the narcotics come in? While you're doing that, I'll tell the Brits – although they're preoccupied with that microchip machine today."

"Someone ought to pay this Daniel Drinkwater a visit."

"I'm sure the Brits will check him and his place out fast. Well done, by the way; I know this is a real tough time for you."

"Thanks. I'll go on checking until Wazz gets back from hospital." She ended the call.

After that, Leonard sat musing for a while. He looked for Mike's message giving him Daniel Drinkwater's details and spent even longer thinking about what to say before pressing some buttons on the phone and putting it on speaker mode. He waited for Gordon Overton to answer.

"Gordon, I've got a name to give you that's likely to be Jan the Dutchman."

"Excellent news. Have you told the Dutch boys?"

"He's a Brit. He lives near Stratford-upon-Avon. You know it?"

"I've been to the Royal Shakespeare Theatre a few times."

"His name's Daniel Drinkwater. Mean anything to you?"

Gordon thought for a second and said, "No, it doesn't ring any bells. How did you find him?"

"Mike Kingdom found him. He's a pet-food importer from China. I'm guessing this is the route in for the narcotics from the labs. We're still checking."

"I'd never have thought of Stratford-upon-Avon as a drug capital. Stratford in London, more like."

"Can you put him under surveillance? Tap his phone? It might save time." Leonard was enjoying having one up on Gordon.

"As you know, we have rules. You'll need to give me a bit more for me to get the clearance."

"Really? Tell them that the Yanks are certain and can't reveal their sources. I'll send you the address."

Leonard knew full well that Gordon would find a way around any regulation. He was adept at it, and he would want to be seen to crack the case and for any kudos to be his. He would try to keep it in MI6 and keep MI5 and the police at arm's length for as long as possible.

Within an hour, Gordon had put a small team on monitoring and investigating Daniel Drinkwater. Once he had enough solid evidence, he would pass this on, and Daniel would be arrested.

Keith Herring could tell by the expression on his young staff member's face that things had gone wrong. Everyone in the room at the factory stopped talking and were listening to one side of a conversation.

Even before it had finished, Keith had stood up. "It's not going to make it, is it?" he asked the second the communication with the airship pilot ended.

"No, he's requested to divert to RAF Covingham. He'll be there in less than an hour. The winds are forecast to get stronger and stronger over the next hour, and he would be flying straight into it. He's going to conserve his fuel for tomorrow."

"Great." Keith's face gradually became set, and he went into management mode: "What do we have to do?"

"Keith, it's not so bad. Covingham is a base with excellent security. It's a squadron base and a training establishment with branches of the Defence School of Aeronautical Engineering and Defence School of Photography. We'll get the two roving units to drive there and patrol overnight. The helicopter and the SAS unit will also be there," the RAF man reassured, "I'll speak to the group captain in charge of the base now."

"I'll see if we can send some more bodies up there. It's not far away. What is it, Jack? Fifty miles by car?" Major Phipps was also trying to reassure Keith, but he was conscious of the man from the Cabinet Office who'd be feeding this all back to the government. The major picked up his phone and began to call up some more resources.

"What's the weather forecast for tonight and tomorrow?" Keith was thinking about his precious cargo.

Someone replied, "Tonight, the winds will go on increasing substantially from the south," and then added rather pointlessly, "the ones currently blowing it northwards."

"And tomorrow?"

"Much better. Even in the morning."

The RAF officer hadn't begun his call to the base. "They have a hangar empty and ready to receive the airship. They know the airship is rigid and can't stay outside. It's one of the reasons we chose Covingham as a back-up."

"It'll only take less than an hour and a half to get here tomorrow, so it isn't all bad. Keith, it's done the difficult bit getting from Holland to Shropshire." Major Phipps smiled in an attempt to soothe Keith further.

"I'm not so worried about the airship; it's the bloody machine I care about. I really don't want it outside all night."

"It's waterproof, and they'll lower it into a sheltered and safe place. It's all been prepared; we just have to put the plan into action."

"And don't forget that any terrorist also won't have planned for this temporary diversion," the RAF officer consoled.

Keith wasn't sure if he was helped by hearing this or not.

"It's drifting northwest." Doug was following the airship's progress.

"What does that mean?" Lucky had been noticing that the wind, even at a low level, was picking up, with the branches above their heads swaying and the leaves rustling.

"Well, at the moment, I'm not sure, but one thing's for certain: it ain't heading towards the factory."

"Oh shit."

Doug began flicking through social media, but there were no useful posts. He checked the weather reports, especially the radar predictions; it did not look good. "I don't think the airship will make it to the factory today."

"So where's it going to land?"

"An airfield, I'd guess."

"Are there many?"

"Two or three. There's an RAF base not far in front of it if it stays on its current heading."

"Will they put it on a lorry from there tomorrow?"

"I doubt it. The weather forecast tomorrow is for light winds. I think they'll stay there overnight and take off in the morning. It'll only take them an hour or a bit longer. I expect the pilot is low on fuel and wants to conserve it for tomorrow or fill up."

"Right, so we have to stay here until tonight and finish the job in the morning."

"It's not as simple as that. RAF Covingham is miles from here, and the airship will be outside the ten-mile range of these drones on the route south to the factory."

"Shit." Lucky was having to think on his feet.

"We have a choice, I think: either we drive nearer and take it out this evening while it's landing or while it's at the airfield overnight, or we move nearer to the new flight path ready for tomorrow morning."

"Bollocks." Lucky had begun to sweat despite the wind. "We haven't got time to get to the airfield before it lands, pick a spot and escape without getting caught or tracked."

"I guessed you'd say that."

"We could go down and attack it overnight, but we don't know what cameras and defence will be in place. I don't know the airfield, but I'm guessing there'll be a lot of security. I suppose it's possible. It's probably better to find a place this afternoon that's nearer to the new flight path and take it down tomorrow morning ... if it flies."

"OK, let's do that. We can't stay here."

"Shall we put everything back in the Range Rover with my bike and head off? I need to ring the missus."

"Looks like I'll be sleeping in the car. It won't be the first time."

"OK, we have a plan."

"I need to make two calls before we leave. You start loading up the car." Lucky threw him the keys and walked out of earshot.

He leant on the top rail of a fence and started dialling.

Daniel picked up straight away on seeing Lucky's number. "What's happening?"

"Houston, we have a problem. The wind has got strong and is blowing it off course. You can probably hear the wind now on the phone. It'll have to land at an airfield and leave in the morning."

"Are you staying there?"

"Of course, my friend is staying as well. We're moving our location, but we'll be ready."

"Why are you moving?"

"Long story, but we need to be nearer. There are limits, understand?"

"OK, I get it. Just don't fail."

"We won't."

The call was ended.

Lucky became conscious that the cows had returned to shelter in the lee of the wood, a sure sign the wind was picking up. The clouds had morphed from white to grey, against which gulls were being highlighted as they were blown inland.

Lucky rang his daughter. "Hi, babe."

"How's it going?"

"Could be better; the bastard thing has been blown off

course. It'll be on an airfield overnight. We'll have to relocate and do it tomorrow."

"Oh ... that's a bummer."

"I won't be home tonight ... obviously."

"I'll survive. Everything is fine here, by the way. Take care ... I miss you."

"Don't worry, it's what your mum used to call a 'minor inconvenience'."

He ended the call, put his phone away and walked back to help Doug lift the two drones into the back of the Range Rover. The electric bike, however, proved problematic. The drones were the priority, and there was no way that the bike would fit on top of the blanket without damaging them.

"I'll ride back to the caravan and leave the bike there. Will you follow me there and pick me up? I can't use the bike where we're going anyway."

"No problem; we aren't in a hurry. We have until tomorrow to find a new base."

Doug described how to get to the caravan site. Lucky said he would sit by the trees for twenty minutes before setting off; he didn't want to hang around the site with what was in the back of the Range Rover. Their plan in place, Doug left.

Lucky stayed in the car after Doug had cycled off, as it was too windy to stand outside. He looked around the interior and particularly at the leather seats. If he had to spend a night in a car, he was glad it was this one and not his first vehicle – a beaten-up minivan with a plank of wood across the collapsed driver's seat.

CHAPTER TWENTY-SEVEN

It was after 6pm by the time Lucky had driven to a village called Cupstone, guided by Doug, who was using a combination of the car's satnav and his phone. They hadn't raced and hadn't drawn attention to themselves. The village wasn't their final destination, but it was within a five-mile-square area Doug had identified as likely to be under the flight path.

"Somewhere around here would be good," Doug suggested. "I'd drive on through the village. Look, it shows that there are some woods on the other side."

Lucky drove out of the built-up area and into a landscape of rolling hills and fields bounded by unkempt hedgerows. They weren't close to RAF Covingham, having decided that the place would be crawling with military, all on high alert. The village of Cupstone was about ten miles away to the south of the airfield.

There was no traffic, and therefore they meandered slowly along the lanes until Doug said, "Let's check that out." He was pointing at two rows of what appeared to be derelict chicken sheds.

Lucky pulled up at a gate, which Doug leapt out to open. He had to turn into the wind, which was blowing dust up into his eyes. Lucky drove through and pulled up alongside a wall. Doug closed the gate and walked twenty paces around the back of the first shed while Lucky parked behind the wooden buildings so the Range Rover was hidden from the lane.

Their first impressions were right; it was long abandoned, with broken windows and a metal grain silo that had tipped over and was lying on its side. The floors of the sheds were covered in decades of old chicken shit, which had turned to dry and flaky pellets, liberally peppered with rat droppings. The remains of a dead pigeon was the only other feature besides the grey cobwebs that hung down like gothic Christmas decorations.

"Can we open those doors and get the Range Rover in here? I don't want to take the risk that a helicopter flies over and spots us."

They heaved the doors wide open, and Lucky reversed deftly inside, the tyres crunching on the shed floor. It was good to be out of the wind, which was buffeting the buildings, and even better to be inside the car.

"Perfect. I think it's time to eat," Lucky said as Doug jumped into the passenger seat.

They had stopped in a village shop to buy some provisions, which included a six-pack of cans of lager. Doug ripped open a packet of crisps and looked behind himself. "We'll leave the drones and kit in the back in case we have to make a speedy exit or our plans have to change."

"No problem."

They opened two cans almost simultaneously and clinked them together – or perhaps clunked them would be more accurate.

"Cheers," they said in unison.

Doug took a rechargeable battery pack out of his rucksack and sat his phone on it. "I want to monitor social media to see what's happening."

"Fine." Lucky had moved his seat backwards to give his legs

room to stretch and to create some space between his stomach and the steering wheel. It would be a long evening and night. The time was going to drag.

Eventually, feeling the effects of three cans of lager, he needed to get out of the car.

Doug went on checking for updates and found that the airship had landed successfully at RAF Covingham, which was captured on several clips of mobile phone footage. Also captured were several Land Rovers patrolling and making sure no one tried to breach the security fence. They had made a good call staying away from the airbase.

He was looking at the weather forecast for tomorrow, worried that this strong wind might continue and disrupt the plans even further. He didn't trust any one website, so he flicked from the Met Office to AccuWeather and meteoblue; they all showed the windspeed beginning to diminish after about 4.00am.

Lucky opened the driver's door and climbed back in. "I've got six fucking bathrooms at home, and here I am, shitting in the corner of a chicken shed."

Now was probably not the time for Doug to remind him that they shouldn't leave traces of anything with their DNA, if possible. It was a very long shot that anyone searching for the perpetrators afterwards would hit upon these chicken sheds. However, he wasn't sure what retrospective tracking of mobile calls was possible.

It was only twenty minutes later that Lucky had to go for a pee – so much for the joy of drinking three cans of lager.

At around 9.30pm, it began to get dark, and Lucky took the blanket from on top of the drones and draped it over his body. He was only wearing a long-sleeved tee shirt. Doug, in his dark green fleece, was quite comfortable; this being one of the benefits of years in the army not knowing where one might end up sleeping. In fact, this was the first time he had been on an active job with Lucky, who's lack of military awareness and discipline was ever more apparent.

Doug turned off his phone and suggested Lucky did the same. Doug had already told him to turn off location services and not call or message anyone. He was asleep before Lucky had finished tucking the blanket around his body.

On Friday morning, Mike had driven Wazz's van to Salisbury District Hospital.

He had recovered enough that he could return home to convalesce. The medical team were pleased with his progress and confident no internal organs had seriously been damaged. He was dressed in clean clothes, which Mike had brought in. They were having to take the bloody ones back to be washed.

Wazz was apprehensive about the journey home as Mike had only driven the van half a dozen times. In fact, his nervousness had begun from the second she began pushing him in the hospital wheelchair with a small bag on his lap. Going up and down kerbs was especially painful.

He slid into the passenger seat, and she went off to return the wheelchair before getting into the driver's seat.

"Right, no comments on my driving." Mike started the engine.

He changed the subject: "Anything from the police?"

"Nothing."

"Have you told your bosses?"

"Relax, I've found out who did it. I've passed his name and details to Leonard, who's liaising with the Brits," explained Mike, leaving out that she hadn't told Leonard about the knifing.

"We need to be careful until we know those guys are out of circulation."

"We will be."

"I'm surprised the big guy could even walk after I hit him."

"I think you frightened them off, but I promise you that neither of us is going anywhere until it's sorted, and they're behind bars."

Wazz tried to enjoy the luxury of being driven, and he stared out of the passenger window at the gentle curves of the landscape. He saw lakes and a hotel he had never noticed before. They passed a burger van in a layby, and he almost asked her to stop; he was starving. After a mercifully uneventful journey, Mike drove into Rodbourne, The Green Feathers came into view, and his hunger grew. Unfortunately, the pub was closed. She drove past and into Church Lane, stopping right next to the footbridge over the ditch.

"Let me open the front door of the house for you," she said while jumping out.

While she was doing this, he had pushed against the van door, swivelled and had his feet on the ground. He heard her scream. "*Mike!*" he shouted, unable to run to her.

By the time she was coming back out of the house, he had made it across the footbridge. Terror was etched into her face, and she was trying to control her breathing.

"It's the man repairing the back door. He frightened me."

"Oh Mike."

"Sorry, I'm on edge."

They walked inside and on into the kitchen through the lounge.

Despite the adrenaline coursing through their bodies, it felt good to be back home; because of the excitement, his hunger had temporarily disappeared.

"Morning," the man in the brown overalls said as Wazz entered the kitchen.

"Good morning." Wazz lowered himself gingerly onto a chair.

Mike closed the front door and brought Wazz's small bag into the lounge.

"Nearly finished," the repairman said. "I had to fit a new frame, but the door was fine." He pushed the door open and shut a couple of times by way of demonstration.

Twenty minutes, later he had cleared up and was heading back to Wilton.

"Shall I cook?" Wazz's hunger had returned.

"Sit down. I've bought some eggs and bacon as a welcome-home meal. You can have baked beans as well."

"Sounds great. Is this the new regime?"

"Don't get used to it, and woe betide you if you milk the situation."

On Thursday evening, the Home Secretary and a judge had been involved, but in all honesty, Gordon Overton hadn't waited. His team had begun investigating Daniel Drinkwater on several fronts. One person was looking at his financial situation and, in particular, his pet-food business. Another had been checking his travel history, while a third was remotely monitoring his property outside Stratford-upon-Avon.

The team who'd enter the property was gradually being assembled, ready to support the police when the search warrant was finally issued. Some of the officers had already travelled up from London.

Gordon wasn't aware of the fine details of how the warrant was achieved – it was done by a senior colleague coordinating several departments and bodies – all he needed to know was that they could monitor any phone calls and the police could search the place.

After a long evening of phone calls and Zoom meetings, all the planets aligned and a multi-agency team was nearby and would enter the property the next day – Friday, 10th July – at 7.00am.

Despite having a more junior and peripheral role seven years ago, Gordon was aware of what had happened and that the drug ring was never identified and the apparent ringleader – Jan the Dutchman – was never arrested. Nobody, to Gordon's knowledge, had thought for a second that the boss was British. If he could pull off this arrest, Gordon would be well placed to leapfrog his nearest competition for a significant promotion.

At 7.00am sharp, a group of police officers – one with a sniffer dog – descended on the isolated red-brick house surrounded by its walls and trees.

The door was opened by a woman who seemed to be in a state of shock. She was pale with a disconcerting stare and blinked rarely. If eyes are the windows to the soul, the curtains were closed. This wasn't caused by drugs, legal or otherwise; it looked like she simply found life a constant surprise.

Brenda Drinkwater listened attentively and invited the policemen inside. She knew her husband was involved in property deals that might have involved him not paying all the appropriate taxes either in the UK or Spain, but he had told her never to reveal this and always to say that he wasn't at home. She was oblivious to his real criminal life. "Please, come into the lounge. What's this all about? Would anyone like a tea of coffee?"

The lead policeman had asked her immediately whether her husband Daniel was at home, to which she had replied that she hadn't seen him for twenty-four hours. He was often in London or abroad, she had said.

While one officer stayed with Mrs Drinkwater, the remainder of the team spread out throughout the house and outbuildings. The spaniel was roaming excitedly, but it was finding nothing that would lead to it being given a reward; there were no illegal drugs on the property.

"Does he have a diary or calendar, Mrs Drinkwater?" the lead police officer asked.

"I expect so, but I wouldn't know; he spends a lot of his time in his office running the business."

She stared at the police officer as if he were a ghost, but he realised this was her normal look. He wondered what she looked like when she was really scared. "And what business is that?

"Pet food. He owns pet-food shops around Birmingham."

"And where's his office?"

"In the stable block. He likes to keep business separate from the house. It works well; he doesn't disturb me. Are you sure you won't have a drink?"

Two members of the team had already walked down the path, noting the immaculate lawn, flower beds and vegetable area. They tried the door to the last part of the outbuilding, but it was locked. They peered in through a window, but there was no sign of life. They jemmied the door open using minimal force and stepped inside the two rooms, which were a cross between an office, a bric-a-brac shop and a study. It was cosy, private and quiet.

The first thing they noticed was the two cameras – one in each corner, covering all angles; they were being filmed.

One of the team went back to the house quickly to update the officer in charge. Daniel Drinkwater didn't appear to be on the property, but he might be aware of the police presence via the cameras.

Something about the tidiness and order of the house and garden sowed seeds of suspicion in the senior members, including Gordon Overton's man. Daniel Drinkwater could be hiding somewhere in a roof, basement or other secret place. If not, then he wasn't there and was watching events unfold – wherever he was. He had flown under the radar for so long that he must be well aware of how to hide his tracks and to disappear.

Despite a reasonably thorough search, they had found no phones, no computers, no diaries; in fact, they had found nothing suspicious – which was suspicious in itself.

The officer in charge walked outside to call his superiors. He reported that the suspect wasn't at home and nothing criminal or unusual had been found so far. Brenda Drinkwater had been helpful, but she wasn't the sharpest knife in the box and didn't know where her husband was.

The team would be there for several more hours, but they would find nothing.

CHAPTER TWENTY-EIGHT

Brenda Drinkwater did know where Daniel was; she had driven him to Birmingham airport at 4.00am to catch his usual flight to Valencia.

He had already booked it, based on the assumption that the machine would have been blown out of the sky the day before, as planned. The annoying gradual increase in the strength of the wind had taken many people by surprise, but it had always been a possible factor.

He had heard from Lucky, who appeared to have everything under control. He and Doug would deal with it whenever the airship set off from its temporary stop. Spending a night sleeping in a Range Rover was a small price to pay.

The main reason for him going out to Spain was to cover the next shipment from China; Lucky would be tied up for a couple of weeks, dealing with the machine in the UK and the one en route to Phoenix in Arizona. Daniel didn't really like to be so hands-on – he preferred there always to be one level of detachment – but needs must, and what Lucky was doing was more important and more lucrative. One of them needed to oversee their Spanish manager and make sure he adhered to the rules that had been laid down. It was too easy for anyone at the warehouse to divert packages elsewhere. It had happened once before, and the manager had been relieved of his duties; sadly, he would no longer be needing a reference.

Daniel was now safely ensconced in his villa. He walked onto the terrace, carrying a bottle of wine in an ice bucket, before settling down to read any news reports. It was 11.30am in Spain, an hour ahead of the UK. He was guessing the airship would travel late morning or over lunchtime. Over his first glass of wine, he was fruitlessly pondering whether the airship was intending to stay somewhere on the south coast or whether it would have enough daylight to get back to the base outside Paris. He wiped the condensation from the wine glass and laughed out loud. All that planning would be irrelevant; it would have been blasted out of the sky long before that.

Part of him wanted to see the explosion at first hand, but he would have to settle for watching it on the BBC or CNN. Currently, there was nothing on social media, and he presumed the airship had yet to set off.

He was enjoying having a few hours to himself. This would only last until early evening when Olivia would turn up. She was half-Spanish and half from somewhere east of the Alps. Having originally been married to a man with whom he had come into conflict, she had been abandoned by her husband, who had gone back to South Africa. In dire financial straits and ostracised by her devoutly Catholic family, she had become desperate. In an ironic twist of fate, she had firstly come to Daniel for a job – any job – and more latterly as company for him. He didn't enjoy sleeping in a big bed on his own. Life was too short. He had settled for an enemy with benefits.

Looking forward to his evening, he was halfway through the bottle when his mind floated off to his sister and Henk.

Liam was going back down to the village in Wiltshire tomorrow with his mate, Tommo. Lucky had thought the CIA woman should be there on a Saturday morning, with no chance she might be working in London. Her wedding would have been cancelled according to Liam, and her mate would probably still be in intensive care – if he had managed to survive.

There would be no mistakes this time, and after revealing Henk's killer's name, she would be eliminated.

In fact, it could turn out to be a good couple of days with the first machine blown up and that sodding woman out of the equation, having told Liam the all-important name. He finished the bottle. It was a long time until Monday morning when he would visit the factory ahead of the container being delivered.

Daniel was relaxing and, having been up at some godforsaken hour in the morning, was looking forward to a siesta before Olivia turned up, otherwise it wouldn't be worth her coming over.

He checked the news feeds and main websites and then stared out to the Mediterranean Sea before drifting off to sleep.

It was mid-morning, and Wazz was still in bed, where he found it easier to lie flat out. Prostrate or standing were both fine; it was the intermediate stages of sitting and bending that caused him some pain, despite the prescribed course of tablets. Mike was struggling as his nurse; it wasn't a position that had ever come into her mind or that of her careers advisers at school.

She constantly checked on him and was getting exasperated with herself. She realised how much he meant to her and how close she had come to losing him.

"I'd kill for a cup of tea, but I can't be arsed to sit up to drink it."

"I'm not sure if we've got any straws. I'll bring you a cup anyway."

"If I need to pee, it's your fault."

She went downstairs to put the kettle on.

While waiting for it to boil, she set up her computer equipment on the kitchen table and went over to lock the back door, which was part of a new routine after the break-in. Looking out of the kitchen window, it seemed such a happy and peaceful place as far removed from the world of international narcotics smuggling as it was possible to get.

With the tea made, she went back to the bedroom, and after putting the cup on his bedside table, she kissed the patient and jogged down the stairs that ran across the house, separating the front and back rooms on both floors.

While munching on a pack of biscuits and drinking a coffee, Mike began following up on some ideas that had part-formed sometime during the night. She was almost sure Daniel Drinkwater was Jan the Dutchman, and she knew why he had killed Terry and was after her – it was revenge over the death of his brother-in-law – and this thought had now fully crystallised. It was all very well knowing the *why*, but what was the *how*?

Overnight, she had been thinking that either he had found Terry by gaining access to the forensic evidence at the hotel – perhaps from fingerprints or facial recognition – or maybe someone in the intelligence community had collated the movements of all the undercover agents working on the project. They may have realised Terry had disappeared for the relevant days and changed his phone.

Neither of her theories was very convincing, but they were the best she could come up with. It never once went through her mind that no one had traced or even heard of Terry Bailey; it was her call to Jakob that had triggered everything.

Still confused, she parked the *how* for another day.

Thinking of Daniel Drinkwater, she hoped the police were raiding his home near Stratford-upon-Avon, but she didn't have high hopes that they'd find anything. He had been around too long, was too experienced, and had evaded the police and intelligence agencies of the USA, UK and Holland for a decade. It was as if he had morphed into a new form whenever anyone got close.

Was the fact that she and Terry were getting close to him another reason he was bidding to have them eliminated?

Mike had found no phone details, no social media and no emails. She thought the police would be equally unsuccessful, but she hoped this wasn't true. Mulling over his relationship with his sister and her husband while she drank the coffee, Mike flicked casually through the photographs on Henk's phone. It always helped her if she could see the person she was pursuing rather than aiming at some chimera.

Roger Fortuna caught her eye. Now she knew Daniel was a successful narcotics smuggler and distributor, she looked at Roger Fortuna in a new light. He was patently a thug and had spent time in prison. Why was he at Henk and Ana's wedding? They weren't relatives, as far as she could tell. He could well be Daniel's hard man in charge of the heavy stuff.

With everything that had happened, she had never shown Wazz a photograph of Lucky. She pulled out the power cable on her laptop and carried it upstairs.

He was flat out in bed, staring at the ceiling, having strained himself drinking the tea.

"Is this either of the men who attacked you?"

Wazz squinted at the screen as she held it so he didn't have to sit up. "No, nothing like them; the big man was stockier and the thin man ... well, he was a scrawny, nasty piece of work."

"OK. It was worth a try."

"Who is he?"

"A heavy who's cropped up, but I can eliminate him from my enquiries."

She returned to the kitchen with one less thing to worry about, although there was still the smallest of nagging doubts.

Despite her searches, she also couldn't find any phone number for Roger Fortuna, and this always made her suspicious.

Over the next few hours, she went over his criminal career, his time in prison and the murder of his wife. At the time, it was speculated that this was a turf war, but nothing was ever proven. Knowing who Daniel was and guessing what Roger Fortuna did, Mike didn't doubt that they were mates and in this together. She needed to find a bit more proof.

There was another thing nagging at her. Should she tell Leonard about the knifing? It currently felt deceitful and perhaps counterproductive not to. She was in two minds.

———

A large crowd was gathered outside the security fence at RAF Covingham. The standard 'No photography' signs found outside any such military establishment were being roundly ignored.

Lucky and Doug had laughed at the new 'No drones' signs on the security fence, which they had spotted in photographs on social media.

"It's OK; we're ten miles away," Lucky had said.

A helicopter had taken off and was flying a few circuits around the fenced perimeter of the airbase, checking visually for any suspicion of terrorists. A Land Rover Wolf, quickly followed by another, had driven out of the main gates and past the Spitfire on its plinth; they were heading south. How many Spitfires were left that they could consign one to such an ignominious fate?

Every sign of activity was greeted by a cheer as the waiting horde grew restless. Only the press photographers remained professionally focused.

The weather was fine, and the wind had dropped to six miles per hour or wind force 2, light breeze, on the Beaufort scale. It had turned overnight and was blowing in a south-westerly direction, so it was finally of some benefit to the French captain and co-pilot.

At about 10.40am, the level of activity at ground level suddenly increased, with vehicles and personnel emerging from several buildings.

Those outside the chain-link fence who had binoculars could see the enormous doors of a hangar sliding back, revealing the airship inside. The engines were started, and it emerged into the daylight. Fifteen minutes later, it was in the air and motionless on station over the machine wrapped in its waterproof cocoon. A team attached the cables to the eyelets of the net.

Just after 11.00am, there was much cheering and waving as the airship began to rise and clear the grass-covered hangars built during World War I – ironically, to protect Birmingham and Liverpool from Zeppelin raids. It rotated demurely on the spot and began its journey south-south-west across the Shropshire landscape towards Herefordshire.

The helicopter made one last sweep over the waving crowd before taking up a position to the starboard side behind the airship. An ex-RAF expert on BBC News had said it would only take fifty minutes to reach the factory thirty-nine miles away.

As the airship gradually became smaller against a backdrop of high, white clouds, the onlookers dispersed. However, many groups around the country and abroad were firmly focused on the weather and the progress from RAF Covingham

---

At the factory, Keith Herring and his reassembled team were thrilled that, within an hour, the machine should be hovering over the factory. The men in charge of opening the special roof access and releasing the hooks, which would enable the airship to depart for its return journey, were walking up and down nervously.

As at the airbase, there was a line of people eager to see its arrival. The media and, in particular, the TV channels had set up within the factory fence, but in a tightly defined area. Keith only wanted positive press. A private security company had vehicles driving around the perimeter road and around the outside of the factory itself.

The police also had a sizeable presence, following threats to destroy the machine made online. A demonstration against technological advancement and the rise of AI was being organised.

While this was happening in Herefordshire, Pascal and his team in the hangar outside Paris were in almost constant contact with the captain and co-pilot. They were concerned not only with monitoring the delivery but also with scheduling the return journey. This had to be agreed with air traffic control as times and weather conditions changed.

In London, Gordon Overton was with a number of key participants who, as a group, were having to provide updates to the Cabinet Office, the Home Secretary and the Prime Minister. So many individuals' futures rested on the successful delivery and installation of the machine. From the moment the Prime Minister had made it a cornerstone of his industrial, technological and defence policy, it could be no other way. Nobody wanted to face him should the terrorists – or indeed any party – successfully destroy the machine. It had attained a now almost-mythical significance.

Gordon was looking at his watch every few minutes and would continue to do this until the machine was inside the factory. This was likely to be between midday and 12.30pm.

Supremely confident as always, he had already decided to go to the Commonwealth and Overseas Club for a celebratory drink, which would be something he truly enjoyed and not Kümmel on ice.

Another pair of individuals were very active in their preparations, happy to be stretching their legs and backs after a night sleeping in the front seats of a Range Rover. Lucky was less concerned about his comfort and more worried that there were two drones packed with explosives immediately behind him. He didn't risk putting his seat back.

CHAPTER TWENTY-NINE

Gabby had stayed up late the night before and hadn't been keen to get out of bed; her morning routine had been put out of sync. Now the priority was to have breakfast as she was starving, and so holding a bowl of cornflakes, she walked into the conservatory at 10.00am.

Carmen was shuffling up a branch while squawking something incomprehensible. Lola was looking at Gabby as if expecting an answer to her sister's question.

"Wait a minute, girls; I need to have my breakfast first, then I'll get yours."

They didn't look convinced and clearly felt they weren't being prioritised.

It had been a long evening in which she had been trading in currencies and moving money between accounts and Bitcoin wallets. Happily, it had been a successful session, only disturbed by one call from her father, who – while choosing his words carefully – had explained that he was staying somewhere overnight and was waiting for the cargo to head his way in the morning. He was unlikely to be back until mid-afternoon, he thought.

Once she had finished her bowl of cereal, she began checking the newsfeeds and threads on social media. It looked as if the airship had spent the night at RAF Covingham and would complete its journey very soon. Unsure of the time, she felt her watch and guessed that something would appear on the news imminently. She finished doing her chores. It was going to be a busy morning.

With a tray of pellets topped with green peppers now being devoured by the two macaws, she was about to settle at her computer when there was an incoming call. This, she had also been waiting to receive. She answered it.

"Hi, it's Daniel. I'm in Spain. Any more news from your father?"

"Hi. No, nothing since last night. I think he's sleeping in the car. I bet it will hurt his back."

"No pain, no gain."

"I'm pretty sure he isn't looking at it like that."

"You may be right, but at least it has comfy seats; he's got too used to a life of luxury. He'll probably be back mid-afternoon. When he does get back, I want to get the next tranche of money from our friends as soon as you hear that the job has been completed."

"I set up the wallets last night to receive it. I'm ready."

"Great." He moved on to their more regular business: "I'll go down to the warehouse on Monday. The ship is on time, I think."

"Yes, it's scheduled to dock at just after 9.00am. You may be lucky and get the container in the afternoon, but definitely on Tuesday, I think."

She was pleased Daniel was out there, what with her father tied up on the microchip machine project for a couple of weeks. It meant that somebody would be watching Juan, who wouldn't be left to his own devices unloading the container; this was always a risk. "Has the address label cock-up been sorted?"

"Yes, I've been in contact with them. It shouldn't happen

again. I suggested they could send a list of the names and addresses for us to cross-check, but they didn't fall for that one."

"Nice try."

"If I hear about any dramatic events in Herefordshire, I'll send three thumbs-up emojis, OK?"

"Thank you; you're more likely to find out before me. Now I'm off for a swim."

"It's all right for some."

While Lola was sinking her claws into a green pepper and biting a chunk with her beak, Lucky was standing next to the two drones they had carried from the back of the Range Rover just after daybreak. They had no idea when the airship was likely to begin its journey, and it would only take twenty or so minutes to reach them. They needed to be ready for any eventuality.

Doug had chosen a flat area of hardstanding behind the chicken sheds but with a clear view in the general direction of the airfield. He was using the rear wall of the shed to lean against while holding his binoculars. It made them stable over long periods and was less tiring on the arms. He was scanning the horizon back and forth, while Lucky checked on social media for an indication that the airship had taken off.

A little earlier, for about ten minutes, Doug had been fiddling with the drones. "Right, Lucky, they're primed. Don't go near them."

"I'm scared shitless by them; don't worry. I'm going to bring out the Range Rover so we're ready to make a sharp exit. I'll park it by that wall."

No sooner had he done this and closed the chicken shed doors than Doug said, "I think I can see it."

Lucky hurried to join him in the lee of the buildings.

"Don't worry; it's still ten minutes away, I'd guess."

"Is it coming over us?"

"No, my best guess is that it will be a mile or two to the west, but that's good. We don't want the airship or its escort right above us."

Doug continued to look through his binoculars, giving Lucky frequent updates.

It wasn't long before the sound of a helicopter was brought to them on the breeze, and Doug bent down to pick up his controls, after handing his binoculars to Lucky. Doug put the straps over his shoulders, opened up the small screen and took the joystick in his right hand.

Looking like an usherette at a cinema with a tray of ice creams. He pressed some buttons and the rotors on one of the drones began to rotate, purring gently. It was almost time to send it off on its one and only deadly mission.

Outside Stratford-upon-Avon, Brenda Drinkwater was as white as a sheet and staring into space; this, the police had discovered, was her normal state. Whether she had grasped what was happening or not wasn't entirely clear. She was sitting in her lounge, accompanied by a policewoman who never left her side. At the beginning of the search, Brenda had handed over her phone and been told not to try to contact anyone.

"Why would I do that, dear?" she had asked.

The property was compact, but it had twelve rooms, a large roof space, a cellar and numerous converted outbuildings; it would take a long time to check out the whole place.

An officer had asked for her PIN and disappeared into a separate room to open her mobile. Nothing odd jumped out at him, and he sent the details to a colleague in London, where everything on the phone would be checked further. Two of the numbers in the address book were marked as 'Dan 1' and 'Dan 2', presumably her husband, but they hadn't been used recently. There were no texts or WhatsApp messages. She had downloaded very few apps, and it looked like, rather unusually, she used it basically as a phone.

While the search continued throughout the day, the numbers contained within her mobile had been circulated via Five Eyes, the information sharing group of five English-speaking spy agencies. Having been highlighted as a priority, these numbers were sent hotfoot to the CIA in London.

———

Leonard de Vries had been waiting for these numbers. He had his team undertake a series of searches and checks. Both Morag and Chuck were pulled off their current projects to find anything of interest. Time was of the essence.

Disappointed that Daniel Drinkwater hadn't been caught at the house, Leonard picked up his phone and dialled Mike's number. She answered by the third ring.

"Hi, how's Wazz?" He tried to sound as concerned as possible.

"Asleep upstairs in bed. Some honeymoon, eh?"

"Hey, he's home. That's great to hear." He didn't miss a beat before he launched into the main reason for the call: "As you're at a loose end, I thought that maybe you could do a bit of investigating for me?"

"Do you have no sympathy? I'm a full-time carer."

"Me too; I have to look after myself without any help. I do it out of love." He could play her and disarm her in seconds. "Mike, Daniel Drinkwater wasn't at home this morning when the Brits went in, just his wife, but they got his phone numbers. Take a look, will you?" He knew she would bite.

"Damn, do they know where he is?"

"No, and the wife is out of the loop by the sound of it; actually, out of her mind from what I hear. She's gonna be no help."

Mike went quiet for a second, but she was almost hooked. "What do you want me to do that the Brits aren't doing right at this moment, I suspect?"

"Find him. You're the best at this sort of thing."

"Huh." Flattery wasn't generally well-received by her. "Wazz needs me."

"Sure, I get that, but while you're sitting around between ward rounds, could you take a look? It would be awesome if we could beat Gordon and the Brits." He knew this would do the trick.

"Huh," she said again, but the die was cast.

"I'll send you the link and code to everything we've received."

After the call had been ended, she ran quietly upstairs to check on the patient, but he was fast asleep. She left him alone and went back downstairs, where a long afternoon and evening beckoned.

She wasted half an hour on Daniel Drinkwater's two phones, but she came to the conclusion that he was an arch professional. There was nothing incriminating, and he obviously removed the batteries and turned location services off when he wanted to disappear. He was unlikely to make a mistake. The Brits, especially GCHQ, would already be checking them out more thoroughly than she could do.

After a break to fetch a Coke from the fridge, she turned her attention to his wife's phone. Perhaps she was less discreet or was genuinely not firing on all cylinders. An hour passed while Mike checked out her movements.

"Whammo!" she whispered, as loudly as she dared, through clenched teeth.

There on the screen was proof that Brenda Drinkwater had gone to Birmingham airport at 4.30am and returned forty-five minutes later, only two hours before the police turned up at her door.

"You were dropping off Daniel," she said out loud, "but who tipped you off? If you were tipped off."

Daniel, I bet you're going to Holland; that would be spooky as that's where it all began and would make an appropriate place to end it. My Reichenbach Falls moment, she thought to herself melodramatically.

She pulled up the early departures from Birmingham, presuming that he would be on one of the first flights out this morning. She didn't have weeks to hack into airport or airline systems, so she came at it, as usual, from a different direction. There were no flights to Holland, so that idea was quashed.

Of course, he could have gone on holiday with mates, transited to Timbuktu at the next airport or taken a taxi to Birmingham New Street railway station to lose any followers, as Mike knew too well. He would almost certainly be using a different name and false passport. There was no point looking for Daniel under his real name, and she didn't have time to find him under any other unknown name. The Brits would do this over the coming weeks.

Instead, Mike made assumptions, starting with the thought that he was probably going for work – even if his line of work was narcotics smuggling.

Fortunately, Birmingham wasn't a busy airport, and on looking at the list of early flights, only a few destinations leapt out at her. She guessed he was unlikely to be going to a holiday island in the Mediterranean or a European capital, so she had dismissed such places. He had, however much he varied the locations of his operations, always favoured bringing the narcotics in by container. Which of these flights went to a container port?

It turned out to be two: Gdansk in Poland and Valencia in Spain.

Sticking with her assumption that he was doing something

with his drug business, she began searching for pet-food importers in these two locations. Only one name took her eye in Gdansk, and it looked as if it was a multi-generational family firm. Perhaps she could talk to Wazz about it? He could even phone them.

In Valencia, there was also only one, and again, it was a family firm, but the website looked very different. It was functional and more impersonal with no photographs of the directors.

It was mid-evening by then, and she went back upstairs to check on Wazz, who was awake and hungry. Frustrated at having her search disturbed and the momentum lost, she made him some food.

"I'll sleep in the spare bedroom. I'll be working late into the night, I expect."

He shook his head while chewing on a cold chicken thigh and then told her not to do too much. These words were wasted, of course.

Once back at the keyboard, she picked up her thread involving the Spanish pet-food importers, only to find it was owned by a company in the British Virgin Islands. This struck Mike as very strange, and she couldn't think of a reason for this – the company was small and provincial at best. Why would it warrant transferring to a tax haven?

By 10.00pm, she was mentally exhausted and hadn't made any more real progress. Before retiring for the night, she sent the flight details from Birmingham to Valencia, a photograph of Daniel from Henk's phone and the Spanish pet-food importers ownership to head office in Langley, asking them to check, collate names and send her anything relevant, such as the phone number and addresses in Valencia. She copied and pasted a front page from a previous request to head office from Leonard, changed the status to 'Urgent' and added his signature. Even more cheekily, she requested that she was to be copied in on the reply. This wasn't the first time she had done this, but even if they questioned it, Leonard would back her up. She knew how to play him.

With any luck, the results should be in when she woke in the morning. Tomorrow promised to be a significant day in her life.

She wasn't wrong.

CHAPTER THIRTY

Doug had decided that if the first drone was successful, he didn't want Lucky taking the second one back to Essex. Killing two birds with one stone, he would use the second to destroy the chicken sheds. There definitely wouldn't be any DNA or tyre tracks left after that. There would also be nothing incriminating in the car for the journey back to the Malvern Hills.

"Are you ready? Everything in the Range Rover? Nothing left behind?"

"I've double-checked." Lucky wasn't used to being told what to do, but he knew the importance of the questions.

They were standing behind the sheds and next to the car, with both its front doors open. The drones were a few feet in front of them on the concrete hardstanding, one with its rotors whirring. The sky was reasonably clear, and the wind light.

Timing was everything.

Doug didn't want the drone in the air any longer than was necessary; every second it was aloft would allow the teams on the helicopter or on the ground to spot and destroy it.

The multiple rotors of the first drone began to spin faster, the hum becoming more intense.

The airship came into full view, no longer requiring binoculars to see it. The machine was clearly visible slung beneath it, looking ridiculously large and black compared to the ivory-coloured airship. How could it carry such an object that weighed so much?

It was now a waiting game, and the seconds dragged.

Lucky had no idea how close the airship would need to be before Doug sent the drone off on its attack trajectory. He kept quiet and held the car key fob in his hand, ready to make a speedy getaway.

"Right, hang on," was all Doug said as he pressed buttons on the controls.

The drone rose very slowly and vertically for about fifty feet, providing panoramic views of the Shropshire countryside on his screen before it started to move off.

"*Shit!*" Doug shouted as he waggled the joystick. In several rapid movements, he pushed various levers and again pressed many of the buttons.

The drone seemed to stop in space for a second, like Wile E. Coyote running off a cliff, before plummeting silently out of the sky.

Before the two men could take three paces, it exploded, killing them instantly. The Range Rover had taken a direct hit, turning it immediately into a fireball. Most of the chicken sheds' wall panels were blown sideways or collapsed like dominoes before the dried shit and tinder-dry wood ignited, and the whole site turned into a massive conflagration, pumping black smoke and sparks high into the sky. Smuts and debris fell over a wide area.

The sound of the roaring and cackling flames was gradually replaced by the noise of the helicopter approaching. It was not, however, the first of the security vehicles to arrive at the scene.

A Land Rover Wolf in drab army green pulled up 100 yards

away, its occupants surveying the scene and in constant communication with the helicopter.

The Wolf was one of two special vehicles developed using Ukrainian technology and intelligence. They had left the base ahead of the airship and driven southwards, keeping roughly eight miles apart where possible, giving them a total coverage of about sixteen miles. On board each vehicle were sophisticated jammers that targeted the frequencies used by drones.

The moment Doug had turned on the first one, the jammer had locked on and, within thirty seconds, established a fix on its location. The vehicle had raced in the direction of Cupstone.

Once the device had established that the drone was moving and in flight, it killed the communication between operator and drone. The rotors had stopped turning, and the bomb intended for the airship and its cargo dropped to earth, detonating on impact with the Range Rover. The petrol in the V8 car merely added to the inferno.

(In the weeks of press and social media speculation afterwards, there was no mention of the jammer or the real way that the drone had been located and destroyed. Instead, there were outrageous theories that the terrorists' own phones had interfered with communications with the drone and in some way triggered the explosion, or it had been activated by the Range Rover's key fob. However, gross user incompetence [GUI] was the theory most widely offered by the talking heads on all the news programmes. The military simply made no comment.)

As the smoke billowed upwards, the helicopter landed two fields away and disgorged its contingent of armed soldiers, who made their way along the hedgerows, checking constantly for any terrorists still alive. Their colleagues in the Wolf continued to monitor the site of the explosion, having sent up a small reconnaissance drone of their own, which fed live pictures to everyone. No one, it appeared, had survived what was still a fierce fire.

Doug also need not have worried about leaving small amounts of DNA behind in the corner of the chicken sheds. Both his and Lucky's were spread across a very large area.

The airship continued on its course, with thirty miles left to cover. Everybody on board had already been on edge before they heard the explosion and were treated to a bird's eye view to the east from the wide glass windows of the gondola. The plumes of black smoke were impressive and ominous.

Now at full speed, it was travelling at sixty miles per hour and would be over the factory in thirty minutes. The captain wanted to get away from the area as quickly as possible.

Major Phipps took the call that gave him an update on events. All eyes in the room were on him, although his face betrayed not the slightest emotion.

"There's been an explosion at ground level, but nothing has happened to the airship," he told the expectant group. "The teams are at the scene, including the helicopter, and are reporting that whatever was there has been destroyed. They picked up a drone frequency, therefore it's safe to assume we came under attack."

"Oh great." Keith Herring had already taken off his jacket and undone his tie. His face was ashen, which – along with his white shirt – accentuated the blue-black shadow appearing on his cheeks. "Do you think there are more drones?"

"Highly unlikely; something like this takes a lot of men and *materiel.*" He emphasised the last word, although it meant nothing to Keith.

Everyone knew the major was guessing.

“Have they arrested anybody?” Keith was concerned.

“It’s thought that they’re all dead, but there are teams combing the area.”

The major continued to give updates for the next twenty minutes, as and when he received them. Keith’s son emerged from the back of the group to tell everyone that the explosion was all over social media with mobile phone footage of plumes of black smoke over the village of Cupstone.

The local media, which had been covering the airship’s departure from RAF Covingham, thought they had finished for the day, but they were now racing to the village, using the black cloud as a marker.

Someone came in through the door to say the airship could be seen in the distance. Everyone left the room to have a good view of its arrival.

Unlike watching a large plane land at an airport, there was no roar of the engines, no fast descent. Instead, there was a certain serenity to the airship’s movements and its ability to pivot on its axis.

For five minutes, it appeared not to be getting any closer, so slow was its approach. Eventually, it crossed the outer boundary of the factory site.

Cheers came from the crowd outside the fence as the pilot manoeuvred to a position directly over the wide opening in the roof of the building. The retractable cover had been activated. For a second, the airship resembled the *Hindenburg* in the apocryphal photograph, but it didn’t burst into flames.

It lowered its load with an impressive precision and was on station for only eighteen minutes while the hooks were removed from the eyelets. It had been such a long and circuitous journey to spend such a short time at the destination.

Once the ground crew had radioed up to the pilot to confirm successful delivery, it began to rise slowly, the cables still dangling beneath it swinging back and forth.

Unseen from the ground, the cover on the roof of the factory began to slide back into place. It would take a day to remove the net, the platform and the waterproof cover from the machine, but it would take two weeks to remove every speck of dust from the inner sanctum – a task as complex as the trip made from Breda.

To even louder cheering and waving, the airship moved away from the factory complex and began its 300-mile flight southwards over Hampshire and out across the English Channel to Paris. The winds were favourable, and there was ample daylight. Air traffic control had been able to accommodate the requests and had offered as direct a route as one could expect.

The pilot had been given the option of making an overnight stop at Southampton, but he had decided that the quicker he was out of British airspace, the better. He was beginning to question his career move, having transferred from Boeing 747s.

It was Friday evening when Liam tried to call Lucky, but he was unable to get through. "Pick up the fricking phone, will you?"

He wasn't to know that this would have been difficult as Lucky's right arm was being put into a bag by a member of the forensic team at the derelict chicken farm in north Herefordshire.

They had agreed to have a late-afternoon call on Friday in case there had been a change of plan. Lucky had said he might have new information about the American woman's whereabouts, and it was a heck of a long way to drive to find that she had gone on holiday for two weeks.

All the preparations had been made. Liam had arranged to pick up his friend Tommo from his house in Colchester at 9.00am on Saturday morning to head off across country to Wiltshire. Harry couldn't make it; he could still barely stand after the punches from the big guy in the American woman's house. Liam hadn't been impressed with Harry; all the lump had to do was grab the big guy, but he had instead let him get in two blows that had crippled him. No wonder they had chucked Harry out of the rugby club.

Liam had himself been barred by a kick boxing club, but his ban had come from an inability to control his temper once he had started fighting. Too much aggression rather than too little had been a problem all his life. It was ironic that he had 'TRUE' and 'LOVE' tattooed on his fingers – probably because 'PSYCHOPATH' wouldn't fit.

He knew how dangerous it was returning to the scene of the crime, but he couldn't let Lucky down. If he did, he would never work again, and he was in too deep. This time, the big guy wouldn't be there, and with Tommo, he wouldn't be in the house five minutes. She would give him the name and address, then he would kill her and drive home. Job done.

Early on Saturday morning, as planned, Liam had set off for Colchester to pick up Tommo; the car was full of petrol, ready for the long drive down to Wiltshire. He pulled up outside an ugly block of flats built of a depressing grey concrete with what looked like a Mohican haircut on top, made up of various mobile telephone transmitter towers. He walked to the communal entrance and pressed one of the doorbells. A deep voice answered, saying that he would be right down and would see Liam in the car.

A few moments later, Tommo appeared, effortlessly carrying a rucksack over one shoulder. He looked like the rugby player he had been most of his life, with a broken nose and shaved head. He opened the hatchback at the rear of the burgundy Renault

Fuego and threw in the rucksack. "Morning," he said before joining Liam in the front.

"What's in the bag?"

"Nosh. I can't last without my lunch."

"Don't worry, we'll stop for a McDonalds and a pee halfway there."

Tommo tried to get comfortable in the front seat, but it was difficult. The car was over forty years old but lovingly maintained by Liam. It may have seemed a strange choice for a man on a mission, but he had changed the plates to a number he had spotted on another red Fuego. If he drove within the speed limits and didn't draw attention to himself, there would be no problem. Killing an American woman didn't factor into this equation.

All went well until they had rounded London, when the car began to make a strange knocking noise.

"What's that?" Tommo could feel the vibration through the passenger seat.

"I don't know; we'll pull over at the next services."

It hadn't taken long before they were driving into a car park with a sailing club on an old gravel pit just visible through the trees. Liam parked far away from the petrol station and the food outlets, where there was plenty of space and the nearest people were a couple walking their small dogs on the grass. He pulled a cap down over his forehead, got out and walked around the car.

Tommo stayed in the vehicle, away from any cameras; he wouldn't be of any use to Liam – he was younger than the car and rarely drove. Through the windows, he watched Liam look underneath and kick each of the tyres.

"Bollocks," he heard Liam say. "Put your cap on and jump out. Keep your face away from the cameras. There's a bulge on the inside of the rear offside tyre; I'll need to put on the spare."

Tommo looked on in amazement as Liam emptied the boot to take out the spare tyre and the jack, which he put under the car and began winding the handle. Once he'd changed the tyre, he put the old tyre and everything else back in the boot and slammed the tailgate shut. "Right, let's get out of here. The last bloody thing I wanted was to spend twenty minutes being filmed at a service station. We've got a job to do."

Liam drove out as sedately as possible, despite the anger that had risen inside him. He tried to relax his tight grip on the steering wheel. Getting Liam angry didn't bode well for his victim.

CHAPTER THIRTY-ONE

Mike brought Wazz breakfast in bed, where she found him sitting up. Staying in one position was fine, but any movement he made was slow and tentative.

"Did you see what happened yesterday?" He was someone who needed to be active every day. Spending days in bed wasn't good for him. He had quickly become bored with scrolling continuously on his phone since waking up.

"What?" Her mind was elsewhere – Valencia to be exact.

"Terrorists tried to blow up an airship with a drone near Hereford."

"Really? Did they succeed?" She had been up an hour, but she was entirely focused on what had come in from Langley overnight.

"No, it looks like they blew themselves up, but they obviously got close."

Mike, for once, didn't know what to say. He had no idea what she had been working on, and she couldn't tell him. "Have they caught anybody?"

"BBC News says that the terrorists are all dead. They've been trying to piece everything together."

This was good news on one level, but catching them alive would have given the authorities a chance to interrogate them. This failed attack showed her that her previous project wasn't closed, and they could still be intending to hit the American machine on its way between Phoenix and the factory. She would check out the *modus operandi* used in Herefordshire and see if anything could be learnt.

"Did the machine make it to the new factory?"

Wazz looked at her askance. "You know about it?"

"Yes, I know about it." She left it at that.

"It made it to the factory, where the airship lowered it through the roof. That was impressive. Want to see the clips?"

"Sure." She sat on the bed and spent a few minutes watching stuff with Wazz before going back downstairs to continue reading what had come in overnight from the team at head office.

The techies at the Farm, as it was called, had gone above and beyond the call of duty – perhaps because of the high-level status she had attached to the request in Leonard's name.

They had found that Daniel Drinkwater used the name Ramón Casas for his shell companies registered in Road Town on the island of Tortola in the British Virgin Islands (BVI). No one had twigged that Gabby had chosen the name of a famous Spanish portrait artist for him.

Even better, the techies had searched for other shell companies and found a property company with two factories, a warehouse and a villa in Spain, all near or in Valencia. There was an address for the villa on a hill above the city.

While Mike was scanning the details of these holding companies, her eyes fell on the names of the BVI solicitors and accountants who acted as ghost directors and also on the name of another director: Gabriella Fortuna.

"What? So that's it!" She had finally made a link between Daniel Drinkwater, his sister, brother-in-law and the Fortuna family, some of whom where in the wedding photographs on Henk Visser's phone. One of her next tasks would be to find out how Gabriella fitted into the Fortuna family. Mike presumed she was Roger's wife, but in this she was wrong.

However, this wasn't her first task, which was to send the villa name and address to Leonard so he could pass it on to the European – specifically, the Spanish – agencies and authorities. She began to compose a message, cutting and pasting the key information.

Her phone buzzed, and she saw it was Leonard. He was obviously using his psychic capabilities.

She answered it: "Oh, hi." She could guess what this was about.

"Did you see that intel from head office?" he asked.

"I did. It's excellent. I'm just about to send you the essential points. The techies were great."

"Yeah, I was so tired last evening that, this morning, I clean forgot about asking them to search overnight for this guy Daniel and his pet-food company. I even marked it 'Urgent'."

"You clearly thought it was important ... and it was."

He had decided not to reprimand her. "What did Langley find?"

"Daniel Drinkwater is known as Ramón Casas in Spain and lives in a villa outside Valencia, where he has another pet-food business. I'm sending you the address now." She paused to do this. "There. Got it?"

"Yes, great; I'll get this off to our team in Madrid and to Europol, the EUDA and the Spanish police."

"They'll need to be quick. I think that Daniel or Ramón or Jan, or whoever he is today, is very clever."

"Don't worry, I will. Don't forget we're all in job-protection mode. The clock is ticking down, and I need to score every point ... and there's no timeout."

"Oh, and another thing, I've made a connection between Daniel and the Fortuna family."

"Who are they, when they're at home?"

"I'm guessing they help Daniel in his operations. It'll be good back-up details for any court case."

"Sure." He paused the work discussion to ask her about her plans: "Do you have a new date for your wedding?"

"Not yet; I've been distracted ... *what the fuck?* Someone's crashed through the back door! Shit! Call the police."

She never heard Leonard's response because she was shouting out Wazz's name and running across the lounge to the front door. She, in turn, was being pursued by a big man in a thin, black jacket who emerged from the kitchen. There was no time to think.

Outside the house, she screamed, but there was no one in sight. After crossing the small footbridge in two strides, she ran up Church Lane with the man ten paces behind her. The pain in her left leg slowed her, but fear and adrenaline took over. She didn't look around.

At the junction with the High Street, the decision whether to turn left or right was taken out of her hands. The local Rodhopper community bus was coming towards her. She stuck out her hands, waving frantically. It stopped, and the door opened.

"*Drive!*" she shouted, "*I'm being attacked.*"

Tommo hesitated, unsure what to do as she clambered on board. The driver had assessed the situation instantly, closing the door and hitting the accelerator. Her pursuer turned and ran back towards her house.

She pulled out her phone and called the emergency services, telling them what had happened and that Wazz was alone in the house and incapacitated. The bus driver, listening to the conversation, stopped the bus 200 yards along the High Street outside the small Methodist chapel.

Back in the bedroom, Wazz had been woken by the smashing of the back door and Mike's shout. Not knowing what was happening downstairs, he had heard her opening and slamming the front door only for it to be opened immediately by a pursuer. Her screams as she ran over the footbridge chilled him, and he could only imagine what was happening to her.

While Tommo chased Mike, Liam paused in the kitchen, wondering why she had shouted. He decided to walk up the cross stairs to find out if anyone was above him. If necessary, he would sort them out before Tommo brought the woman back.

Another terrible scream reverberated through the house. This time it came from Wazz.

He had swung the baseball bat with such force that it had torn the stitches in his abdomen. He collapsed to the floor of the landing as the full force had hit Liam on the forehead with a frightening crack, which knocked him back down the stairs. He tumbled down to the kitchen door where he had ended up in an unnatural position. He was dead.

Tommo had run back down Church Lane as an elderly couple came out of a cottage opposite the thatched terrace to see what all the fuss was about. He realised that the American woman had escaped, and the job was blown, but he needed to tell Liam it was time to make a speedy exit. He went back in through the open front door to see his mate with a broken neck and his legs propped up against the kitchen door.

He ran over, but knew immediately that it was hopeless. He looked up the stairs to see Wazz sitting holding a baseball bat. Wazz began to stand up unsteadily, and Tommo made his decision. He took the car keys from Liam's pocket and ran outside to the Renault. His last thought as he left the village was that he might need to ask Lucky for some help; disappearing abroad for a long while might be a very good idea.

Tears ran down her cheeks.

The two macaws appeared at the window, peering inside, but this wasn't sympathy – they could see their food being carried out to the conservatory. Gabby always talked to the birds when things were bad; it was a form of therapy. Remembering back to the day her mother had been murdered, she thought she would never have a worse day in her life. This proved not to be true.

She had been monitoring the news all the previous day, waiting to hear that the airship had left RAF Covingham and Doug had blown it up. As the morning dragged on, she went back to her other work while listening to BBC Hereford & Worcester. Surely it would be the first to announce that the damn thing had left the airfield?

There had been a newsflash.

On hearing that there had been a huge explosion, but not in the air, her heart had stopped. Had either or both of them escaped? She had tried to phone her father, but there had been no reply. This told her nothing as his mobile would have been turned off anyway with the battery out.

Then came the details in the news reports about a ground explosion at a chicken farm and that it was suspected the terrorists had been killed as their bombs blew up on launch.

She had tried to let out her anger, but there was no one near, and she couldn't run around or hit anything. She just screamed and howled for hours.

As the time passed and the afternoon segued into evening, she knew her father was dead. If he had survived, he would have turned on his phone at least for a few seconds to send her his favourite thumbs-up emojis. Until she was told otherwise, she would cling on to the hope that he was injured, hiding or both. Waiting for a formal identification via the police investigation might take days.

At a low point that evening, her phone rang, and her heart leapt. It was Daniel, who had heard about the explosion and that the airship had made it successfully to the factory. He was wonderfully sympathetic and consoling for the first half of the conversation, giving her hope and assuring her that he would sort out whatever had happened in Herefordshire. It hadn't taken him long to turn the conversation to the consequences of the failure and that the Chinese would want all their money back and may turn off the drugs supply – after they had killed him, that is.

This was not what she wanted to hear at that moment.

Her annoyance grew as he asked her if she knew or could find another person to take over the operation to blow up the other machine in Holland, which was now less than a week away.

"*How the fuck am I supposed to know? Dad dealt with that side of things,*" she shouted down the phone.

"But you pay them. You must have a list?"

She gritted her teeth. "I'll send you some names and numbers, but don't ask me anything about them; I don't know."

"Thank you, and don't worry; I'm sure Lucky has survived and will turn up over the next couple of days."

After the call she was fuming, which at least distracted her from her grief for a while.

She blamed Daniel for turning her father from a local heavy in Essex into a murderer. Whatever happened, Daniel's hands were always clean; it was always Lucky who did or organised the nasty stuff – the wet work. For years, Gabby had been trying to get her father to give up all this and enjoy the money they had, not just that which he had earnt but also what she had made on currency trading.

They had more than plenty, but now she knew in her heart it was all too late.

On Saturday, 11th July, the bulls were running through the streets of Pamplona in Spain. The San Fermin festival was well underway, and the revellers were taking enormous risks as the bulls chased them and, hopefully, ran past. Every year, some of the runners were gored. The line between life and death was thin.

Daniel Drinkwater wasn't aware of the bull-running fiesta; he had his own nightmare and was well aware of how thin that line was.

He had spent most of the previous evening ringing around, cajoling, threatening, pleading and using every tool available to find someone to replace Lucky and Doug on the job in Holland. He really did need to destroy that American machine if he was going to come out of this alive. Fortunately – and it was only a stroke of luck that Lucky had told him – he knew where the drones were hidden near Tilburg in readiness.

Daniel was missing a trustworthy drone operator, and this wasn't something he could put an advert for in the newspaper; he was at his wit's end trying to find someone.

The previous morning, he had been in a buoyant mood, knowing that Lucky and Doug were near the airfield and were well set up to blow the airship out of the sky. He had enjoyed his pre-prandial bottle of wine with one eye on his phone, ready to spot the three thumbs-up emojis when they appeared.

Then, he had seen the newsflash and the bottom had fallen out of his world.

After that, trying to sort out a new drone operator while being completely on edge had ruined his Friday night with Olivia. She would be back at his villa again later, when he hoped he could enjoy her company a little more.

Sadly for Daniel – or Ramón Casas, as the Spanish police called him – this never happened. A team of ten had turned up at his villa to arrest him, while another team simultaneously descended upon the pet-food warehouse.

His days of avoiding capture had ended.

CHAPTER THIRTY-TWO

It hadn't taken the police long to track Tommo driving the Renault. They had been given the registration number and a good description. He had been picked up on every camera up the A303, the M3 and M25. By the time he got to Essex, a police helicopter was above him, directing the officers in cars on the ground. Outside Colchester, he was stopped and arrested.

Liam's body had been carried out of the house in Rodbourne, after the SOCO team had finished, and had been put into a black VW van to be taken away for the autopsy. His knife, jemmy and the baseball bat had also been placed in bags and removed.

The ambulance had turned up within twenty minutes to take Wazz back to Salisbury District Hospital, where he had emergency surgery to repair his torn stitches and to check if he had damaged anything else.

"You'll have to pay council tax if you spend any more nights in here." Mike had walked onto the ward and bent over to kiss him. She had been beyond relieved to find him alive when she had raced back to the house, accompanied by two ex-soldiers who had jumped off the bus with her, having heard and watched the story unfold.

"No jokes please. It really does only hurt when I laugh." He was equally thrilled to see the other attacker hadn't caught her. "Mike, you really should come with a health warning."

"I'll get it tattooed on my forehead."

"Written backwards so you read it every day in the bathroom mirror. You're a danger to yourself."

"I won't do it until we get married, otherwise we'll never drag in a witness from the street."

Wazz raised a hand to cover his eyes; he didn't know whether to laugh or cry – both of which would cause him considerable pain.

Mike was sitting in her kitchen, having finished a call to the door repairman for the second time in a week, when her phone rang.

It was Leonard. "I hear you hit a mean dinger."

"What are you talking about?"

"A home run ... with your bat."

"That was Wazz. He has a career waiting in baseball, I think."

"I'm glad the emergency response got there in time. Is he OK?"

"He's awake and will survive."

"Great, and you're OK?"

"Well, it would be the first time in my life if I am."

"I'll take that as a yes. I wanted to let you know I've spoken to people in high places, here and at home. You'll be interviewed one more time about who the attackers were, but they shouldn't give you too much grief. If they do, call me."

"I think this is the last straw. I'm done with it all."

"Nah, take a week off, do something interesting ... you know, like get married."

"Do you ever give up?"

"Nah, and I've just got the heads-up that all our jobs are safe. You cracking the Chinese lab thing and identifying Jan the Dutchman went down well back home. Even POTUS is impressed."

"He's impressed if he puts his pants on the right way round in the morning."

"No, really; it's all good, and with Jan being interrogated in Spain, we'll tie up a lot of loose ends. Oh, and the Brits have already identified the two who blew themselves up in Hereford-shire." He struggled with the name of the county, somehow breaking it down into five syllables.

"Fantastic." She didn't sound enthusiastic.

"One was that Roger Fortuna you found."

She perked up for the first time "Really? What? Daniel Drinkwater's mate in the wedding photograph?" Mike couldn't bring herself to call him Jan.

"Yeah."

Her mind raced. "Daniel Drinkwater might be behind both. Is anyone checking that link?"

"They are now. I'll put my best analyst on it."

"What? No."

"Hey, it'll take you no time."

"I need a break."

"Nah, you need to keep yourself occupied. It'll stop you going over everything in your mind."

"The last few weeks have been traumatic."

"Sure, but it's over. Everyone's dead or behind bars. Jan the Dutchman will spend the rest of his days in a British jail."

"I sure hope so. I can't go through all this again."

Her mind went back to where this had all started with Terry

– poor deluded, drunk Terry. She now knew he hadn't shot Jan in that hotel room; he had shot an innocent man. Seven years later, Terry hadn't seen Jan driving a car in The Gambia. How could Jan possibly have known about Terry or where he was on holiday?

Yet without Terry contacting her in a blind panic, she would never have begun searching for Jan. If he hadn't had the foresight to keep Henk's phone and given it to her; she would never have come close to tracking Jan down. In this, she herself was wrong, and he hadn't intended her to find the phone. She would never know about his mother's watch, which was what he had actually wanted to give her.

She hoped Terry was resting in peace.

Three days later, the police turned up outside the large gates of a mansion in Essex and were let in by a terrified Agata.

"Who's in the house?" asked a policewoman.

"Just Gabby – Gabriella – and me."

"Is she aware her father is dead?"

"Yes, she knows."

"Then take us to her, please," the policewoman requested as reassuringly as possible.

"OK ... she's blind, by the way," Agata added as she let them into the big hall and led them down the long corridor to the West Wing.

The police had been told that Roger 'Lucky' Fortuna was dead and had been one of the two suspected terrorists who had blown themselves up while attempting to bring down the airship. They wanted to search his house for evidence and to find the organisation or country behind the plot.

Firstly, they needed to meet the daughter and express their condolences. They hadn't known she was blind.

Agata tapped the door and opened it. "Gabby, there are some police officers to see you."

"What?" She turned around from her screens and looked in the direction of the door.

"Miss Fortuna, I'm Detective Inspector Melanie Curtis, and I'm here with Detective Sergeant Griffiths and Mr Quilley from the Foreign Development and Commonwealth Office. We've come to talk to you about your father, but first we'd like to extend our condolences."

Gabby rotated her chair and extended a hand, but she didn't get up. They all shook hands with her rather awkwardly.

"I'm so sorry for your loss, and I know this is a difficult time, but we have some important questions we need to ask." Detective Inspector Curtis turned to Agata. "Would you leave us while we talk to Miss Fortuna? Thank you."

Agata left, closing the door.

There was an odd and uncomfortable dynamic. Gabby couldn't see what they were doing or their expressions, and they felt they were intruding on a daughter's grief. Something was playing on one of the computer screens while the other displayed pages from what looked like a report.

"I need to ... *close my screens*," she said with emphasis, and they both went black.

The officers looked at each other, and the female detective began the questioning. "Miss Fortuna—"

"Gabby, please."

"Gabby, forgive us, but we have to ask these questions. Did you know what your father was doing in Herefordshire?"

"No, we lead separate lives. I have this end of the house; he lives down the other. My mother is dead."

"So you have no idea what he does for a living?"

"He's mostly retired. He ran some local businesses before he sold them ... and had some properties."

"He has been in prison."

"Yes, he told me, but that was before I was born."

"Have you met a man called Doug Fisher before?"

"No. I don't know anyone called Doug."

"It looks as though your father and this man called Doug were killed when two improvised bombs attached to drones exploded, for some reason, late on Friday morning. You have no idea what he was doing with them?"

"No, that's crazy. My father wouldn't have anything to do with bombs." Her eyes began to moisten as the pain of her father's death welled up again. It was a convincing performance.

"And he's never mentioned any terrorist connections or extreme political affiliations?"

Gabby shook her head and reached for the tissue box on her desk. "No, he had no interest in anything like that. I doubt he could tell you who the Prime Minister is. He used to like going down the pub and playing golf. That's about it."

"He appears to have gone to Spain a lot?"

"Yes, to play golf with his mates."

"Do you know where he stayed when he went on these golf trips?"

"All over the place, I guess. How would I know? I never went with him. I can't play golf, obviously."

"No, fair enough. Did he ever mention a man called Daniel Drinkwater?" Quilley, the man from the FCDO, joined the questioning.

"Yes, he's a friend of the family. I've met him at weddings ... and funerals."

"What's he like?"

"You're asking someone who's blind?"

"Not physically; I meant as a person."

"I think my dad met him through work years ago. They stayed friends ... probably played golf together." Gabby was a consummate actor. She needed to be because she had hoped that, with her father and Doug dead, the authorities would close the case quickly and move on without making other connections. She needed to find out how they had stumbled across Daniel. She had set up all the communications for them and thought they were watertight.

"Do you know if your father has phones or computers here in the house?"

"How would I know? Check out his rooms yourself. I've never been in there, but given he can't remember his PIN, I doubt it. If he wanted something ordered from Amazon, he asked me to do it for him." She managed to sound so matter of fact.

"We'll check in a few moments."

"Good luck." Gabby knew that there was nothing in her father's end of the house. She was beginning not to like the sound of Mr Quilley's voice.

"Our warrant means that we can take away any phones or computers from the house for testing by our people. Do you have a problem with that?"

The three visitors were looking at each other as Gabby stared in their direction, her eyes flicking back and forth and occasionally disappearing upwards to reveal only the whites. Something innocuous she had said meant that the computer screens had flickered back into action, and the FCDO man in particular was trying to read what was on them.

"I need my computers. I rely on them. I don't have anything else."

In the conservatory, the two macaws chose that moment to pick an argument with each other, squawking loudly. It distracted the visitors, who had never seen such beautiful birds so close.

"We'll get them back to you as quickly as possible," Quilley reassured her.

"There's nothing on my computers. What are you looking for?"

"Anything that explains what your father was doing in Hereford on the day he died."

"You'll find nothing. He was a hopeless dreamer" – she sounded almost wistful – "he was always ... *tilting at windmills*." She articulated the last three words clearly and loudly; the screens turned black before a series of numbers began cascading down. The hard drive was being wiped, having received her coded instruction.

"Stop ..." Quilley didn't finish his sentence as he realised the futility of saying anything more.

"Please take the computer equipment if you really have to."

The previous evening, she had spent almost four hours completely wiping the drives and memory, removing and replacing small, specific pieces of hardware. Nobody would be able to recover anything of value. She had hit with a hammer what she had taken out and put it in a padded envelope addressed to a fictitious address in Scotland. These had been posted by Agata. She had already downloaded all her data onto two portable hard drives, which she also put in padded envelopes addressed to her aunt Rita and Agata similarly had posted.

Once she had been told Lucky's body had been identified, she had known the police would come calling. They'd find nothing on her equipment. Her final instruction of 'tilting at windmills' wiped the very last data and recent history, but in truth, there was nothing on it that the police could possibly find interesting.

After some more questions and a search of the property, the police team left with all the computers, phones, notebooks, wallcharts and diaries. Gabby didn't see them off the premises.

Inside, she was in a rage. This emotion added to the unimaginable levels of grief, and she began to walk around her room trying to release the tension. A leather armchair caused her to stumble, and she needed to re-establish where she was in the room.

Over a decade, Gabby had gradually assimilated tens of millions of pounds in various currencies, including Bitcoin. In addition, she had control of most of Daniel's business interests via the BVI shell companies. The deposit paid by the Chinese for the destruction of the two microchip machines was already in two cryptocurrency wallets to which only she knew the passwords. As if this wasn't enough wealth, her father had already transferred the Fortuna mansion into her name.

She had the list of all of the users and pushers from the Chinese labs, which she would sell on the dark web. After all that had happened over the last ten years, she didn't intend to be involved in drug smuggling again.

The only person she needed was Agata, who'd be her eyes and would continue to run her home. From this point forwards, she would be paid ten times what she was paid now.

Gabby Fortuna was a very rich young woman, but without her father, what was the point?

Her shoulders rose and fell as she began to sob uncontrollably. She thrashed around and screams came from deep inside as she lashed out, not knowing where she was in the room.

Finding herself at the French windows, she opened them, startling her beloved birds. Unused to having free access to her living room they flew inside, flapping wildly. Carmen attempted to land on the marble mantelpiece, but she skidded. She knocked the blue-and-white Delft urn to the floor where it smashed, spilling its powdery, grey contents onto the floor in a cloud of dust.

Gabby flopped onto a chair, trying to pull herself together.

"I will regroup." She was speaking to the macaws, who were now either climbing up the curtains or walking along the backs of a sofa. "I've done it before, and I'll do it again. It's time for a fresh start. Time to move on."

A point had been reached and a decision made – she would never be Jan the Dutchman again.

ACKNOWLEDGMENTS

I would like to begin by declaring my debt to the late Gerald Pollinger who, with his father, was agent to Graham Greene among others. He represented me in the late 1990s and his support and advice were invaluable, particularly as I began to write the Mike Kingdom series; he never lived to see *The Tip of the Iceberg* completed.

Further thanks go to my wife, Natasha, my sister, Angela, and my friend, Amber, who have shouldered the burden of reading my first draft. Paul and Mandy have also given me great encouragement.

All six of the Mike Kingdom thrillers have been edited by Lindsay Corten and she still has not changed her name and moved abroad. I hear her voice in my ear even as I write this. She has been the most wonderful critical friend.

Jem Butcher has produced the stunning covers for the series picking up on all of the subtleties as only a gifted designer can.

My thanks go to Adrian Hobart and Rebecca Collins at Hobeck Books whose advice, support and friendship are what every writer needs. It only took me twenty-nine years to find them.

Finally, a big thank you to the reviewers and bloggers who have all been so generous and who have, unwittingly, given me the strength to follow Mike Kingdom wherever she takes me.

David Jarvis

ABOUT THE AUTHOR

David Jarvis went to art college, and then ran his design and planning practice for forty years, working all over the world. He ended up planning countries. His canvases just got bigger and bigger.

HOBECK BOOKS – THE HOME OF GREAT STORIES

We hope you've enjoyed reading this novel by David Jarvis. To keep up to date on David's fiction writing please do follow him on Twitter/X, Bluesky or Instagram.

Hobeck Books offers a number of short stories and novellas, free for subscribers in the compilation *Crime Bites*.

- *Echo Rock* by Robert Daws
- *Old Dogs, Old Tricks* by AB Morgan
- *The Silence of the Rabbit* by Wendy Turbin
- *Never Mind the Baubles: An Anthology of Twisted Winter Tales* by the Hobeck Team (including many of the Hobeck authors and Hobeck's two publishers)
- *The Clarice Cliff Vase* by Linda Huber
- *Here She Lies* by Kerena Swan
- *The Macnab Principle* by R.D. Nixon
- *Fatal Beginnings* by Brian Price
- *A Defining Moment* by Lin Le Versha
- *Saviour* by Jennie Ensor
- *You Can't Trust Anyone These Days* by Maureen Myant

Also please visit the Hobeck Books website for details of our other superb authors and their books, and if you would like to get in touch, we would love to hear from you.

Hobeck Books also presents a weekly podcast, the Hobcast, where founders Adrian Hobart and Rebecca Collins discuss all things book related, key issues from each week, including the ups and downs of running a creative business. Each episode includes an interview with one of the people who make Hobeck possible: the editors, the authors, the cover designers. These are the people who help Hobeck bring great stories to life. Without them, Hobeck wouldn't exist. The Hobcast can be listened to from all the usual platforms but it can also be found on the Hobeck website: **www.hobeck.net/hobcast**.

ALSO BY DAVID JARVIS

The Mike Kingdom Thrillers
The Tip of the Iceberg
This Is Not a Pipe
The Violin and Candlestick
The Mongoose and the Cobra
The Green Feathers
Jan the Dutchman

The Collation Unit

Buy online, from your local bookshop or from the Hobeck Books website.

www.ingramcontent.com/pod-product-compliance
Ingram Content Group UK Ltd.
Pitfield, Milton Keynes, MK11 3LW, UK
UKHW040944110326
468872UK00003B/794

9 781915 817990